THE RAIN CATCHER

THE RAIN CATCHER

BUCK TURNER

Page & Vine
An Imprint of Meredith Wild LLC

Paperback ISBN: 978-1-964264-46-2

To those who dare to dance in the rain.

PROLOGUE

Life isn't about waiting for the storm to pass...
It's about learning to dance in the rain.
—Vivian Greene

PART I

CHAPTER 1

DIANE

March 1996

"Maybe today is the day," I tell myself as I stare at my laptop and its glowing screen. My fingers hover just above the keyboard, suspended between intent and paralysis. On the monitor, my manuscript seems to yawn back at me, its blank page akin to the emptiness I feel inside.

A gust of wind whips through the open window, and every so often, a stray grain of sand stings my ankle as the breeze flicks it off the warped floorboards. The ocean is less than a hundred yards away, but today's wind muffles the sound of the surf beneath a ceaseless flutter of windblown grass and gull cries.

In the distance, Cassie sprints along the shore, trailing a ribbon of laughter behind her. Our little dog, Rolo, darts around her in playful loops, kicking up the sand with his quick, eager paws. Cassie's yellow T-shirt, the one with the faded sea turtles, flaps around her skinny frame as she races from one clump of seaweed to another, stooping every few seconds to inspect whatever treasure has surfaced overnight. I can just make out the edge of her profile when she turns, head bowed over a shell or crab, as absorbed as any scientist in her research.

I try to translate the image into words, the way I used to, but every sentence I type unravels into something brittle and obvious. I delete, rewrite, delete again. My novel is a black hole, consuming hours and yielding nothing, while the digital afterimage of my journalistic peak refuses to be ignored. The line of Cassie's back, curved with intent, her single-minded joy—how would I even begin to pin that to the page without flattening it?

A gust slams the window, and a loose paper from my notebook cartwheels to the floor. I bend to pick it up, more out of habit than necessity, then run a thumb along the dog-eared edge of the pad. My notebook is a collage of dialogue overheard at Wink's grocery store, dreamscapes from late-night insomnia, wishful outlines in blue ink that fade by morning. Each page is another failed experiment, evidence of the thing I can't yet name.

I close my eyes and inhale the mixture of old cedar, sea spray, and damp laundry that is our home. The cottage, with its long, slender porch with flaking paint, rockers aimed at the water, and windows streaked with salt, is all thresholds. There are only a handful of rooms—kitchen, living room, two bedrooms, and a study—but the boundaries between them feel half-hearted, as if the cottage never quite made up its mind to be anything more than a waiting room for the sea.

Somewhere behind me, the clock on the stove ticks in steady opposition to the pulse of the waves. Time here is both elastic and relentless, stretching as the sun drifts over the water, then snapping back when I realize another morning has slipped by without a single usable paragraph. I rub my temples and glance at the browser tab, where my name, DIANE MONTGOMERY, leans into the masthead in solid, confident type.

I hate her a little. Or maybe I just miss her. That girl who could spend an entire day lost in a single thought, a single phrase, and come out on the other side with a piece so raw and beautiful it still takes my breath away. She was invincible, a word magician with a silver-tongued pen, and she existed in the world she wrote just as much as the one she lived in. But she seems like a stranger now. That girl had a vigor and fluidity that I can't seem to muster anymore. A sudden pang of nostalgia creeps in as I remember the old office, the smell of newsprint and fresh coffee, the background hum of chattering colleagues and ringing phones. The thought adds another layer to the complex tapestry of my emotions, a dull thread woven through the bright hues of this new life and its wild, undulating surrounding.

There's a crash outside, followed by Cassie's shriek that is pure mischief and not a hint of alarm. I stand and press my forehead to the window, which is cool and wet. On the beach, Cassie has abandoned her shell hunt in favor of chasing gulls, which scatter in outraged formation, their white wings flashing like handkerchiefs. She's been in Kitty Hawk for only two summers, and already she moves through the dunes like a native, as comfortable on shifting sand as she had ever been on concrete. She's had to grow up fast, my Cassie, and even now, barely a teenager, she carries herself with a careful, conscious ease, as if she knows the world is a floor where any board might give way.

Watching her, I remember my own childhood summers on a different stretch of coast. The sweet ache of sunburn, the taste of chlorine and plastic ice pops, the slick, dizzy feeling of being underwater and holding my breath as long as I could stand it.

I turn back to the desk, bracing my elbows on either side of the laptop. My screen is now blank except for the angry cursor, pulsing with expectation. I force myself to type:

> *Cassie runs the beach, all knees and elbows, hair in a dark stream behind her. Rolo bounces from one shell to the next. Cassie collects them as fast as she can in a mesh bag, refusing to settle for the broken or ordinary. She has learned the names of the birds and can mimic their calls with an accuracy that startles the real thing. She is not afraid of the wind or the gray water or the deep, empty sky.*

I stop, read, delete. Too clinical. Too precious. I can't decide if I'm writing for an audience or just trying to convince myself that this exile is a form of progress. Every day I promise to lower my standards, and every day I fail.

The heat kicks on. The cottage's ancient ducts vibrate, then settle as the space fills with warmth. I take off my reading glasses and rest my chin in my hands, eyes drifting to the notebook. Half-formed ideas crowd its margins, jostling for attention: *write about first love, memory as migration, Cassie's spiral shell = recursion.* I remember scribbling these lines on the ferry, at the dentist, waiting for Cassie to finish swimming lessons at the rec center. The process was always messy, but at least there was momentum. Here, every thought splinters on arrival.

A shadow passes the window, and for a second I imagine it's Sara, back from her walk. But it's just a bank of clouds, tumbling out to sea ahead of the next cold front. The horizon goes a little blurry, the sunlight thinning to the consistency of skim milk. I picture Sara out on the wet part of the beach, her gait slow but stubborn, the way she will stop to examine a broken sand dollar or the ribbed exoskeleton of a horseshoe crab. She's promised to bring back cookies from the bakery if she's feeling up to the walk, but I don't expect her for another hour.

It occurs to me that the world beyond this cottage is both larger and more permanent than anything I might manage to articulate. A single feather floats past the window, and the sight of it fills me with a vague and unfamiliar longing.

I reach for the notebook, run my fingers over the spiral binding. The top page is half-filled with yesterday's effort, a paragraph about the sound Cassie's laughter makes when amplified by wind and water, a simile about kites, a metaphor I immediately regret. I tear it out, crumble it, then flatten the sheet again before placing it face-down on the desk. The act is almost ceremonial. Maybe tomorrow it will feel more true.

Outside, the rain catcher starts to rattle, an early warning of an impending storm. I imagine Cassie's feet and Rolo's paws on the porch soon—sandy, probably wet, trailing bits of beach through the tidy kitchen. I imagine her voice, higher than mine, telling me about the gulls or the shells or the strange jellyfish that washed up near the pier. I try to imagine the future, our future, here, or wherever we land next, but the picture blurs at the edges, a watercolor left out in the rain.

I glance again at the laptop, the blank screen reflected in the window. For a moment, I allow myself to believe that every blankness is just a prelude, a surface tension waiting to be broken. I watch as the shadow of a gull passes over the sand, and then another, and then nothing but wind and water.

I exhale, long and slow, and rest my hand atop the notebook, hoping to find the rhythm of the story within.

CHAPTER 2

DIANE

Cassie barrels up the porch steps like a stray bullet, nearly colliding with the screen door. Rolo is right behind her, his paws clattering on the wooden boards in his scramble to catch up. Cassie flings open the door, tracking a comet-tail of sand across the entryway, then stands there on the runner, hands on hips, grinning through a drift of hair and salt. In her right hand she clutches a lopsided bouquet of cockle shells and augers, fragments of moon snail, and even a full sand dollar miraculously intact.

"Mom!" she yells, the word echoing off beadboard and old glass. "Look what we got! Can you believe it?"

I spin in my chair, heart leaping the way it always does when her voice is pitched that high, as if every ordinary day might contain its own small catastrophe. But she's beaming, cheeks chapped, freckles spread across her nose.

I meet her at the threshold, brushing sand from her arm. "Let's see," I say, examining the shells. I let her guide me to the kitchen where the light is better, the faucet ready for rinsing. Cassie dumps her haul onto a folded paper towel and begins arranging them by size and species, her tongue poking out in concentration.

"These are so pretty," I say, holding up the sand dollar between thumb and forefinger. It's veined with hairline cracks, the whole thing impossibly fragile.

"It was just sitting there, like it was waiting for me. Do you think it means something?"

"Maybe. Or maybe it just means you're good at noticing things."

She grins again, but her fingers are already busy, washing grit from a conical shell with exquisite care. "Actually, Rolo saw it first. He's getting good at finding these things."

"Maybe we should change his title from 'house pet' to 'professional seashell detective." I fill a small bowl with tepid water and set it beside Cassie, handing her the soft-bristled toothbrush we keep for just this purpose. She scrubs the shells, narrating the adventure as if I hadn't been watching the entire time—how the gulls led her to the wrack line, how she found a jellyfish shaped like a melted ice cube, how the wind almost stole her hat.

I listen, a little awed by the density of her memory. At thirteen, Cassie has an archivist's sense of detail. Her discoveries are cataloged, cross-referenced, stored in the permanent record of her mind. She can remember the exact pattern of stars from a single night in third grade, the names of every dog she's ever met, the taste of last summer's wild blueberries. The contrast with my own daily amnesia is embarrassing. I can barely remember what I did last Tuesday.

She finishes cleaning the shells and lines them up on the towel. I reach for another, a whelk, and roll it in my palm. The ridges are worn smooth, the colors faded almost to bone. Still, there is something beautiful about its ruined symmetry.

I wonder what Cassie will remember about this season

of our lives. This borrowed house, this stretch of sand, these mornings when the world feels suspended and incomplete. I want her to remember joy, or at least a kind of possibility, but I know memory doesn't work that way. It's less about narrative, more about accidents of weather and smell. Besides, she's at that age where the world expands in boundless dimensions, more than any mother can contain. Soon, her eyes will begin to turn outward, peering at the horizon, yearning for what lies beyond these sun-drenched days. She'll start to carve out her own path, molding the world to fit her dreams and desires.

I swallow back a sudden lump in my throat as I watch her, this beautiful girl of mine who's no longer a child, yet not quite a woman.

She tugs my sleeve. "You okay?"

"Yeah," I say, tucking a loose curl behind her ear. "Just thinking."

"You always say that." She leans against my side, a little damp and shivery but solid. "Is it a grown-up thing?"

I laugh, surprised. "Yes, it's a grown-up thing. But you can do it too."

She considers this, then shrugs and starts stacking the shells in an old peanut butter jar, her favorite storage system. The morning has a momentum I can't quite match. I busy myself wiping down the counter, arranging the stray shells that didn't make the cut, rinsing out the toothbrush. It feels almost ceremonial, this small act of order.

Cassie's voice floats up again, softer this time. "I checked the rain catcher before I came in. It seems to be filling up pretty quickly. The garden will be happy."

"That's good," I reply, glancing out the window where our little vegetable garden basks in the early morning sun. "It'll need plenty of watering as the days get hotter."

She hums in agreement, her attention still on the shells she's meticulously arranging inside the jar. "Good thing Sara taught us how to build one. Now, we won't have to worry about wasting water from the tap."

"Indeed," I say, remembering Sara's lessons on environmental conservation. "Every bit helps, doesn't it?"

She nods, and there's a seriousness in her gaze that makes me feel both proud and a little sad. It's strange to see my own concern for the world reflected in her younger eyes, as if she's taken up the mantle far too early. I want to tell her that there's time, that she doesn't have to shoulder the world's worries just yet, not while there are still shells to discover and stars to count.

"Do you think she's lonely?" she asks, breaking the tempo of our conversation.

"Who, sweetheart?"

"Miss Sara."

"Oh, I don't know... Why do you ask?"

"She's always staring at the water. Even when she's talking to us, her eyes kind of...go past." Cassie demonstrates, gazing out the window with exaggerated vacancy.

"She's lived here a long time," I say. "Maybe it's just habit."

"Or maybe she misses Andrew." Cassie's attention is already drifting back to the jar, where she's arranging her favorites in concentric circles. "The way you miss Dad."

The mention of Kyle steals the rhythm from my heart and throws a shadow over our otherwise bright morning. "I suppose," I finally manage. "Maybe we all miss something."

She nods, serious in the way only a teenager can be, then turns her attention back to her treasures. "I wish we could stay here forever."

The words hit me with the force of a sudden current. I want to say, *Me too*, but I don't want to lie. Cassie has adapted to Kitty Hawk as if she'd always belonged to the place, while I feel like a sand crab awkwardly transplanted, skittering sideways, never quite able to dig in.

A knock on the front door startles us both. Cassie bolts upright, the jar nearly tipping, and races to the entryway, shouting, "Sara! You're back!"

Sara Hastings stands in the doorway, cheeks windburned, hair pulled into a haphazard knot. She carries a paper sack in one hand and a thermos in the other. For a moment, I see the outline of her old self. The sharp, angular elegance of her posture, the mischief still alive in the corner of her smile. Then her left hand trembles, the thermos rattling, and she steadies it against the frame with a practiced, almost invisible motion.

"Delivery for the young scientist," she calls, stepping over the threshold. Cassie nearly tackles her, burying her face in the crook of Sara's elbow. Sara wraps an arm around her, balancing the thermos expertly despite the tremor.

"What'd you bring?" Cassie demands.

"Guess." Sara holds up a paper sack, as if auctioning it.

Cassie inhales. "Cookies?"

"Not just any cookies. Chocolate chip with pecans. And there's a treat in there for Rolo, too." Sara hands over the bag, then glances at me. "And you, Diane, look like you need caffeine."

I smile, trying to ignore the queasy relief that always comes when Sara's symptoms are mild enough to be easily disguised. "You know me too well."

She crosses to the kitchen, her gait steady but measured. As she sets down the thermos and mugs, I notice the subtle pauses in her movement, tiny hesitations where her muscles don't quite fire right, little gaps the untrained eye would miss. She pours tea into the mugs with a steady hand, then grins at Cassie, who's already inhaled two cookies and has crumbs dotting her chin.

"Don't tell your mother I'm corrupting you with sugar before lunch," Sara says, winking.

We settle at the small kitchen table, which Sara wipes compulsively with a damp cloth before sitting. Her hands are more still when occupied. Cassie bounces on her chair, talking through a mouthful of pecan cookie about the morning's adventures and the relative merits of different shell shapes. I watch Sara as she listens, her head tilted, a slight smile softening her features.

I take a sip of the tea. It's black and unsweetened, sharp enough to make my tongue curl. "You went all the way to Manteo for these?" I ask, gesturing at the bag.

Sara shrugs. "The drive's not bad early. More pelicans than people."

Cassie beams. "Pelicans are my favorite."

"They always look like they're thinking deep thoughts," Sara says, and Cassie immediately imitates a pelican, folding her arms and sticking out her chin in dramatic contemplation.

Sara laughs. For a moment, she seems lighter, untethered. But when she reaches for her tea, her fingers spasm, and a few drops slosh onto the table. She dabs at them with a napkin, face impassive.

Cassie doesn't seem to notice, but I do. I notice everything now. The careful way Sara moves, the way she holds her wrists close to her body, the way she swallows twice before drinking. There's an awkwardness to it, but it's also fierce, a refusal to be limited by her condition. She's still herself, even as the perimeter closes in, inch by inch.

Sara looks at me, and for a moment I think she knows exactly what I'm thinking. "You're quiet today."

I shrug, embarrassed by how easily she can read me. "Just frustrated. The novel is going nowhere."

"It's going somewhere," she says. "You just can't see the path yet."

Cassie, still fixated on her cookies, pipes up. "Mom says writing is like searching for shells. Sometimes you have to get your feet wet."

"Wise words. You've got a real philosopher here."

"I keep telling her," I say, and Cassie rolls her eyes.

The three of us linger at the table, the sunlight shifting through the kitchen window, pooling in honey-colored patches on the wooden floor. For a while, the conversation drifts. Cassie discusses her favorite birds and the upcoming science project, while Sara tells us stories about time spent on the lake in her younger years. Each anecdote comes with a punchline, a little wink, as if Sara is gently reminding us that every story, every life, is a kind of performance.

The more time I spend with Sara, the more I realize how much she is teaching me about the art of the present tense. Not the grammatical kind, but the lived kind, the ability to hold a moment without demanding it add up to something later.

At one point, as Cassie disappears to wash her hands and feed Rolo, I catch Sara's gaze lingering on the edge of her mug. She rubs her thumb along a crack in the glaze. I want to ask her if she's scared, or angry, or both. I want to ask if she regrets letting us stay here, if she finds our company a comfort or an annoyance or just a distraction. But I don't.

Instead, I say, "Thanks for this."

Sara's eyes brighten, as if she's been startled out of her reverie. "You're welcome, dear. I'm glad you're here. Both of you." She glances at the kitchen window, where the wind is picking up again. "Life is better when it's shared."

I nod, not trusting myself to answer. My chest is tight, the words I want to say compressed into something small and sharp.

Cassie returns, her hands still wet. Sara pretends not to notice as she reaches for another cookie, and the moment passes.

Later, when Sara gets up to refill the mugs, she sways slightly, just enough for me to notice the edge of her hand gripping the back of the chair. The tremor is a flicker, a warning shot. She waits, then straightens, smiling as if nothing is out of place. Cassie is oblivious, but I feel the gravity of it all the way down.

We finish our tea, the kitchen heavy with the smell of cookies and ocean air. Cassie asks if she and Rolo can go back to the beach, and I say yes, watching as she bolts out the door, peanut butter jar in tow.

Sara and I stand in the empty kitchen, the residue of our conversation settling around us. I reach for the thermos, pouring the last of the tea into my mug. The steam rises, curling into the space between us. For a moment, I imagine us years from now, older, maybe braver, the past less urgent. I imagine Sara still here, still herself, and Cassie grown and strong.

But for now, it's enough to stand in this kitchen, the shells on the counter, the air tinged with salt and sugar, the present holding steady.

CHAPTER 3

DIANE

The porch faces east, which means by late afternoon the sun is behind us, making the air soft and gold. Days like this make me glad we decided to stay in Kitty Hawk, even though we could have easily gone back to Albemarle, left Sara and the coast behind. But here we are, still testing our roots in sandy soil, waiting to see how far down they'll go before the water table or the wind knocks us sideways. My mother would call it sentimental. She would use that word with a little breath, a faint shake of the head, as if it were an affliction particular to me, as if she didn't cry at every dog commercial or the sound of "Blue River."

Sara says I just have an affinity for nostalgia. I haven't told her that's what I'm most afraid of. Not that we'll get stuck, or bored, or that we'll lose ourselves in the repetition of this life. Those are risks, sure. But I'm scared that if I set the past down and turn away, even for a minute, it will dissolve behind me like a sandcastle in a high tide, and I'll never remember how Kyle used to burn dinner at least once a month, or how Cassie once fell off her bike and said, "It was worth it, Mom," because the wind felt faster than her fear. That if I don't keep an inventory at the ready, measuring out the days in teaspoons, bundling the years into small storable containers, there won't be anything left between the leaving and the version of myself that waits at the next threshold.

Cassie is first to claim her seat, knees tucked beneath her chin, the peanut butter jar of shells rattling every time she shifts. She has named the porch chairs. Hers is officially the Queen's Throne, though the only thing regal about it is the way she insists I announce her presence. "Her Majesty requests more lemonade," she declares, and I am both butler and loyal subject, fetching the sweating pitcher from the kitchen while she and Sara negotiate the best vantage point for birdwatching.

Sara settles into the rocker nearest the railing. Her hands are steady now, but I notice the effort it takes, the subtle drag of muscle memory over muscle reality. She's dressed in a faded T-shirt and old jeans, looking as much a part of the cottage as the peeling paint or the creaking steps. The ocean stretches out in a long, undisturbed plane, brown pelicans skimming just above the water line, their shadows flickering over the glassy surface.

I set the lemonade on the little wicker table and pour for everyone, ignoring Cassie's exaggerated sighs of anticipation. My laptop is open but dormant on the porch rail, next to a yellow legal pad weighted down by a conch shell. I keep telling myself that writing out here will feel less like work and more like breathing, but I haven't typed a word since breakfast.

Sara notices. She always notices.

"No luck?" she asks, chin nodding at the computer.

Cassie answers for me, voice muffled by her glass. "Mom's stuck."

Sara's laugh is dry but kind. "Stuck is sometimes just a detour. You'll get there."

I look at the paper, the half-baked sentences and circled metaphors. "I'm starting to think the only thing I can write about is not writing."

"You'd be surprised how many people would pay for that," Sara says, and her smile is lopsided and irresistible.

Cassie laughs, then launches into an animated story about a gull that stole a french fry from her hand at lunch yesterday. I listen with half an ear, my attention caught by the way the light outlines every movement on the porch. Sara's fingers tapping the armrest, Cassie's bare feet swinging over the boards, the invisible boundary where the screen door separates indoors from out.

There is a peace to this moment, but also an undercurrent of urgency. I feel it in the way Sara steers conversation to the here and now.

When Cassie darts down the steps to investigate a ghost crab near the dunes, Sara leans closer. "She's growing up fast, isn't she?"

"Yes, she is," I reply, tracking Cassie as she crouches down in the sand, her sun-streaked hair falling over her face as she giggles at the crab's sideways scuttle. "Sometimes I wish time could stand still just for a bit. Let her be this age, right on the cusp of childhood and growing up, a little longer."

Sara hums beside me, her blue eyes rimmed with the same melancholy that's been coloring my own thoughts. "It's a precious age. Full of wonder, curiosity...innocence. I remember when I was that age, exploring the woods with Jack, thinking the summers would last forever."

Looking out at the shifting dunes, the ceaseless dance of the ocean, I feel that innocence spread out before us. Yet just as these grains of sand slip through our fingers without pause, I realize time is relentless, always moving forward. And the ebb and flow of the ocean reminds me that change is inevitable.

"Perhaps that's the beauty of it," I say. "The fleetingness. It makes these moments even more precious."

"There's wisdom in that, you know," Sara says, the corners of her mouth tugging upward in a wistful smile. "You're right, of course. We must cherish these moments because they are ever so fleeting."

The moment hangs in the air between us, a shared sentiment that wraps around our hearts, as delicate and as substantial as a sea breeze. Her words feel like a nudge, a gentle push to reminder that there's writing to be done.

"I was thinking," says Sara, her gaze shifting to the lighthouse in the distance, "of commissioning a painting. One of that old lighthouse I love so much. Maybe you could even write it into your novel. To give it life beyond the canvas."

The suggestion takes me by surprise, but as I look at the lighthouse, gleaming white in the afternoon sun, a spark of inspiration flickers within me. Yes, I could do that. Slowly, the gears of my mind start to turn again, the rusty edges of writer's block beginning to grind away.

Cassie's excited squeal pulls me back from my reverie. "Mom, look! The crab is dancing!" Her cries of delight pepper the air, bringing with them a renewed sense of joy. I watch as she skips back toward us, holding an imaginary dance partner in her arms. Her face is flushed with excitement, her eyes aglow with a childlike glee that is contagious. I can't help but laugh as she twirls around, her feet leaving small indentations on the sandy ground.

"Miss Sara is thinking of having a painting done of the lighthouse," I tell her as she joins us on the porch. "What do you think of that?"

Cassie's face lights up at the idea. "Really? That would be amazing. I could do it," she adds, her fingers already sketching shapes in the air. "I'll use all the colors, bright ones that sparkle just like it does in the sunlight."

"That sounds wonderful," Sara replies. "But I was thinking it might be nice to have a professional do it. Someone who could really capture the spirit of the place."

"Okay, but I'll make one too. That way we can have two paintings, and they can be friends just like us."

Sara laughs, her eyes mirroring the mirth in Cassie's. "That's a brilliant idea. I can't wait to see your masterpiece."

"Who are you thinking of commissioning?" I ask, turning my attention back to Sara.

She crosses her legs, the faded denim of her jeans catching the dying sunlight. "There's a man in town... someone new to the area who has a studio down by the boardwalk. Apparently, he specializes in seascapes. I thought it might be worth approaching him."

"What's his name?" Cassie asks, as if she is already planning to personally vet him.

Sara chuckles, shaking her head at Cassie's eagerness. "I believe his name is Nathan. Ever heard of him?"

Cassie shakes her head, her brows furrowed in deep thought as if she's trying to mop up a trace of this stranger from the fabric of her memory. "Nope, not ringing any bells."

"Well, that's understandable," Sara responds. "He only moved into town recently."

"Then we should meet him," Cassie says. "Maybe he can teach me how to paint the lighthouse right."

Sara smiles at Cassie's energetic optimism. "Perhaps he will.

And who knows, maybe he could even help your mother with her story." She winks at me. "Artists see the world differently, you know. He might just provide the inspiration she needs."

CHAPTER 4

NATHAN

The first thing I notice about the new studio is the way the light migrates, hour by hour, from the far-right window to the left, dragging the horizon with it. I've spent the morning tracking its path, aligning easels and half-unpacked canvases to catch the blunt yellow spill. The room itself is twice the size I'm used to, complete with echoing floors, scuffed walls, the faint smell of old turpentine and fresh paint.

I set a row of empty jars on the edge of the worktable, rinse them under the sink, and towel them dry. My hands still remember the move from Charlotte, bubble-wrapping my entire life into boxes, labeling them in a handwriting I barely recognize. *Fragile, Bedroom, Studio.* Each word a minor betrayal, a reminder of what I'd left behind and what I still owed to someone who had once considered me indispensable.

The seascape waits for me on the easel, half-finished. I circle it like a suspicious dog, stepping back, squinting, testing my own resolve. The sky is wrong. Too clean, too sterile, a digital blue that doesn't exist for screensavers and airline brochures. I load the brush with cerulean and titanium, drag it horizontally, then vertically, then horizontally again, trying to pull some weight into the upper third of the canvas. I want it to look like it feels outside, which is to say, not beautiful but urgent, the whole world threatening to evaporate in a single gust.

Charlotte is still with me, of course. Not the city itself but the phantom ache of the life I'd assembled there. The high-rise apartment, curated down to the mid-century credenza and the bowl of unripe fruit. The assurance at parties of always being "Nathan, the finance guy, but also an artist, did you know that?" The clockwork precision of waking at six, running before work, the Friday gallery crawls, the occasional weekend trip to the mountains. None of it had survived the rupture.

Now, the only clock is the one inside my head, and it runs on guilt, regret, and the occasional surge of panic. A palette knife falls to the floor, and I crouch to retrieve it, knees popping in protest. On my way up I catch a glimpse of my own reflection in the studio window. My hair is longer than it's ever been, shirt spattered with Prussian blue, mouth set in a line I don't remember learning. I look older, which makes sense, but I also look something else. Less domesticated. I try to decide if I like it.

Back at the easel, I tackle the horizon line. It refuses to sit still, keeps threatening to slide up or down, obliterating the illusion of depth I'm supposed to be creating. I realize that the ocean doesn't have a horizon. It's all horizon, an infinite plane of division. Maybe that's why I came here, to stare at a boundary that never resolves, to stand on the edge of something and not be asked to cross it.

When the paint begins to congeal, I switch to the smaller brushes, detailing the foam and the suggestion of wind in the grass. I lose track of the hour, which is both a relief and a threat. The longer I stay here, the more likely I am to convince myself that this, the act of making and remaking the same strip of coastline, is enough. The jar of turpentine turns a cloudy blue. I swap it for fresh, then set the dirty liquid on the windowsill where it will catch the light and refract into a watery prism.

It's only when I reach for the palette that I see the old watch sitting in the supply bin. The band is leather, or was, once. Now, it's cracked and blotched with oil paint, the face frozen at 7:04. I don't remember putting it there. I pick it up, trace a finger around the bezel, then toss it back in. It lands atop my old business card holder, which now does service as a tube squeezer for the more stubborn paints. I like to think this is progress.

The last time I saw her—Melissa, not the watch—we met in a park halfway between her office and my apartment. It was August, still fever-hot, and we sat on separate benches like defendants at our own trial. She wore her black glasses, the ones that made her look both severe and heartbreakingly young, and talked about "next steps." I nodded, and apologized, and tried to remember when exactly I'd become so replaceable.

Now, I fill the silence with the drag of brushes and the shifting palette of the morning. Outside, the wind threatens rain. The colors on the canvas darken in anticipation. I'm losing the battle for realism but gaining something else, a rough vitality that I don't quite know how to name. I step back and try to see the work as a stranger might. I fail.

The sound of footsteps catches me off guard. The boardwalk is mostly empty. The locals are still bundled up against the spring chill. A moment later, a knock at the door. Not a polite, social knock, but a determined three-count. I consider pretending I'm not here, but curiosity wins out, as it always does. I set my brush down, wipe my hands on my jeans, and move to answer.

On the other side of the gallery door, I find a woman

leaning on the jamb, chin lifted in appraisal. She wears a pea-green windbreaker and old jeans cuffed above hiking boots, her salt-colored hair tucked behind her ears. Up close, you can see the tiny tremor in her left hand, the way she corrects for it by clutching the handle of her oversized tote. She smiles at me, businesslike, suggesting she's already mapped out the next several minutes of our interaction.

"Mr. Garner," she says, as if she's been here dozens of times before. "May I come in?"

"Of course." I motion her inside. "And it's just Nathan." I try to sound casual, but the paint on my forearm and the mess of brushes on every available surface conspire to make me appear more feral than professional.

She steps into the room and introduces herself. "I'm Sara Hastings. I live just down the coast. Where the lighthouse is."

I remember the tall, white-and-black-striped beacon jutting out from the earth just a few miles away. "That's a lovely area, Mrs. Hastings. Very scenic."

"Please, it's Sara," she corrects, turning back to me. "So, do you actually paint here?"

"Yes, sometimes. I prefer being outdoors, but the weather doesn't always cooperate."

She moves past me to the easel and stops. I watch her take in the unfinished seascape, her gaze flitting between the brushwork and the actual shoreline visible through the windows.

"This is incredible." She has the earnestness of a teacher or a nurse, someone whose compliments are a form of labor. "How do you do it? The way the light hits the water, the movement. It's alive."

I shrug. "Mostly it's just staring at the real thing until I go cross-eyed."

She laughs. "There are worse places to go blind." She shifts her weight, favoring one leg, and sets her tote on a stool. "You're new to the area, aren't you?"

"Yes, I am," I reply, scratching the back of my neck, a nervous gesture that has followed me from childhood. "Moved here over the winter. Finally getting settled in."

"Ah, welcome then." Her gaze is now steady on me, and there's a curiosity in her eyes that seems to peer into my very soul. "Do you mind if I take a look around?"

"Be my guest." As she moves about the studio, I find myself watching her as much as she's examining my work. She's not like the patrons I was used to in Charlotte. There's an authenticity about her, a realness that is refreshing. "Sorry for the mess. I'm still in the process of getting everything ready for opening day."

She waves off the apology without turning, her attention caught by a sketch pinned to the cork board. It's a rough study of a girl on a beach with her hair whipping about, her arms spread wide as if to embrace the oncoming wind. Sara pauses before it, her finger hovering mid-air as if tempted to trace the lines. "Who's this?"

"My niece, Jordan. I sketched her last summer when we were at Kiawah Island."

"Ah." She lowers her hand from the sketch and continues perusing. "I suppose you can paint just about anything, can't you? Figures, landscapes, seascapes."

I shrug, a modesty reflex. "I guess. I paint whatever catches my interest, or whatever I'm commissioned to paint."

Without turning away from the sketches and canvases leaning against the wall, Sara asks, "Have you ever painted a lighthouse?"

"I can't say that I have," I reply, upturned corners of my mouth betraying curiosity. "Why do you ask?"

Sara turns back to me, her eyes gleaming with an idea. "Our lighthouse," she starts, "has been standing tall for over a century. It's an emblem of this town. Moreover, it holds a lot of personal significance for me. Believe it or not, I've lived in its shadow for more than half my life, and each day, it gives me something new to admire. I think it would make a wonderful subject for a painting. You have an incredible talent, Nathan, capturing moments and emotions in your work. I'd love to see what you can do with our lighthouse."

I'm stunned by her proposal. Remembering my manners, I manage to stammer out, "I'd be honored."

"Wonderful," she exclaims, clapping her hands together in anticipation. "When can you start?"

I scratch my chin thoughtfully, casting a final glance at the gallery still in disarray. There is a sense of urgency in her request, as if time is of the essence. "Soon. I just need to finish getting the gallery ready for next week's grand opening. But after that, I could start right away."

"Of course. Take your time. I wouldn't want to interfere with your big day. When you're ready, why don't you come by for tea? I'll give you a tour of the property and you can get a feel of the place." She hands me a card with her address and phone number written in neat, elegant script.

"Sounds good. I'll give you a call in a few days."

"Excellent." She gathers her tote bag from the stool, adjusting the strap on her shoulder. "I'm looking forward to it."

As she starts toward the door, I find myself watching her go. There's a grace to her movements, a steady undercurrent that speaks of a life deeply interwoven with this place. "Sara,"

I call out, prompting her to turn. "Thank you. For dropping by and for sharing the idea. It's... well, it's been a while since someone appreciated my work like this."

"It's my pleasure. And thank you for accepting. You don't know how much this means to me."

CHAPTER 5

NATHAN

After spending the weekend unpacking and getting the gallery ready for opening day, I call Sara first thing Monday morning. I tell her I'm ready to visit whenever she is. Her voice sounds airy, her mood light as she accepts the invitation.

"Can you be at my place by ten? Bring your sketchbook. We'll do a tour, maybe get some ideas in your head."

I try not to sound overeager. "Of course. Ten is perfect. Just let me take care of a couple of things here, and I'll be on my way."

The drive is shorter than I think. Sara's house sits at the far edge of the island, a quarter-mile of sand path winding through beach plum and thistle, the air glittering with the salt haze of evaporating surf. I follow the directions she texted, right at the wind-scoured mailbox, left at the dilapidated fence with its collection of seashells and driftwood. The house is visible from a distance, a hulking block of green and gray against the dun-colored hill, the lighthouse looming in the background like a silent sentinel.

Sara is waiting for me on the porch as I pull to a stop, a mug balanced on her knee. She's swapped the windbreaker for a cashmere sweater and is wearing a pair of faded jeans. She waves me up, then disappears inside, leaving the door ajar.

"I brought muffins," I say, following her into the foyer.

"Bribery. Smart man." She sets the basket of muffins down on the side table, then says, "Let's give you the grand tour."

The house is a tangle of cozy rooms and vaulted hallways, each wall packed with paintings, sketches, and multicolored mosaics. A library is crammed with volumes of literature, from Shakespeare to Huxley. There's even an entire section dedicated to art history.

"Wow. So, you're an enthusiast of both art and literature," I say, taking in the enormity of her collection. "Quite impressive."

"Actually, my late husband was the art aficionado. I, on the other hand, am the book worm."

"I see. Well, you know what they say—'art and literature often go hand in hand.'"

"Indeed they do."

Sara moves with a practiced efficiency, sliding between the narrow spaces like she's memorized the obstacles.

"This is the main house. My husband and I designed this together. This part"—she gestures around—"this is where we lived and loved. Our little sanctuary."

She leads me past the kitchen to the sunroom, where the entire eastern wall is glass. Beyond it, you can see the dunes tumbling down toward the water, the lighthouse steady on its outcrop.

"There it is," she says, setting her mug on the windowsill and gesturing to the lighthouse.

"It's stunning."

She leans against the counter, studying me. "There's a tenant in the guest cottage," she says. "Her name's Diane. Writer, former journalist. Keeps to herself."

I nod, not sure what response is appropriate.

"She's nice...and quiet. She's working on a novel, something about second chances and reinvention. You'll probably cross paths if you're here long enough." Sara says it with a deliberate casualness, like she's laying down a chess piece and then glancing away.

I follow her to the back porch, where the world opens to a ragged sweep of wind-torn grasses, the blue-white concussion of the ocean, the sky already bruising with the promise of afternoon storms. Sara points toward the lighthouse.

"Want to walk up? Or do you want to sketch from here?"

I hesitate, tempted by the idea of staying in her sunroom and just watching the water mutate by the minute. But the horizon tugs at me. "Let's go see it up close."

The path to the lighthouse is not a path so much as a succession of trampled grass and soft sand, interrupted by splintered driftwood, and the occasional skeletal remains of a crab. The wind batters us from the south, smelling of salt and tar. Sara walks slower than before, careful and deliberate, but never complains.

"You're probably wondering about the gait," she says. "It's called chorea. Latin for 'dance.' My brain thinks I should be dancing all the time, so my legs don't always listen. It's supposed to get worse, but the experts keep revising that timeline, so I just live in the here and now."

I feel a prickle of embarrassment for noticing, but she waves it away. "If I didn't mention it, you'd be staring anyway. This way, you can just watch the lighthouse instead."

Passing by the cottage, I catch a glimpse of a woman on one of the Adirondack chairs, her fingers dancing over the keys of a laptop. Diane, I presume. She doesn't look up from her work, completely engrossed in her own world.

We continue our walk in silence. The sand becomes finer as we approach the lighthouse, each step sinking into the grainy surface. We reach the base, a squat cylinder striped in black and white. Sara touches the worn brick, then tilts her head up to the windows at the top. "My husband used to bring me here on storm days. Said the building was luckier than most. It never even lost a shingle." She looks over at me, her eyes sharp and amused. "He was wrong, by the way. It lost plenty. But sometimes it's better to let the legend win."

I get out my sketchbook, trying to keep my lines loose, fluid. The light keeps shifting, cloud and sun dueling in the high air. Sara watches, occasionally pointing out the way the doorframe tilts, the green stain where moss creeps up the foundation. She tells stories as I draw, about the volunteer who once camped here for a week during hurricane season, about the teenagers who spray-painted a proposal on the seaward face.

We circle the building, then start the slow walk back. The conversation slides from local gossip to the history of the island, to Sara's own biography in fragments. She tells me about her time in law school, her years in Tennessee, and her marriage to Andrew. She edits her life as she narrates, making the worst parts sound either funnier or less important.

We pass the cottage once more. Diane has abandoned her laptop and is now standing on the porch with a raised hand in greeting.

"Sara," she calls out, her tone warm and familiar.

Sara answers back with an equally friendly wave. "Diane! Meet my new friend."

Diane's eyes land on me, and there's a slight pause as she takes me in. As she approaches, I notice the way she appraises me, with the clinical detachment of someone who's probably spent too much time interviewing strangers.

"Diane, this is Nathan Garner," Sara says. "He's the one I was telling you about... The artist. He's agreed to paint the lighthouse for me."

"Oh, how lovely. Well, it's nice to meet you, Nathan. I'm sure Sara's been regaling you with tales of the island and its interesting inhabitants."

"Interesting is certainly one way to describe it," I reply.

"Diane is from Charlotte too," says Sara.

"Really?"

"Albemarle, actually," Diane says. "But close enough."

I blink at the coincidence. "Well, I guess what they say about small worlds is true."

"Indeed," Sara says, her eyes crinkling in amusement. "Well, Nathan, shall we continue?"

The three of us part ways, Diane returning to her porch, while Sara and I continue back toward the main house.

"Sara, this place... It's incredible. I can't wait to get started on some sketches."

As we ascend the hill, Sara gives me a wily smile. "She's quite a sight, isn't she?"

The way she says it, I'm not sure if she means the lighthouse or Diane.

We settle at the porch table, and Sara pours tea into mismatched mugs. The conversation stays easy, as if we've known each other longer than a few hours. She asks about my family, my last job, my earliest memory of the ocean. She doesn't judge, just catalogues, storing each answer for later. Occasionally, her gaze drifts to the guest cottage, as if tracking the passage of its elusive inhabitant.

I ask her about Diane, and her expression turns thoughtful. "Diane... She's a good woman, still finding her footing after some personal setbacks. But she's resilient. She's been here a couple of years now. I invited her here to write my memoir, then asked her to stay." Sara sips her tea, glancing toward the cottage. "She and her daughter. And I'm glad I did. I think they've found a certain peace here on the island."

"Daughter?"

"Yes, Cassie. She's thirteen. Bright as a button and just as sharp. She has dreams of being a scientist one day."

"That's a wonderful dream. My mother was a scientist. A biologist, actually. She used to take me to the ocean and explain all about the mysteries beneath the surface."

"Is that why you chose Kitty Hawk for your gallery? Because of your mother?"

"In a way, yes. The ocean was always her place of peace. It's where she found her inspiration, her joy. I guess I wanted to feel close to her somehow. Even though she's gone, I wanted a piece of that peace, that joy."

We finish our tea, and Sara stands, gathering the empty cups. "You should come back tomorrow. If the weather holds, you'll want to catch the light just after sunrise. It's when the whole island glows, even the ugly parts."

She walks me down the porch, then pauses. "Diane's single, by the way." It catches me off guard, and I'm not sure how to respond. But before I can, she continues. "In case you were wondering."

With that, she turns back to the house and leaves me standing there, watching the swirl of sea and sky, the lighthouse steadfast in the distance. The words "Diane's single" echo in my mind, mingled with the crash of waves and the distant call of a seagull. I'm not sure why Sara thought it necessary to share that information, but it adds another layer of intrigue to my day.

CHAPTER 6

NATHAN

Morning at the lighthouse is a private kind of quiet, filtered through mist and the hush of water on sand, the world subtracts itself down to just what matters. I claim the weathered bench at the base of the tower, a slab of sun-worn driftwood perched above the dune grass, the perfect spot for studying how the old lightkeeper's house leans into the wind.

I arrange a hard-bound sketchbook half-filled with failures, two drawing pencils, though I only ever use the finer one, charcoal sticks in a recycled jam jar, and a kneaded eraser shaped into a rabbit's ear from nervous fidgeting, and prepare to work.

The first order of business is always the horizon. You'd think it would be easy, a straight line where the sky surrenders to the ocean, but out here it buckles and flexes, refusing to stay true for more than a minute. Today it's blurred by the marine layer, a gauze of pale blue, and the top of the lighthouse hovers above it like something airlifted from a different reality. I make the first mark, graphite on toothy paper, and the rest of the world recedes.

Ten minutes in, I'm deep in the muscle memory of shading when I sense movement at the edge of my vision. Not the sly, territorial shuffle of gulls, but something shorter, wilder. There is a faint metallic rattle, then a sharp sneeze.

I don't have to look up to know it isn't Sara. It's the unmistakable noise of a child, and she's not alone. A chocolate colored Maltipoo trails behind her, his tail wagging enthusiastically and his nose buried in the sand. The girl sneaks up beside the bench, her mesh bag of shells slung like a satchel over her shoulder. Her sneakers are soaked through, a muddy camouflage to the white laces, and her hair, almost the same dark as the damp sand, sticks in wind-blown clumps to her forehead.

"Hi," she says. Not a question, not even a greeting, just a flat announcement of presence.

I tip my chin in acknowledgment. "Morning. Who's this?"

"This is Rolo," she replies, beaming down at the little dog who has now taken to sniffing my art supplies. The girl glances at my sketchbook, then at the lighthouse and back again, rapid as a shorebird. "Are you drawing that?"

I flip the page so she can see the emerging contour of the tower, the rough scaffolding of where the lantern room will go. She makes a sound somewhere between a gasp and a snort. "That's...really good. You got the little chips in the bricks and everything."

"Those are called spalls. The lighthouse is covered in them."

She leans in until her hair brushes the edge of my page, peering at the shading like she's looking for a magic trick in the paper grain. "Did you bring paint, too?"

"Not today. I like to start with pencils."

She considers this, then nods with a gravity far too old for her years. "I like pencils better, too. You can erase if you mess up."

"That's the hope," I say and erase a smudge for effect.

She sets her shell bag at my feet, the mesh sagging with weight. "I'm Cassie," she says, extending a hand with such solemnity that I actually wipe my palm on my jeans before shaking it.

"Nathan," I say, and it feels unexpectedly important.

Cassie swings her legs over the bench and parks herself at my elbow, picking at the frayed seam of her jacket. The dog settles in beside her, curling up into a ball, his head resting on her worn sneakers. "I bet you could draw shells, too. I found a really weird one this morning."

She digs into the bag, her whole arm vanishing as she reaches for the best specimen. When it emerges, she's holding what looks like a perfect miniature conch, spiral intact, the aperture lined with a faint lavender.

I take it, turning it over in my hand. "Scotch bonnet. State shell of North Carolina."

Her eyes go wide. "I'm surprised you know that. Most people don't."

"Spent a lot of time looking at the ground," I say, though that's only half the truth. I did my homework, sure, but part of me is just eager to impress.

"Mom always says I should learn more names for things. She thinks if I know what something's called, I won't break it."

"That's smart," I say and set the shell carefully on the bench beside us. "Want to see how to draw it?"

She nods, tucking both knees up to her chin. I open the sketchbook to a fresh page and, with a few deliberate lines, capture the long axis first, then the tight, mathematical spiral. Cassie leans in, absorbing every gesture, her own fingers twitching with the urge to try. I hand her the other pencil without saying a word.

She takes it, hesitates, then mimics my movement. Her eyes narrow in concentration, tongue peeks out from the corner of her mouth. Her lines are hesitant at first, but then she goes over them, dark and decisive, filling in the shadow where the spiral tightens.

"Nice."

She beams, then starts flipping through the remaining shells, setting aside a tiger-striped clam, then a shark tooth, then a broken piece of whelk. Each time, she asks the name, and I do my best to provide it. It becomes a kind of game, one I didn't know I wanted to play.

"You're not like other artists. You talk to people."

I snort. "Sometimes I even listen."

She cocks her head. "You don't have to. I just like being around people who make things."

I sketch another horizon, this one just for her, letting the pencil skate along the paper. Cassie reaches down to stroke behind Rolo's ears, her eyes never leaving my sketch.

"Do you ever mess up?"

"All the time. Most of my drawings end up in the trash."

"Do you ever try again?"

"Sometimes. Sometimes it's better to just start something new."

She takes this in, mulling it over the way only a kid can—seriously, like it might change the trajectory of her day. "I mess up a lot. Mom says it's called 'learning opportunities.'"

"That's a nicer way of saying it. But she's right."

Cassie watches a pair of gulls bicker over a fish scrap at the waterline, then turns back, her mouth set in a line of fierce determination. "Will you teach me how to do shading like you did with the lighthouse?"

"Sure. It's all about pressure. The harder you push, the darker it gets. Watch." I shade a small patch beside her shell, then hand the pencil back. "You try."

She does, and the effect is instant: the lightest touch, then a bolder swipe, the gray deepening. "Cool."

From somewhere above, the wind shifts, and the lighthouse's shadow creeps closer, darkening the sand at our feet. Cassie stares at the tower, then at me. "Do you ever get lonely out here?"

I pause, caught off guard. "Not really. There's always something to look at."

"I think I'd get lonely. But maybe it's different if you're drawing."

I think of the hours I've lost in sketchbooks, the way time collapses when I'm chasing a line. I almost say yes, it is different, but Cassie is already flipping to a new page in the sketchbook, eager to start again.

As the sun climbs higher, the mist begins to lift, revealing the sharp edge of the sea and the wind-ruffled line of the dunes. Cassie sketches in silence, utterly focused, her brow furrowed in concentration. I watch her, then turn back to the lighthouse and pick up where I left off, adding crosshatch to the bricks.

We work side by side for a long time, neither of us in a hurry to finish. The bench creaks under the shifting weight, the graphite shavings dust the page like ash, and the only sound is the low, contented hum Cassie makes when she's happy. It's a quiet I haven't known in years, and I'm surprised by how much I want it to last.

By the time the tower's shadow falls across the dune grass,

Cassie's hands are streaked with pencil, and her shell drawing has evolved into a menagerie—every specimen labeled in her spiky, determined print. She signs her name at the bottom, then looks up at me, her eyes bright and wild.

"Can I keep this?"

"It's yours," I say, tearing off the paper and handing it to her. "You earned it."

She rolls the sketch and tucks it into her jacket pocket, careful not to crease it. Then, with a final, triumphant grin, she hops down from the bench, landing with both feet in the soft sand.

"See you later, Nathan," she says, and she and the dog sprint off toward the low fence that marks the lighthouse property. I watch them go, the mesh bag swinging like a lantern in her hand.

For a while I just sit, the echo of her presence lingering like sea mist. I pack up my supplies, brush the last flecks of graphite from my fingertips, and stare out at the horizon. It's perfect and unbroken when I hear the crunch of footsteps on gravel behind me, crisp and purposeful. Cassie has only just vanished into the haze, but I know immediately it's not her retracing her steps. This tread is too even, too adult, careful not to dislodge more than is necessary from the earth.

I look up. There, picking her way along the path toward me, is Diane. She has on olive pants and a faded T-shirt with the sleeves rolled up. Her hair is down today but held back by sunglasses perched atop her head.

"Cassie!" she calls, her voice bouncing off the lighthouse stones. "Rolo!"

I wonder how long she's been watching, if she saw the impromptu sketch lesson, the gravity that held her daughter to the bench.

I clear my throat and offer a small wave. "They're down by the fence."

Diane relaxes almost imperceptibly, the tension in her shoulders evaporating as she steps off the rock and onto the packed sand. "Thank you," she says. "Cassie tends to...adopt people."

"She's welcome to," I say. "She's got a sharp eye."

Diane squints at the sketchbook balanced on my knee. "Can I see?"

I hesitate. Showing unfinished work is always a risk, but something about her curiosity feels different from the hungry attention I'm used to at gallery shows. I hold out the book, open to the current page.

She takes it delicately, turning it so the spiral faces her. For a second she studies the lines, tracing the spiral of the shell Cassie insisted on, then the harder angles of the lantern room. "You caught the shadow just right," she says, running a fingertip over the dark crescent at the tower's base. "It's not what I expected."

"Most people want the postcard version," I say, self-conscious. "Blue sky, stark black and white stripes. This morning, I just liked the way the mist made everything look softer."

Diane's gaze slides up from the sketchbook to me. Her eyes are the color of driftwood, storm-tossed and a little wary. "Sara's right. You see things differently."

I shrug. "It's a hazard of the profession."

She smiles, just for a heartbeat, then sits beside me on the bench, folding her hands in her lap. "Did Cassie tell you she fancies herself as an artist too?"

"I got the feeling," I say, recalling the intensity with which she applied pencil to paper. "She's already better than she thinks... Better than I was at her age."

"She's obsessed. Half the time, I can't get her to do her homework because she's sketching. She even doodles on her math worksheets. I keep telling her that even great artists have to know their math and history, too."

I chuckle. "Yes, they do. But it's also important to nurture that spark. Who knows? Maybe you have a future Picasso or O'Keeffe on your hands. She's got the right patience for it."

The compliment seems to land somewhere between pride and embarrassment. Diane stares out at the sea, her foot tapping a soft rhythm on the sand. "We moved here so she could have more of this. The wild, the space." She pauses, as if considering whether to say more. "It hasn't been easy, but I think it's worth it."

"Definitely worth it," I agree.

She turns to me, tucking a strand of hair behind her ear. "So, how long have you been in Kitty Hawk?"

I think about a real answer, not the practiced, tourist-board version. "Not long. I left Charlotte after I quit my job. I needed to see something else, somewhere different. This town... It felt like the right choice."

She nods, as if this makes perfect sense. "Are you planning to stay?"

"Maybe." I don't say that every day feels temporary, that I still haven't unpacked half my life. "I'm opening a small gallery at the boardwalk next week. I figured I'd try selling my work, instead of just keeping it in storage. If it does well, who knows?"

Diane smiles, bright and genuine. "That sounds wonderful. Cassie will be thrilled. She adores art galleries...and the boardwalk. She'll probably want to spend all her time there now."

"Your daughter is always welcome," I say, my words sounding more sincere than I expected. "You too, if you like. I'd be honored if you'd come. Both of you."

A soft blush creeps into her cheeks. "You don't know what you're getting yourself into with Cassie. She might just take over the place."

I laugh, thinking of Cassie's enthusiasm that morning. "I think I can handle it. Would be nice to have a friendly face or two in the crowd."

Diane studies me, as if she's trying to see the prospect of that future. Then, she gives a small nod. "All right. We might just take you up on that."

From the slope below, Cassie's voice rises in a triumphant whoop. She's found another shell. This one, judging by the size and color, is a horse conch almost as long as her hand. She sprints up the sand toward us, waving it like a trophy.

"Look!" she shouts, then, "Mom, I found a rare one. Nathan, what's it called?"

I take the shell from her outstretched hand, and examine the heavy, orange coil. "Horse conch," I say. "A good one."

Rolo barks in agreement, leaping around Cassie in a circle of excitement.

Cassie beams, then jumps onto the bench between us, her sand-caked knees bumping mine. "Want to see my drawing?" she asks Diane, then unfurls the drawing.

Diane's pride is transparent. "It's beautiful, Cass. I'm going to put it on the fridge when we get home."

Cassie grins up at me. "Told you Mom would like it."

We sit like that for a while, the three of us in the lighthouse's shadow, the breeze rifling the pages of the sketchbook. Diane rests her hand on Cassie's shoulder, steadying her as she leans forward to peer at the horizon.

After a few minutes, Diane stands, brushing sand from the back of her pants. Her expression is softer now, less guarded. "Well, it was nice seeing you again, Nathan, and don't worry, I'll make sure Cassie doesn't monopolize all your time while you're out here."

"Not at all. Her company was a pleasure."

With a soft nod of acknowledgement, Diane turns to leave but not before reaching down to ruffle Cassie's hair affectionately. They walk off, side by side, with Rolo bounding ahead, their shadows meandering over the dunes.

I watch them disappear, their voices drifting back on the breeze—a soft laugh from Diane, the high pitch of Cassie's excited chatter. I sit there for a while, listening to the distant clack of shells on the kitchen table, the soft closing of a door, the heartbeat-pulse of the tide.

And for the first time since I arrived, I'm aware of a sense of belonging, a quiet vibration deep within me, a feeling that maybe, just maybe, I've found a place I want to hold onto.

CHAPTER 7

DIANE

There's a ritual to entering a new space that I still haven't mastered. I hover just inside the gallery's front door, feigning a casual interest in the guest book while Cassie tugs at the sleeve of my cardigan.

"Mom, look!" Cassie's voice is high and bright, slicing clean through the bubble of laughter in the vestibule. "There's actual shrimp cocktail. With the tails and everything."

I nudge her gently away from the hors d'oeuvres, my heart already drumming. "Let's keep our hands to ourselves for a bit, okay?"

She bobs her head, but she's already forgotten the rule, because the gallery is a field of color, and she's a pointer dog, nose leading her from one canvas to the next. I follow, running my fingers over the soft braided strap of my purse, a nervous habit as ingrained as the pinched set of my mouth. A line of strangers filters past us—a man with sun-leathered cheeks, a trio of college girls with hair in matching buns, an elderly woman in a nautical blazer and pearls. They all look like they belong, which is to say, they all look like they've read the unwritten manual on how to behave at coastal art openings.

Cassie presses her face close to the first painting, her nose almost touching the brushstrokes. "Whoa," she says.

It's a seascape, all raw energy, the sky a slurry of dark blues and the sea below it heaving, almost angry. I recognize the view, but there's something about the light, the way it creeps through the bank of clouds and slicks the surface of the waves, that makes the moment feel fragile, as if the whole scene might blink out if you looked away for too long.

I step up beside her. "Do you like it?"

"I do. It looks like it's moving but also like it's standing still. Does that make sense?"

"Yes." It's exactly right, and I feel both envy and admiration for the man who can make time collapse on a canvas.

"Mom, are you nervous?"

I force a little laugh, try to sound as if I'm only nervous the way anyone would be at a gallery opening hosted by the man whose face you haven't stopped picturing since you met him. "It's just...crowded," I say. "A lot of new people."

She grins, exposing the gap where last week's molar used to live. "You mean you're nervous about Nathan."

I fix her with my sternest teacher glare, but she's impervious. "Cassandra Jade," I whisper, "I will revoke your cookie privileges for the week."

She snickers and runs off, ponytail flying. I watch her go, then survey the room. The gallery is longer than it is wide, the floor a tongue of scuffed pine running from the front windows to a rear alcove where the lights are lower and the paintings more intimate. The walls are a muted driftwood gray, the trim blanched white as sun-bleached bone. Hung at eye level, each canvas seems to pulse with a life that the crowd only amplifies. Wet sand reflecting the violent gold of sunrise, the muscular weight of storm surf, dune grass whipped sideways by wind that you can almost feel, if you squint.

I move slowly, reading the tiny placards with their polite bios and the titles: *Return Current, Suspension, Liminal Hour.* I'm not sure if I love or hate the way artists name things, but I can't deny the prickle of awe that comes from seeing so many versions of the world gathered in one place. Nathan's world, anyway.

He's easy to spot, even from across the room. His hair is a little longer than I remember, and he's shaved, which gives his jaw a blunt, unfamiliar geometry. He's posted up near the refreshments table, talking with a tall man in a dark-green Barbour jacket. He laughs at something, full-throated and reckless, the sound of someone who's still surprised to find joy in public. Cassie is already orbiting him, making deliberate figure-eights between the food and the tall man's elbow, as if staking a claim.

I linger near the periphery, smoothing my dress over my hips, then immediately wish I hadn't. It's a nervous tell, and Cassie's right; I'm not fooling anyone. I focus on my shoes, the left one scuffed from a careless step on the boardwalk, and try to tamp down the urge to bolt. It would be so easy to invent an emergency—an allergy attack, a forgotten medicine—but there's no one here to believe the lie, and Cassie would see right through it.

"Are you going to say hi, or are you just going to stare at him all night?" Cassie's voice is a whisper at my side. She's doubled back, arms crossed in a parody of adult exasperation.

"I don't stare," I reply, smoothing the dress again. "I observe."

She rolls her eyes, which I'm certain she's been practicing in the mirror. "He keeps staring at you, Mom."

"No, he doesn't," I say, and then immediately, "He does?"

She gives me a smug, knowing grin and hooks her arm through mine. "Come on. You said you wanted to support the arts." Before I can resist, she's pulling me into the glow of track lighting and toward the table where Nathan is laughing, red-cheeked, a glass of something pale and sparkling in his hand.

He spots me, and his smile softens at the edges. "Diane," he says, and my name sounds right, as if he's dusted it off and set it gently in front of me.

"Nathan," I reply, matching his nod, hoping my voice doesn't betray the tremor under my sternum.

He sets down his glass and takes a step forward. "I'm glad you could make it. And you, too, Cassie," he adds, with the easy warmth of someone who actually remembers children are people.

Cassie offers a regal wave, then zeros in on the food, transferring three cheese cubes and two shrimp to a napkin with surgical precision.

Nathan gestures toward the nearest canvas, a muted study in gray and white. "What do you think?" he asks, and I realize he's genuinely interested, not just filling space.

I step closer, tilting my head. "I think..." The words snag, and for a second I can't remember how to talk about art, only how to drown in it. "I think you made the wind visible."

He laughs, softer this time, not performative, just pleased. "That's a new one. Usually people tell me it's depressing."

"It's not depressing," Cassie says, through a mouthful of cheddar. "It's dramatic. Like a hurricane, but not scary."

Nathan looks at her, then at me, and suddenly I'm aware of the width of my shoulders and the possibility that my lipstick has migrated to my teeth. "You've got a sharp one," he says, tipping an imaginary hat.

"She takes after her father," I joke, and then immediately regret it.

Nathan doesn't seem to notice. "I'm going to grab some more wine," he says. "Would you like a glass?"

"Yes, please," I reply, and this time my voice is steadier. Cassie shoots me a look—approval or amusement, I can't tell—and vanishes, presumably to find more food.

I trail Nathan to the bar, watching the way he moves, deliberate but never slow, as if every muscle in his body is attuned to the idea of being useful. He pours two glasses, hands one to me. Our fingers brush for a fraction of a second, but it's enough to send a jolt up my arm, so sharp I almost drop the glass. I try to recover with a joke. "I always thought artists were supposed to be tortured and reclusive. But you seem remarkably well-adjusted."

He cocks his head. "I save my brooding for after hours. It keeps the paint from drying out." He lifts his glass in a gentle salute.

"To brooding," I say, tapping the rim against his. The wine is cheap, probably from the grocery store, but the sweetness of it is a shock after the briny air of the gallery.

Nathan leans against the wall, arms folded. "So, how's the writing coming? Sara said you were working on a novel. Very ambitious."

I wince, though I know he's not being cruel. "Not as ambitious as you'd think." I swirl the wine in my glass to give my hands something to do. "It's more an exercise in futility at this point. I get a couple paragraphs down, and then the tide pulls them out again. Honestly, I thought I'd be further along by now."

"You'll find it," he says, matter-of-fact. "Sometimes you just have to stand in the water and let it knock you over a few times."

"Is that an Outer Banks proverb?"

He shrugs. "It is now."

I laugh, and the tension dissolves a little. "You know, if you're going to plagiarize regional wisdom, you should at least charge for it."

"I'll add it to your tab."

From across the gallery, Cassie is deep in conversation with the woman in pearls, who's listening with a patience I haven't seen since my mother used to read me the Sunday comics. I take a sip of wine, letting the silence linger.

Nathan clears his throat. "You know, I was nervous about this. The opening, I mean. I haven't done the public thing in a while."

"Could have fooled me. You seem in your element."

"That's a lie. I kept waiting for someone to throw a drink or ask for their money back."

"Maybe after the second glass," I say, and he grins, wide and delighted.

We drift along the wall, stopping at another painting, a study of the sound at low tide, herons balanced in the shallows. The brushstrokes are urgent, almost desperate, and I find myself leaning in, trying to see how the illusion holds together.

"Do you miss Charlotte?" I ask, surprising myself.

"Not the city, really. More the routines, I suppose. And the people—friends, family, neighbors. It's the familiar faces you get used to seeing every day that you miss most when they're gone."

I glance at him, curiosity tugging at me. I want to ask about his past, about what had driven him away from the familiarity of home to this secluded stretch of coast. But the question feels too intimate, too invasive for our casual conversation, so I let it hang in the air between us.

Someone else approaches, a neighbor or a casual friend, and Nathan excuses himself with a gentle touch to my elbow—a small, protective gesture that lingers long after he's gone.

CHAPTER 8

DIANE

Cassie is a phantom limb. I still sense her presence even when she's yards away, cataloging every painting as if she's running a museum audit. There's a knot of nervous energy inside me, the habitual worry that she'll break something or say the wrong thing, but I watch her for a minute and realize she's perfect, exactly herself, and the crowd has accepted her as ambient decor: a local kid with sand-scabbed knees and opinions about art.

Nathan returns with another round of wine. He tilts his glass in salute before settling beside me on a high-top table. The din of conversation is less intense here, and I let myself believe I could get used to this—the murmured speculation about technique, the gentle heat of alcohol, the awareness of someone else's nearness.

"Your daughter's a force of nature," Nathan says, voice low enough that it's meant only for me.

"Sorry, she gets that from me," I reply, then laugh.

"Don't apologize. I think she's doing a great job." Nathan lifts his chin, gesturing toward Cassie as she quizzes a gray-haired woman about the provenance of a particular cloud formation. "She's got the crowd eating out of her hand."

I try to hide my pride, but I know I fail. “She’s the only extrovert in our gene pool. It’s both terrifying and impressive.”

The conversation slides easily, surprisingly so, considering how little we know about each other. Nathan asks how we like the cottage, and whether Cassie enjoys the local school. I tell him about her growing shell collection and how she’s managed to charm half her class into trading fossils with her. He seems genuinely interested, occasionally weighing in with a question or comment, but mostly letting me steer.

The evening continues in much the same way, a steady ebb and flow of people and conversation. Every so often Nathan glances at Cassie, a softness in his gaze that speaks more than any words he could say. It’s clear that he’s taken a liking to her, and I can’t help but feel grateful for this unexpected new ally. The blend of curiosity, respect, and genuine fondness that he shows Cassie strikes a chord within me. I find my gaze lingering on him more often than I’d anticipated, drawn to the way he carries himself with an easy grace.

Suddenly, I am acutely aware that he is looking at me, and when I meet his eyes, they hold steady for a breath longer than expected. There’s a softness there, but also a sharpness, like the edge of a wave before it breaks.

He shifts, sudden as a sandpiper. “Can I ask you something?”

“Of course.” I brace myself, though for what I’m not sure.

“Why did you move here?” He doesn’t ask it like a challenge, more like a fellow exile, curious about what wind blew me off course.

I swirl the wine, watching the legs crawl down the inside of the glass. “Honestly?” I shrug. “I came here to interview Sara. I had every intention of returning to Albemarle, but then... She asked us to stay, and so we did. That was two years ago. Now, I find myself unable to imagine a different life. This town..." I take in the crowd, the familiar faces and the comfort they bring. "This town has a way of crawling under your skin and staying there."

"And what about this book you're writing—Sara mentioned something about second chances?"

"Yeah," I say, tasting the admission like salt on my tongue. "It's about reinvention, I guess. About a woman trying to rewrite her story." I expect a smirk, or at the very least a deflection, but Nathan listens, as though I'm not boring him or risking something by sharing. The unearned attention destabilizes me. I start to fidget, the wine glass an awkward appendage.

"Maybe that's why people come to places like this. Not to disappear, but to see what happens if they let themselves be different." His words are gentle, like he's handling something delicate. Me, maybe.

"I think you're onto something."

When he smiles, a dimple appears at the edge of his mouth. I want to touch it, to see if it's as deep as it looks.

"You mentioned the book progressing slowly. Is it safe to say you're suffering from writer's block?"

"That's the polite term." I take a sip, then lower my voice. "It's more like a drought. Words used to flow so easily. Now they hide from me."

He nods, as if this is the most logical thing in the world. "It happens in art, too," he says. "Sometimes I stare at a blank canvas for days, and it's like trying to will a boat to shore by sheer staring."

"Does it help?"

"Not even a little." He laughs, then sobers. "But sometimes

if you just stand there long enough, the tide comes in anyway."

I catch myself tracing the rim of my glass, a nervous tic that betrays my interest. "Were you always a painter?" I ask, eager to shift focus.

He shakes his head. "I started as a numbers guy. Accounting, of all things. But I liked the patterns more than the people. Painting was a hobby, until it wasn't."

"I love that." There's something reckless about quitting certainty for uncertainty, and I respect anyone who can manage it.

He shrugs, face red. "You say that now, but you haven't seen my student loans."

We both laugh, and the tension that's lived in my neck for a year seems to dissolve by inches. I almost want to tell him everything—about the newspaper job, the accident, the improbability of being chosen to write Sara's memoir and the cascade of events that happened as a result—but there's a comfort in not laying it all out, in savoring the ambiguity.

Cassie returns, arms full of brochures and a plate of crackers. "Did you see the one with the pelican?" she asks, cheeks flushed with conquest. "It's enormous, Mom. Like, scientifically implausible."

I smile. "Let's go look."

Nathan follows as we thread the room, stopping in front of a canvas that's all wing and shadow, the pelican perched atop a weathered piling. The bird's eye is rendered in such detail that it seems to pierce through us.

Cassie points to the plaque. "It says it's from your first month here."

Nathan nods. "There was a storm. Lost power for three days. I started painting by candlelight."

"It's weird," Cassie says, and I brace for rudeness, but she finishes: "The feathers look fuzzy but also sharp. Like, the edges are blurry but the shape isn't?"

Nathan's face splits into a delighted grin.

"That's a compliment, by the way," I assure him.

He crouches so he's at Cassie's eye level. "That's exactly what I was going for. You know how, when you wake up too early, and everything outside the window is kind of washed out? I wanted the pelican to appear like it was halfway between a dream and being awake."

Cassie nods, utterly serious. "My teacher says that's called liminality."

Nathan's eyes flicker to mine. He's impressed, or just amused. "Smart teacher," he says.

She shrugs. "Mostly she lets us watch videos in science class."

There's an ease to the way Nathan talks with Cassie, a willingness to meet her logic on its own terms, that's both comforting and a little disarming. I can tell he's not humoring her. He's interested.

After a few more paintings and a running commentary from Cassie ("That one's definitely a nor'easter," "Is the beach ever really that color?" "If you painted a tsunami, would people be mad?"), she spots the makeshift dessert table and darts off again.

Nathan straightens, exhaling as if he's been holding his breath. "She's something else."

"Yes, she is. Sometimes I feel like I'm just following her around, trying not to slow her down."

"Isn't that what good parents do?" The word "parents" lands with a quiet weight. I find myself wanting to tell him about the long nights Cassie spent at my bedside after the accident, the ways she took care of me when I couldn't take care of myself, but I don't. Not yet.

We wander the room again, this time less like two halves of a nervous equation and more like, well, not quite a couple, but something parallel to it. He tells me about his latest series of seascapes, how he's trying to capture the essence of the ocean in different lights, seasons, and moods. I talk a little about my own work, dancing around the confession that most days I don't write at all.

"It's like I'm waiting for a sign," I say and then flush. "That sounds ridiculous."

"Not at all. I think we're all looking for signs. Most of us just ignore them when they show up."

We reach the end of the gallery, where a final painting hangs alone. It's smaller than the others, a study in near-white: surf breaking over a sandbar, sky and sea almost indistinguishable except for a single, blurred shadow that might be a gull, or maybe just an accident of the brush.

"This one's my favorite," Nathan says. "It reminds me that sometimes it's okay for things not to be clear."

I look at the painting, then at him, and I'm grateful for the ambiguity.

Cassie rejoins us, breathless from her dessert sprint. "Can we go home soon?" she asks, leaning heavily into my side. "I need to finish my math homework before it gets too late."

Nathan looks at me, a question in his eyes, but I can't read it. Instead, I gather Cassie under my arm and thank him for the invitation, for the conversation, for making the wind visible.

"Anytime."

As we head for the door, Cassie tugs at my sleeve. "He likes you," she whispers.

"Don't be ridiculous," I say, but I'm smiling, and my chest feels lighter than it has in months.

Outside, the cold air is bracing, and the night sky is scattered with stars I never saw in the city. Cassie skips ahead, collecting stray shells and bits of gravel from the sidewalk.

I watch her, and I think of that pelican, half in a dream, half awake, both states impossibly, beautifully true at once.

CHAPTER 9

DIANE

The ocean is all silver and shadow, the air sticky with the threat of a squall, when I find myself again on Sara's porch. The invitation had been casual—"Drop by anytime, if you need a break from your head"—but the urgency in her voice left little doubt that she wanted company. Or maybe I'm projecting, because I want it too. Cassie is at the pool with her best friend, Amaya, the house is empty except for my failure to write, and the walls of the guest cottage feel suddenly too thin to contain all my thoughts.

Sara's house perches at the edge of the bluff, gray clapboard with a tilt like it's inching toward flight. The porch is sunstruck, boards softened to gray by decades of salt and weather, and from here the ocean is a full 180-degree panorama. A chime made from old teaspoons rings lazily above the door, and I think I see a ghost of my mother in the shape of Sara's silhouette behind the window. It's a trick of the glass, but it sets my chest humming all the same.

I clutch my empty notebook against my ribcage and raise a tentative fist to the screen door. Sara answers, her good hand steady on the frame, the other cradled close to her body like a bird she's coaxing back to health. She's in a faded linen blouse and navy-blue pedal-pushers, her hair pinned up. She smiles, wide, as if I'm the answer to a riddle she's been dying to tell.

"You made it," she says, as if I'd scaled Everest and not just walked the two hundred yards from my front door.

"I made it," I echo, voice already two octaves too high. "You said anytime, so...."

She gestures me inside but then pauses. "No, wait—weather's perfect, so let's use the porch." She hooks her elbow through mine, gentle but directive, and leads me to the table set just shy of the sun's reach. The table is dressed in a cotton cloth, blue with tiny white anchors, and there are already two cups, a creamer shaped like a cow, and a glass pitcher of what appears to be hibiscus tea gone opaque with ice.

The centerpiece is a plate of oatmeal raisin cookies, the edges ragged and uneven in a way that assures me they are homemade.

"Sit, please." She waits until I do, then lowers herself into the opposite chair with a sigh that sounds more relieved than exhausted. "I hope you don't mind," she says. "I'm not much of a caffeine drinker anymore. Doctor's orders. But the cookies are legal."

"They look amazing." I am suddenly very aware of my own hands, how they hover indecisively over my lap. I try to relax my shoulders, but the sense of occasion has them fixed in place.

Sara notices, because of course she does. "You're nervous. Is it the cookies, or the company?"

"Neither," I say, wishing the porch chair wasn't so squeaky. "I just...didn't sleep well last night. Tossed and turned."

She nods as she pours the tea with her left hand, slow and deliberate. The pitcher shakes, but only a little. A single drop falls onto the cloth, where it beads and rolls toward the edge.

When she sets it down, her hand lingers on the rim, as if unsure whether to let go. "I keep telling myself I can still manage this much. Some days it's true. Some days it isn't."

"It's a beautiful morning," I offer, hoping to divert the conversation. "I mean, not that the other mornings aren't beautiful, but there's something about today..." My voice trails off as I wave a hand vaguely toward the ocean. "I don't know."

"You're right. There's a stillness to it today. Like the world is waiting for something wonderful."

"I like that. The something wonderful part."

"You would." She sets her cup down, leans forward, voice conspiratorial. "I saw you come home last night. From the gallery." She doesn't say the word, but Nathan hovers like a drawn breath between us. "So, how was it?"

"It was good. Interesting." I fiddle with the edge of the notebook, trying not to let my gaze stray too far from her face. "Nathan's work is...different. Not what I expected."

"Different how?"

I hesitate, trying to find the right phrase. "It's intimate. Like...he's teaching you to see the world as he does." I recall the muted grays and whites of his canvas, as if recalling a dream. "They were somehow calming but also...full of emotion. It's hard to explain."

"If I didn't know better, I'd say you were smitten."

"Smitten? With what, the art?"

"Perhaps. Or the artist."

I blink, trying to deflect with a sip of tea, but the heat catches me off guard and I cough a little into my napkin. Sara lets me recover, the silence filling with seagull chatter and the distant percussion of a hammer from some construction down the road.

Finally, I say, "Nathan? He's... I don't know. I mean, I barely know him."

Sara nods, her gaze falling back to the sea. "Just an observation, dear. Sometimes, we don't need to know someone very long for them to make an impression."

I notice a faint smile tug at the corner of her mouth as she watches me. It's a knowing smirk, one that only comes with wisdom and experience. I find myself blushing, suddenly feeling like a teenager. "I guess you're right," I say. It's not really an admission, but it's not a denial either.

Sara chuckles. "Honey, life's too short not to appreciate the good impressions. Whether it's a piece of art, or a piece of ass." She winks and takes a hearty sip of her tea, pinky finger extended in a way that somehow manages to maintain her elegance.

The teasing bluntness of her comment seems out of character, a sharp contrast to the woman who has always been so composed and gentle around me. Yet, the flash of humor in her eyes seems earnest, and I can't help but laugh. The sound tumbles out of me, the tension of the encounter breaking away like a wave.

"Is that so?" I ask, recovering my composure.

"Well, it's not something I'd put on a bumper sticker, but yes, that's my personal belief." She reaches for a cookie, breaking it in half with a careful, two-handed maneuver. The cinnamon aroma is so intense I can almost taste it from across the table. "Let me guess, you're a little scared of having your heart touched again, aren't you?"

I take another sip of tea to hide my surprise. It's like Sara has read me better than any book she's ever picked up. "Maybe. Or maybe I'm just nervous about how to proceed. Honestly, I'm a bit rusty."

"Want to know a secret?" she says, lowering her voice. "Nathan is probably scared, too. And nervous. Men are always afraid they'll break those they care about most. Or that they'll be broken by them."

I think of the way Nathan held the wineglass at the opening, pinched at the stem like it might shatter. The way he kept his hands busy, always moving. "He seems..." I struggle for the word. "Untamed. Not in a bad way. Just—like he's still running from something. Or someone."

Sara's smile grows soft, maternal. "Aren't we all?"

The sounds of the coast fill in. Wind rattles the window panes, and I can smell the first notes of coming rain, that sharp mineral edge that always precedes a change in weather.

"You could write about him," Sara says. "That's what you do, right? Convert the messiness into something permanent."

I flip open the notebook, exposing a page so white it aches. "Lately, I just stare at the blank page. Or worse, fill it with things I can't use."

Sara studies me, and I know she's assembling some great theory, the kind that only ever emerges in late-night kitchens or sunlit porches. "Maybe you need to stop trying to write about the future and just be in the damn present."

"That's the thing," I say. "I don't think I've ever been good at that. Even as a kid, I was always jumping three steps ahead."

Sara laughs, and this time it's all throat, no hesitation. "Then you need practice. Start small. Write about the next ten seconds." She raps the table for emphasis, causing the spoons in the chime above to jostle in sympathy.

"Ten seconds?"

"Yes."

I fumble for a pen, find one tucked into the spiral of the notebook, and touch nib to page.

Sara's smile is wicked. "No metaphors, no cleverness. Just what happens."

I want to argue. My whole brain is a tangle of cleverness and metaphor, but I force myself to follow the rules.

I write: *Sara blinks. Her left eye goes first, then the right. She sips tea, then sets the cup down, missing the saucer by half an inch. The tablecloth is blue, with anchors.*

I read it aloud, and Sara beams, as if I've just solved a particularly difficult math problem.

"See? That's all it is. Watch. Record. React. If you do that enough, the future will take care of itself."

I chew on this, then try again. This time, I write: *I'm on a porch with a woman I admire. My hands are shaking, and I pretend they aren't. All around us, the wind keeps changing its mind. Somewhere, someone is hammering nails into something that will outlast both of us.*

I don't read this one out loud, but Sara must sense the difference in me, because she reaches across and, with a touch so light it's almost imaginary, pats my wrist.

"Better," she says. "Now eat a cookie before I make you write a poem."

For the next hour, we talk about everything but Nathan. She gives me the lowdown on Judy and her book club, about her late husband's stubbornness, about the battle she's fighting with her own body and the bargains she makes each morning to just keep going. She tells me about the time a hurricane turned this whole stretch of coast into a saltwater lake, and how she can't sleep if the house is too quiet.

Eventually, when the cookies are half gone and the tea is

mostly ice, she leans back and folds her arms, satisfied.

"I'm glad you came," she says.

"Me too. This has been...enlightening."

When I leave, she insists on walking me to the edge of the yard, her arm looped through mine. At the end of the shell path, she pauses and faces me, her expression serious.

"Diane," she says, "all jokes aside, don't let fear keep you from the things you want. Not for one more day. You deserve to live out loud. To draw attention, make noise. To love fiercely, without apology."

I want to promise her, but the words stick. All I can do is nod and hope it's enough.

I walk back to the cottage, notebook heavier now with a few honest sentences. Above me, the clouds have thickened, dark and threatening, but I can still see the faintest line of blue, stubborn and bright, waiting for its moment to break through.

CHAPTER 10

DIANE

April

The wind is strongest in the evening. It combs the dunes into long animal spines and tugs the hem of my skirt with insistent, invisible hands. I've taken to walking the shoreline before dinner, telling myself it's to "clear the head," but really I'm hoping the ocean will drop a sentence or two at my feet, the way it coughs up blue crabs and sand dollars after a storm.

The sky over Kitty Hawk is in a mood, the clouds gathering and thinning in lopsided armies. Far out, the horizon is a smudged charcoal line, and every so often, the sun slices through and throws a shimmer over the tidal pools. I walk with my head half-cocked, alert for the next cracked clam, starfish, or a gull with the audacity to scream in my direction.

The beach is almost empty except for a young couple, their arms entwined in a way that says "new love." Further up, a man walks his dog, the leash slack, both of them scanning the surf. The only other figure is a speck near the water's edge, hunched over a spread of white. I squint, shielding my eyes from the low angle of the sun. The silhouette is angular, a stick of a man, but the set of the shoulders, the reach of the arm—I know the shape of someone intent on getting things right.

I slow down when I realize it's Nathan. He's camped on a narrow outcrop, close enough to the water that his sneakers are spotted dark with spray. A large pad of paper is balanced on his knees, anchored with his left hand while the right darts in quick, surgical movements. I think about veering inland, giving him his privacy, but then he sees me. He lifts the pencil in greeting, then pats the sand beside him as if inviting a stray cat to investigate.

I hesitate, heart shifting a gear, but the inertia of the day propels me forward. I pick my way over the ripple-ridged sand, careful not to step on the rocks. As I approach, Nathan flips the pad closed with a practiced gesture. The cover is already flecked with dots of pigment, a stray thumbprint of indigo. I realize with some embarrassment that I am about to see him in his element, and there's nothing to hide behind.

"Hey," he says, voice carrying over the wind. "You're out late."

"It's not even five," I say, settling onto the cool sand beside him. "Unless you're still running on Charlotte time."

"Nah, I gave up the city clock. I just meant most people avoid the wind at this hour. They don't like getting sandblasted."

"I like it," I say, and it's mostly true. "Makes you feel small in a good way."

Nathan's eyes go distant for a second, as if cataloging the sensation for future use. He taps his sketch pad. "You working?"

"Trying to," I say, shaking my notebook as if the words might rattle into place. "So far it's just shopping lists and half-assed metaphors."

He laughs, a quiet, companionable sound. "Could be worse. I have a notebook that's just grocery ads and directions to places I'll never go." He opens his pad again, but instead of sketching, he angles it toward me. "Want to see?"

I do, and I don't. But I nod, and he flips to the top sheet, a sweep of coastline, rendered in hard pencil, with a flock of birds sketched above the horizon in loose, offhand gestures. There's something kinetic about it, like the whole thing is about to be whisked away by the next gust. Below the drawing, he's written a date and two words: *breaking weather.*

"It's beautiful."

He shrugs. "It's honest. Sometimes that's all I'm aiming for."

I search for something clever to say, and while I do, I can feel my own heartbeat in my fingers, so I busy them by digging a shallow furrow in the sand, tracing the edge of an old tide pool now gone to memory. "Cassie has been going on and on about the gallery opening. She won't stop talking about the paintings she saw... And the man who painted them."

Nathan scratches his stubbled chin, a faint blush creeping up his cheeks. "Yeah? What did she say?"

"She was fascinated by how you captured the essence of this place. She said your art made people see the world the way she sees it, and how that made her feel less alone."

He stops, pencil hovering over the sketchbook like a reluctant seagull. His smile is slight but genuine. "You know, Cassie has quite a talent herself. That girl can draw."

The wind picks up, spinning a flurry of sand around our ankles. Nathan shields his pad with his arm, then offers it up for me to use as a windbreak. I accept, and the back of his knuckles brushes the heel of my hand. The contact is brief, but my skin registers it like a pinprick.

"So, what are you writing now?" he asks.

"Nothing, really. That's the problem. It's like my brain only wants to regurgitate the past, not actually process it."

"You want to talk about it?"

I let out a slow breath, the kind you only take when you know someone's actually listening.

"I keep trying to write about the move here, about what it means to start over after..." I trail off, not trusting myself with the specifics.

Nathan doesn't push. Instead, he stares at the surf, watching the way the light fractures across the water. "After what?" he asks, gently.

I touch the notebook, thumbing its frayed corner. "After my husband died."

Nathan's hand stills on his sketchbook, and he looks down at his feet buried in the sand. He doesn't offer words of pity or awkward condolences, just a small nod of acknowledgment. It's unexpected, but it offers a comfort I didn't know I needed.

"I'm sorry," he says finally, his voice so soft it almost gets lost in the sound of the waves crashing on the shore. "That's... I can't even imagine what it must be like."

I shrug, looking out to where the sky meets the sea. "Most days, I can't either. It's been almost three years, and sometimes it still feels like a dream. Only when I wake up, he's not there." I draw a shaky breath, trying to steady the tremor in my voice. "Sometimes I just...miss him. We both do. I just thought if I could...transplant us somewhere new, it would stop the ache. But it doesn't. It just moves it around, gives it a new landscape to dwell in."

"I get that."

"You do?"

He shrugs. "My ex and I—long story—I thought relocating would wipe the slate. Turns out you can't outrun your own story. It follows you, like sand in your shoes."

"Yeah. Or like glitter from some party you left early. It shows up in your laundry months later, and you're never sure who left it there."

"You know, when I was in finance, everything was about closure. Balancing ledgers, making things add up. But art isn't like that. Life isn't either. It's messier, and you have to live with the leftovers."

I study him, the way he's sketched his own hands on the edge of the paper—quick, sure, but not idealized. "I'm not used to the mess. I used to think if I organized things enough, they couldn't hurt me."

"How's that working?"

"About as well as you'd expect."

He shifts, drawing one knee up to his chest and wraps his arms around it. The gesture is oddly vulnerable, almost childlike. "You don't have to be perfect. Not out here. You can let it be ugly. The ocean won't judge you, and neither will I."

I want to ask him how. How do you let the world see you messy and uncomposed, when every instinct is to curate, smooth the rough spots, stay ahead of the audit? But the words catch, and all I can do is nod, blinking against the wind.

Nathan seems to sense it, the way good listeners do. He sets his pad aside, pushes his hands into the sand, and stares out at the horizon. "Sometimes I imagine the ocean as a giant etch-a-sketch. Every tide wipes away what came before."

"Except the plastic," I say, too quick. "That sticks around forever."

He laughs, and the sound is like a spark in the gathering dusk. "Fair enough. But you know what I mean."

I do. And for a second, I let myself believe that maybe it's possible to reset, to let the constant scrape of the world grind things into something new.

The sun dips lower, the sky turning the color of old peaches. A line of pelicans glides overhead, wingtip to wingtip, perfect in their ugly grace. The wind tugs at my hair, and I tuck it behind my ear, then realize my hand is trembling a little.

"Thank you," I say, quietly. "For not making it weird."

Nathan tilts his head, genuine confusion on his face. "Why would I?"

I want to explain, but the words seem less important than the feeling of not being alone on the sand, of not having to curate every molecule of myself.

He opens his pad again, tears off the top page, and folds it in half with careful precision. He hands it to me, the paper still warm from his hands. "Here. In case you need a fresh horizon."

The drawing is better up close. There are corrections, ghost lines, the suggestion of something erased and tried again. I trace the edge of the cloud bank, the birds skimming just above the waves, and wonder what it would feel like to draw a new line every morning.

When I look up, Nathan is watching me. Not expectant, not searching, just present.

The wind shifts, stronger now, and sand needles at my shins. "I should head back," I say, even though I don't want to.

"Okay," he says, but there's a reluctance in the way he packs up, careful not to crush the remaining sheets. "Will you be around tomorrow? At home, I mean."

"Yes. Sara's teaching Cassie how to make saltwater taffy. Apparently it's an essential life skill. Why do you ask?"

"I thought, if it's not too much trouble, I might drop by with some art supplies for Cassie. She seems to enjoy drawing, and I have way too many lying around."

I smile at the thought of Cassie's excitement at such a gift. "That would be wonderful. She'd love it." I stand, brushing sand from the back of my calves, and for a split second, I want to say something brave—invite him to dinner, suggest a future, even a small one. But the thought is too raw, so I just thank him again, tucking the sketch into my notebook.

He watches me go, a solitary figure etched against the breaking surf, and for the first time in a long time, the walk home feels less like a retreat and more like a beginning.

CHAPTER 11

DIANE

I'm halfway back to the cottage when I hear my name, stretched out like a gull's cry, carried by the wind. I turn, and there's Cassie, barreling down the beach like a torpedo. Her sneakers throw clumps of wet sand, and her hair fans out behind her like a victory banner. She moves with a lawless energy, redirecting the world to follow her lead.

She zeroes in on me, arms windmilling, and then skids to a breathless stop. "Mom! You missed it! There were like a million comb jellies on the north side... And Rolo found a skull, a real skull... I think it's a seagull, but it could be a tern—" She blinks up at me, cheeks ruddy, and I feel a complicated knot in my chest begin to untangle.

"Did you bring it?" I ask, a little wary of what "skull" entails.

She produces a plastic baggie from her jacket pocket. Inside is a beak and a fistful of feathers, less creepy than I expected. "See?" She's already forgotten the point of the display and is scanning the horizon for the next interesting thing.

"Wow. That's...impressive," I say, trying not to sound horrified.

Before I can redirect her, she's already spotted Nathan,

still perched on his sketching rock. "Hey, Nathan!"

I watch the shift in his face. The reserved lines of adulthood soften into something like delight. He stands, brushes sand off his jeans, and meets us halfway.

"Look what I found!" Cassie says, thrusting the bag in his direction.

Nathan reaches down to pet Rolo, then takes in the skull with the solemnity of a museum curator. He holds it up to the fading light, rotates it, then hands it back. "Definitely a gull. See the hook at the end? That's for grabbing fish."

Cassie examines it, her brow furrowing in concentration. "Do you think it's the same gull from yesterday, the one with the missing foot?"

"Could be. They're tough birds, though. Probably just lost a scuffle."

I watch them, the way Nathan addresses her, not as a child but as an equal, each exchange a transaction of shared respect. Cassie responds in kind, her usual squirming replaced by an intent, almost scholarly posture.

"What are you guys doing out here?" she asks, then, "Mom, did you make any progress on the book?"

"Some. Not a lot."

Cassie nods, as if this is an acceptable answer. "Nathan, did you finish your painting?"

"Not yet," he says, gesturing toward the sketch pad under his arm. "I needed a break. Sometimes you have to let things settle before you know what's missing."

Cassie absorbs this, then tugs at my sleeve. "Can we walk with you?"

We fall into step, three abreast, the surf chewing at our toes. I find myself between them, a buffer and a bridge, and for once, I don't mind the role. Rolo and Cassie race ahead, pausing every few yards to examine a shell or a piece of driftwood, then doubling back to present their findings.

"Is this a slipper shell?" she asks, holding up something oblong and cream-colored.

Nathan inspects it. "Yep. Good eye."

Cassie beams, then points to another fragment. "What about this?"

He leans in, then shakes his head. "That's just a broken clam. But see the ridges, how they're close together? That means it lived in deeper water, where the waves are stronger."

Cassie looks up at me. "Did you know that?"

I shake my head. "I didn't."

Nathan shrugs, modest. "I'm a walking encyclopedia of useless facts. Comes from years of pretending to pay attention at work."

Cassie giggles, and the sound is so sudden and so bright that I feel it in my molars. We keep moving, the beach growing emptier as the light tilts toward evening. The conversation shifts from shells to sharks to the physics of skipping stones. Nathan demonstrates, launching a flat pebble into the surf where it bounces three, four, five times before sinking. Cassie cheers, then tries to outdo him, her throws wild but improving.

It's easy, this rhythm. Easier than I expected. I'm used to managing Cassie's enthusiasm, translating it into a language adults can tolerate, but with Nathan, there's no need to filter. He matches her stride for stride, matching her curiosity with his own, letting her interrupt and steer the topic as if it's the most natural thing in the world. Even the dog doesn't seem to mind, happily tailing the two explorers as they claim the beach as their own.

We walk for a while, the wind dying down, the only sound the hush of water and Cassie's ongoing taxonomy of every shell she finds. Eventually, she tires of the game and drops back, wandering in and out of our slipstream. Nathan slows, matching my pace, and for a few minutes, it's just the two of us.

"You're good with her," I say, surprised by the rawness in my own voice.

He glances at me, then away. "I like kids. They don't bullshit you."

I think of all the times I've envied Cassie's ability to say exactly what she means, even when it's inconvenient or embarrassing.

"She likes you," I say, softer.

He smiles, but it's different from before. There's a flicker of something like fear behind it. "I'm not sure I deserve that."

I want to ask why, but the words jam up. Instead, I focus on the tide line, where the sand is dense and studded with chips of shell.

We walk for a bit, letting the questions hang unasked. It's comfortable, interrupted only by Cassie's intermittent yelps as she discovers a fossilized shark tooth, or a fragment of sea glass polished to an improbable sheen.

The sky has gone full Technicolor now, streaks of orange and pink smeared above the black edge of the ocean. Cassie slows, then stops, crouching in the sand to build a miniature fortress of shells and driftwood. Nathan and I linger nearby, both of us watching her in that way parents do when they're not sure if they're supposed to intervene or just let the magic happen.

"She's lucky," Nathan says, after a while.

"Who? Cassie?"

He nods. "To have you. Most kids don't get a mom who listens."

"I don't always. Sometimes I just fake it."

"We all fake it. That's half of being alive." He digs the toe of his sneaker into the sand, drawing a slow, deliberate line. "My mom used to say you can't teach someone to care. You can only show them and hope they catch on."

Before I can respond, Cassie pops up, holding two identical shells in her palms. "Match!" she says, then shoves them toward Nathan. "You get one."

He accepts, turning the shell over in his hand. "You know what this is called?"

Cassie shakes her head, already invested in the answer.

"It's an angel wing. They're rare. Usually you only find one, but never a perfect pair."

She holds hers up, examining it with new reverence. "Angel wing," she repeats, then slips it into her jacket pocket like a talisman.

I watch them, feeling the shift in the air. We keep walking, now and then stooping to collect more shells, our hands brushing as we pass them back and forth. The light fades, and the breeze returns, but it's gentle now, a nudge instead of a shove.

When we reach the old pier, Cassie is exhausted, her eyelids heavy despite her protests that she's "not even tired." Nathan offers to carry her, and she accepts without hesitation, looping her arms around his neck and resting her chin on his shoulder. He lifts her with an ease that surprises me, and I feel a pang—part gratitude, part longing, part something else I can't name.

We walk the last stretch together, Cassie half asleep, Nathan silent. At the dune that leads to our cottage, he sets her down, and she trudges the rest of the way under her own power.

"Thank you," I say, as we stand at the foot of the porch, the house behind me glowing with the promise of warmth and rest.

Nathan smiles, and for a second, it's just us.

"Anytime," he says. "Seriously. I mean that." He turns to go, hands shoved in his pockets, shoulders relaxed in a way I haven't seen before. I watch until he disappears down the path, then shepherd Cassie and the dog inside. She drops her treasures on the kitchen counter, then vanishes to her room.

I linger, taking the angel wing and tracing its ridged surface with my thumb. I set it on the windowsill, a placeholder for all the things I don't have words for yet. I stare at it until the house is quiet, and for once, the silence is something I want to keep.

CHAPTER 12

DIANE

There's a moment just before dawn when the world is suspended, as if the ocean, the sky, the waking earth have all agreed to hold their breath for a single heartbeat. I'm at my writing desk for it, hunched in my chair, feet bare and cold on the planks, laptop screen a pale blue rectangle in the gray. The house is silent except for the hiccup of the fridge and the muffled tick of the stove clock, whose digits advance with a stubborn optimism I can't seem to muster.

My hands hover above the keys. I flex my fingers, crack my knuckles, and type the first sentence:

It is a truth universally acknowledged—

No. I'm not clever enough for parody today.

Backspace, backspace, backspace.

Try again.

Sometimes, the future arrives like a storm—implacable, uninvited, intent on reshaping the coastline of your life whether you're ready or not.

Ugh. Too on-the-nose, and besides, there's something desperate about invoking meteorology when you live one windstorm from obsolescence. I hit delete and watch the words recede into oblivion, leaving only the blinking cursor.

The morning light catches in the salt crust on the glass. It blurs the world, turns the shrubbery into watercolor smudges, renders the ocean a single band of silver. I could lie and say I find this inspiring, but mostly it makes me want to crawl back into bed and cocoon myself in the scent of yesterday's shampoo and the faint, improbable hope that I'll wake up with a finished novel.

Instead, I push back from the desk and wander the little cottage, tracing the seam where the ceiling slopes, avoiding the board in the living room that shrieks like a murder victim when you step on it. I do a circuit, from my room to the kitchen, to the half-bath, then upstairs to Cassie's nest at the end of the hall. The girl sleeps like she means it, face mashed into her pillow, mouth slightly open, the outline of her shoulder rising and falling beneath the comforter. Rolo is beside her, stretched out on his side, tiny paws twitching as if chasing squirrels in his dreams.

I tiptoe past, then go downstairs and stop at the fridge. On it, Cassie has arranged an army of construction-paper sea creatures, every one of them with googly eyes and a personality. Some have dialogue bubbles—"I'm a cool clam!" or "Beware the crab!" or, my favorite, a narwhal with a speech balloon that just says "WHY?" There are two recent sketches, taped side by side: one is a pencil lighthouse, stark and monolithic against a scribbled sky; the other is a freehand drawing of me, holding a steaming mug, with *SuperMom* written in comic-book font across my chest. The rendering is not technically accurate (I have never in my life possessed visible biceps), but it's accurate enough in spirit to pinch at the base of my throat.

I take down the lighthouse drawing, running my thumb over the graphite, remembering the day she brought it home.

She'd been so excited—"It's for your desk, so you don't get lost," she'd said. I told her I loved it, but in truth, I envied how she could set down an entire universe in half an hour, while I spent days circling a blank screen, unable to even begin.

Coffee. That's what I need. I fill the old kettle, strike a match, and hold it to the gas burner. The flame blazes up, blue and hungry. I watch the water come to a slow boil, savoring the microsecond of peace before the day's first obligations muscle in. While I wait, I run my hands over the countertops, smooth and cool beneath the tips of my fingers, then press my forehead to the window above the sink. The ocean is still out there, just past the dunes, invisible but vast. I remember the first night we arrived, how I'd stood at this very window, half-dazed with exhaustion, and tried to imagine a future here. Tried and failed. Some days, I still do.

The coffee is harsh, but it kicks my neurons into sufficient motion. I return to the desk, set the mug on the surface, and open a fresh document. I stare at it, the way you might stare at a wound you're not sure is healing.

I type:

> *If there is a difference between loneliness and solitude, I have yet to discover it.*

Not bad. I leave it. I add:

> *Three years is a long time to live in the shadow of an absence, and longer still to convince yourself it's not your own fault.*

I pause, breathing shallow. The words are true, but I can feel the old reflex, a surge of guilt, as if naming the pain might conjure it back. This is the pitfall of writing. You risk making the imaginary real, or worse, making the real even more inescapable.

I notice the picture of Cassie at the corner of my desk—grinning, hair windblown, the tip of her tongue poking out between missing teeth. The photo was taken the last time we were at the zoo, just after we'd fed the giraffes. We'd shared a cotton candy larger than her head. The candy is long gone, but the image lingers, a reminder of small victories, of a time when my biggest worry was making sure she didn't get a sugar high before dinner. I wonder if this whole exile was a colossal misjudgment, an overcorrection for a tragedy I couldn't control. But the past is a locked door, and regret is a key that turns in circles without ever catching.

I shut the laptop and walk to the porch, coffee in hand. The boards are slick with dew and sea film, and a low fog hugs the dunes. There's a rocking chair that I've claimed as my own. I sink into it and let my head loll back, closing my eyes.

I think about Nathan.

This is a new habit, and one I haven't quite learned to control. He appears in my mind as if summoned, standing at the water's edge with his sketch pad, or hunched over a canvas in that oversized shirt, hair a mass, lips pursed in concentration. Sometimes I recall the way his fingers curled around the wine glass at the gallery, or the way his voice dropped when he said my name, like he was testing its flavor, not quite trusting it to be real.

I remember the first time I noticed him watching me. No one's looked at me like that in years. I'm equal parts drawn and terrified, a dangerous chemistry that would have thrilled me at eighteen but now feels like a fire hazard.

What am I supposed to do with this? Cassie is only just starting to adapt. She still wakes at night, sometimes, and calls out for her father before remembering he's gone. Am I supposed to graft someone new into her life? Into mine? Would it even be fair, to either of us? The thought makes my stomach fizz.

I remember a conversation with Sara on her porch. "You don't owe the world your misery," she'd said, pouring me tea as if it were a secret potion. "You're allowed to want things." I'd nodded, but the wanting was the hardest part. It felt like a betrayal, even in the best light.

And then there's the writing. Or, more precisely, the failure to write. Is Nathan a distraction, or an excuse? A reason to defer confronting the possibility that I have, in fact, lost the one true thing I was ever good at?

I think of the lighthouse, the way it stands, inert and patient, waiting for a reason to light up. Maybe I'm the same, waiting for permission. Maybe there's no such thing.

I sit with my coffee until the chill sets in, then return inside, back to the page. I stare at the screen, hands poised. The words hang just beyond reach, quivering with possibility.

If there is a difference between loneliness and solitude, I have yet to discover it.

I type it again, slower this time. I let it linger.

I wonder if that's what I want, someone to share the silence, not just fill it. The thought is so raw it almost glows.

I save the file, close the laptop, and lay my forehead on the cool, closed lid. The world tilts. I am neither more nor less certain than when I started, but the simple act of naming the problem is a step in the right direction.

Maybe tomorrow, I'll know what to do with it.

CHAPTER 13

NATHAN

The studio smells like old turpentine, wet canvas, and metal I only now realize is coming from the rusted heater in the corner. Morning seeps in through the bank of windows, the pale light bending around the cheap paper shades and puddling across the hardwood. There's a half-eaten granola bar next to my mug, a dried paintbrush stabbed into the empty sleeve like a flag of surrender.

I'm supposed to be painting the lighthouse, but what I am doing instead is staring at the mail. It's scattered across the drafting table, bills and junk and a single envelope addressed in a familiar, tight script. My name, full and formal. No return address, but I know the handwriting. I'd know it in the dark.

I sit and stare at the envelope for five minutes before touching it. Even then, I use the tip of my palette knife to nudge it off the stack. It flips, lands facedown, the seal a perfect triangle of expensive paper. I remember the way she used to buy stationery, never the cheap stuff, always with a watermark or a heavy linen finish that left ridges in your fingers. I wonder, briefly, how many details like this I've been hoarding in the attic of my head.

When I finally pick it up, my hands are stained blue and

raw, nails ragged from tearing open tubes of oil paint. The contrast is absurd. I break the seal with my thumb, inhaling that faint perfume of ink and memory, and unfold the sheet inside. Her writing slants right, aggressive, almost falling forward:

Nathan,

I don't know if you want to hear from me, but I couldn't stop myself. There are so many things I didn't say, and even more I wish I hadn't. I hope you're well. I hope the new coast feels like home. I'm sorry for all the mess—mine, yours, ours. If you ever want to talk, I'm here, day or night. I think about you. Sometimes I think about us.

Melissa

That's it. No "love," no "sincerely," not even a postscript. Just the raw-boned fact of her in my mailbox, sudden as a thunderclap.

I read it three times, each pass more surreal than the last. The words slide around, refuse to sit still. I want to believe the message is simple—she's sorry, she's moved on, she's releasing us both into the wild. But I know her better than that. Every apology is a loaded gun. Every "I hope you're well" a dare.

My hands are trembling, so I set the letter down and wipe my palms on the thighs of my jeans. A faint blue streak trails after, smearing her signature. I curse, then try to dab it with a rag, but it only spreads. Now her name is a smear across the page.

I turn my attention to the painting. The lighthouse stands center canvas, thick with underpaint, the palette still blocked out in heavy strokes of white and cobalt. I squint at it, trying to see what Sara saw, but all I can see is an empty tower, a warning. I pick up a brush, dip it in linseed, then set it down again. The thought of painting is suddenly suffocating, as if the smell of oil has turned toxic overnight.

I circle the studio, inventorying tubes, knives, balled-up paper towels, sketches of the same coastline at different hours of the day. I stop at the window and peer out. There are a couple of gulls fighting over a crab shell, their shrieks hollow and victorious. Past them, the ocean rolls on, gray and ugly and stubborn.

I think about Diane. The way she watched me on the beach, like she was trying to memorize the exact temperature of my voice. The way she said "thank you" when I handed her the sketch of the horizon, as if I'd given her a key instead of a piece of paper. I think about the way she never tries to finish my sentences, or correct my jokes, or make me feel small in the name of efficiency.

Is it fair, I wonder, to start something new when the old thing is still bleeding out? Is that what Melissa's letter is, an invitation to wrap a tourniquet around our history, to see if there's anything left to save?

I rub my eyes, hard, as if I can erase the memory of the envelope. I wish I could call my mother. She'd know what to say. But she's gone, and besides, I'm too old to need a referee for my own feelings.

I grab the letter and fold it, deliberately creasing the blue smear. I set it in the drawer with the other things I've kept—ticket stubs, a single earring, a photo booth strip from a wedding neither of us remembered past the third drink. I close the drawer gently, as if the contents might spill out if I'm not careful.

Back at the easel, I force myself to mix the paints. White, Prussian blue, a dab of ochre for the light. I load the brush and bring it to the canvas, but at the last second, my hand falters. The stroke goes crooked, cutting a diagonal through the horizon. I stand back, brush limp in my grip, and wonder if this is what all my art has been, a series of interrupted lines, never quite reaching the shore.

I think about Diane, again, and how she's probably sitting at her own desk, wrestling with ghosts of her own. I picture her in the morning light, hair still damp from the shower, eyes narrowed at her screen as if the force of her focus might will a story into being. I remember the way she smiled, like maybe she, too, wanted to believe in something unfinished.

The heater sputters, clicks off. I pick up my phone, hesitate, finger hovering over the numbers. I put the phone down, then pick it up again, the urge to connect almost physical.

Maybe I'll call. Maybe I won't.

I turn back to the lighthouse, and with a deliberate hand, add another layer to the sky. The horizon line is ruined, but it doesn't matter. Sometimes you have to let the mistakes stand. Sometimes you even paint over them, let the old color bleed through.

I work until my arms ache, and when I finally step back, the lighthouse isn't finished, but it feels truer than before. It's battered, off-kilter, but still upright. Still holding the line against the weather.

I wipe the brush clean, set it aside, and walk out onto the boardwalk. The air is sharp, the wind restless. I breathe in, let the sting of it clear my head.

The ocean isn't going anywhere, and neither am I.

CHAPTER 14

DIANE

May

It's the last week before summer, the kind of morning that can't decide between rain or sweat, and the backseat is dominated by a box bigger than my daughter. Cassie is wedged in beside it, knees up, eyes flickering between the window and her hands. The box—her science project—is swaddled in towels, buckled in with both seatbelts and the kind of maternal hope that expects the universe to spare this one small, precious thing.

I merge onto the causeway, first in a parade of minivans and golf carts, each one loaded with poster boards, paper-mâché planets, neon trifolds sprouting with motivational stickers. The science fair is today. Technically it's the "Coastal Ecology and Innovation Expo," but everyone just calls it the science fair because that's what it is, a bloodsport for overachieving eighth-graders, a panic attack for their parents.

Cassie leans forward, craning to see if her project's still upright. "Can you go slower? You hit that bump like we were on the moon."

"We're at fifteen miles an hour, sweetheart." I glance in the rearview. "Is it tipping?"

She lifts the edge of the towel, a surgeon prepping for a

high-stakes reveal. "I don't think so, but if the coral shifts, the whole reef will collapse. I glued it three times, and it's still not stable."

"That's science for you. The ocean's a volatile system." I try to sound reassuring, like the calm parent in a cereal commercial, but my own hands are sticky on the wheel.

Cassie exhales with the force of a deflating raft. "I wish you could come in with me. What if the gym is locked? Or if I drop it and it breaks, and everyone sees and—"

"Cass." I meet her eyes in the mirror. She's got my brow, too serious for thirteen, but her dad's sharp, skittish mouth. "Nothing is going to explode. Even if it does, the world keeps spinning."

She nods, but I can tell she doesn't believe me.

The project is a diorama, but it's more than that. She's modeled the entire Outer Banks in a shoebox so large we had to cannibalize four pairs of shoes. There's a sandbar built from oatmeal and glue, a ring of tidal pools painted with nail polish, and in the center, a salt marsh constructed with the delicate precision of someone who's spent hours studying the real thing.

Every creature is accounted for, each labeled with a spiky tag in her neatest handwriting. Blue crab, sanderling, diamondback terrapin, the rare and always elusive piping plover. She's even painted miniature jellyfish on a cellophane overlay, so that when you peer inside, the light refracts and the jellies seem to drift, weightless, over the rest of the world.

I love the project, but what I really love is the way she cares about it, like she's building something that might survive where she won't. I remember the night she started it, after dinner, huddled on the living room floor with a paper plate and a lump of modeling clay, determined to get the shape of the sandbar "just right." She said it with a finality I recognized from my own mother. "Just right" is how we survive.

We hit the four-way stop in front of the high school, and traffic thickens. SUV doors yawn open, kids spill out like marbles. There's a knot of teachers herding students toward the gym, each child armed with a cardboard representation of their own interior world. In the soft light, the line of children reminds me of nesting dolls, each smaller and more vulnerable than the last.

Cassie bounces her heel against the seat. "Mom, do you think the judges are scary?"

"They're teachers, not judges. Their job is to love every project."

"That's not true," she says, and I'm startled by the certainty in her voice. "Some of the parents said last year there were only three trophies, and everyone else just gets a ribbon."

I try to think of a lie that doesn't sound like one. "Well, ribbons are cool, too."

She hugs her backpack to her chest. "Not really."

The gym is visible now, brick-red and boxy against the flat blue of the sky. In the parking lot, mothers in yoga pants wrangle hot glue guns and last-minute touch-ups, while clusters of boys in mesh shorts shout about volcanoes and bottle rockets. I pull into a spot, engine idling.

Cassie sits still, her anxiety coiled so tight I can practically hear it buzzing.

"Do you want help carrying it in?" I ask. I want to walk her to the door, to stand over her like a forcefield, but I know she'll say no.

She shakes her head, then yes. "Actually, maybe just to the sidewalk?"

We both get out, the door slamming with a sound like a challenge. She slides the diorama out, arms straining beneath the weight. We walk together through the gauntlet of other parents, who are busy comparing their own children's genius.

At the gym entrance, the air hums with voices, the flapping of banners, the hollow thunk of sneakers on wood. I see two girls from Cassie's class, one with a solar system model that's bleeding glitter, the other with a paper-mâché tornado whose funnel is already listing starboard. Cassie stares straight ahead, white-knuckling the box, but her voice is steady when she says, "You can go now, Mom."

I crouch to eye level. "You've got this," I say, because I can't say, *I want to stay with you until it's over.* "Remember, the most important thing is that you learned something."

She makes a face. "That's what people say when they know you're not going to win."

"Maybe. But I still mean it."

She nods quickly, and before I can even stand up, she's gone, project held like a shield.

I watch through the streaked glass as Cassie threads her way through the chaos. *Careful, careful, careful.* She holds the diorama close, shoulders hunched against the onslaught of elbows and poster boards. She looks smaller than usual, compacted by fear and the weight of expectation.

It happens fast. Maybe it's the gust of air when the main doors swing wide, maybe a jostle from a kid with a foam rocket. I'll never know. All I see is the project lurch, the back panel catch the edge of a table, and—before she can rebalance—the painted cardboard splits with a sound like ripping skin. The ocean backdrop, weeks in the making, tears clean down the center.

I can't hear her, but I see her freeze. Her mouth is open, hands clamped at the edges of the box, eyes wide and unblinking as the top half of the reef folds in on itself like a closing book. For a full second she doesn't move, as if she might rewind the moment by sheer force of will. Then her face crumples. The tears come all at once, hot and obvious, and she just stands there, boxed in by the wreckage while the gym keeps spinning around her.

My own body moves before my mind catches up. I'm through the doors, dodging a paper-mâché planet, nearly tripping over a tangle of extension cords. By the time I reach her, she's surrounded by two other kids and a teacher's aide, all of them talking at once, offering advice or pity or both.

I crouch next to her, taking in the damage. The backdrop is torn nearly in half, the sandbar has shifted, and the cellophane overlay that once shimmered with jellyfish is wrinkled and askew, smeared with a dot of what looks like grape jelly from someone else's breakfast.

Cassie's hands are shaking, not with rage but with something deeper, more tectonic. Her breaths come in little choked gasps. "It's r-ruined."

"No, no, no. It's not. We can fix this." I'm lying, but it's automatic, the first line of defense in a long parental history of improvisation. I scan the gym for a roll of tape, a tube of glue, anything. There's a supply table near the entrance. I grab scissors, markers, and a few strips of blue painter's tape and return, peeling off a length and smoothing the panel together. The tape sticks, but the seam is jagged and obvious, a suture that refuses to be invisible.

A girl at the next table, her own volcano already half-collapsed, watches us with a mixture of relief and sorrow. "That happened to my sister last year," she offers. "She still got second place."

Cassie doesn't look at her, or at me. She's staring straight ahead, eyes shiny and furious. "It's not the same. It's not right."

I reach for her, but she pulls away, hugging the box to her chest.

Behind us, parents and kids steal glances, then look away. I hate them for it, and I hate myself for hating them, and I hate the universe for letting this be the thing that matters today.

"Cassie, listen to me." I keep my voice low, meant for her alone. "You made something amazing. No one else here even thought to do a whole ecosystem. It's still beautiful, even if it's a little...wounded."

She doesn't answer, but her grip loosens just a little. The teacher's aide tries to help, offering a glue stick and a sympathetic smile. "These things happen," she says. "It's all part of the process."

Cassie's jaw tightens. "That's what losers say."

I wince but can't disagree. Sometimes the world gives you nothing but ugly choices.

We spend the next ten minutes patching what we can, but it's a lost cause. The background won't lie flat, the jellyfish overlay keeps sagging, and the sandbar, once so precise, now tilts into the marsh, a miniature disaster that mirrors the real one.

Every time I look at Cassie, she's watching her project like she might will it back into perfection. But the more we work, the more obvious the damage becomes.

Eventually, she sits beside the diorama, shoulders rounded, hands resting in her lap. She doesn't cry anymore, but the shock is still there, a glassy film over everything. I want to hold her, to gather her up and flee the gym, but I know it would only make things worse. She wants to face this down, and she wants to do it alone.

I hover at her side, useless and desperate, waiting for the next blow to land. I want to tell her that none of this matters, that there will be other projects and other chances. But I also know that right now, to her, this is the only thing that matters. And that helplessness, the inability to fix what's broken, is a special kind of heartbreak.

Around us, the science fair pushes forward, oblivious. Other parents snap photos, judges consult clipboards, the distant echo of a soda can rolls across the floor. But at our table, everything is still.

Until I hear my name.

"Diane?" The voice is off a little, uncertain, as if he's not sure he belongs here.

I look up, and there's Nathan at the gym entrance, framed by a shaft of sun and the blurred commotion beyond. He's holding a paper grocery bag, his hair windblown and his shirt just a little crooked at the collar. His eyes dart between Cassie and me, then to the project, and he puts it all together before I even say a word.

He's here to deliver art supplies for the fair—he mentioned it in passing, said he'd offered to set up a painting demo for the sixth graders. I'd forgotten, or maybe I just didn't expect to see him in the middle of this crisis. But now he's walking over, navigating the obstacle course of folding chairs and emotional landmines, zeroed in on our disaster.

He crouches next to Cassie, careful not to crowd her. "Rough morning?" he asks, gentle.

"It's broken," she says, voice flat. "It's not going to work."

Nathan examines the damage, hands on his knees, and whistles low. "Oof. That's a bad one. But I've seen worse. My first gallery show, the paintings got delivered upside down, and the frames exploded. I had to glue them back together with chewing gum."

He glances at me, eyebrow raised, as if asking permission. I nod, desperate for any lifeline.

He sits back on his heels and addresses Cassie directly. "You know, I'm not sure if they're judging for creativity or just for survival. But you've got both covered." He opens his bag, rifles through the contents, and emerges with his sketchbook, its cover peppered with coffee stains and old, dried paint. "Let me show you a trick," he says, flipping through until he finds a blank page. He tears it out clean, then finds another, stacking them together until he's got a surface big enough to cover the ruined ocean scene.

He leans over the gym table, right in the chaos, and starts to draw. At first it's just the hush of pencil on paper, quick and effortless, lines blooming into the shape of water. Then the pace slows, and his whole body seems to fall into the rhythm. His left hand steadies the paper, the right shading in layers of blue and gray, then switching to a stubby marker for the deeper creases of the sea. He doesn't bother with straight edges or rulers, just draws.

Cassie watches, seemingly captivated despite herself. With every sweep of the pencil, the ragged gym, the failure, all of it blurs into background. Nathan is fast but not rushed, narrating his process in a low, soothing voice. "The trick to water is to let it be messy. The more you try to control it, the less it looks like water. Kind of like life, right?"

Cassie nods, barely perceptible, but I see the tension in her jaw loosen.

A small crowd has started to form—a couple of kids, a teacher, the girl with the volcano from earlier. Even the judges, their clipboards held like shields, drift closer to see what's happening. Nathan doesn't notice, or pretends not to. He reaches into his bag for a pack of colored pencils, hands one to Cassie. "You want to help with the marsh? I bet you remember all the names."

Cassie hesitates, then takes the pencil. She draws in the tufts of grass, the curve of the sandbar, a flock of sanderlings racing the tide. Her movements are cautious at first, but soon she's adding tiny details, labeling species, pointing out where the fiddler crabs hide. Nathan shadows her, filling in the water behind her strokes, letting her lead.

I stand back, barely breathing, afraid to disrupt the spell.

In ten minutes, the two of them have conjured a seascape even better than the original. The colors pop, the horizon is clean, and the marks of disaster have been transformed into a wild, dramatic sky.

"Tape it over the rip," Nathan says. "No one will even know."

Cassie mounts the drawing, and when she's done, she sits beside it, breathing deeper, her shoulders no longer curled in defeat.

Nathan wipes his hands on a napkin, stands, and gives me a lopsided grin. "Not how you planned your morning, huh?"

I shake my head, too full to speak. For a second I think I might cry, but then Cassie grabs Nathan's arm and hugs him, quick and fierce. "Thank you," she whispers.

He hugs her back, careful and gentle. "You did most of the work."

The judges approach. Cassie straightens, ready. She starts her presentation, voice clear and strong, while Nathan and I stand to the side, just far enough away to let her have the spotlight.

I lean close and say, "I think you just saved the day."

CHAPTER 15

DIANE

I hover near the back row of parent seating, where every other mother seems to be equipped with a camera or camcorder, tracking their child's every move.

Nathan sidles up next to me, cradling a pair of Styrofoam cups of coffee. He hands one to me and says, "She's a natural."

"She's petrified," I whisper back, afraid the force of my hope might jinx her.

Onstage, Cassie begins her pitch. I can see the muscles in her jaw clench and unclench as she pushes through her opening lines, eyes flickering from judge to project and back. She's prepared, but she's also thirteen, and the words trip over themselves in their hurry to be worthy. The judges lean in, peering at the sandbar, the swarms of tiny hand-drawn sanderlings, the reconstructed ocean scene. One of the women asks a question, and Cassie's answer is a little too loud, like she's surprised to find her voice still functioning. The words tumble out—facts about brackish marshes, why piping plovers nest on the leeward side, how jellyfish stings don't actually kill you, but it really hurts, and here's a fun story about my last summer vacation. The narrative wobbles but never falls.

I study her posture, the way her hands start to move as she

gets comfortable, sketching the shape of the ocean and wind in the air. Her hair has come loose in the front, and a thin sheen of sweat is already forming at her temples. The judges are smiling, not condescending but genuine, taking notes with their school-issued pens.

"She's killing it," Nathan says.

The pitch ends, and the judges thank her, moving on to the next table. Cassie stands rooted, then slides down into the folding chair behind her project, face in her hands. I can't read her expression from here, but her body language is pure relief, the aftershock of surviving an avalanche.

Nathan and I walk the perimeter of the gym, pretending to admire the other projects, but our attention is fixed on Cassie's corner. When we finally approach, she looks up with eyes red and shining.

"I said 'fecal matter' in front of everybody," she stage-whispers.

"Honestly, that's the most accurate term," says Nathan. "You'd be surprised what passes for scientific language in the adult world."

Cassie giggles, then covers her mouth, cheeks bright. "Do you think they liked it?" she asks, her gaze darting between us.

Nathan smiles, cool and easy. "Are you kidding? They ate it up."

I want to hug her, but the gym is full of witnesses. I settle for a hand on her shoulder, squeezing just enough for her to feel my pulse through the bone. "You did amazing, honey. Really."

She looks at the project, at the place where the repair is obvious, and traces the blue seam with one finger. "Do you think it matters that it's broken?"

"Nah," he says. "I think it makes it better."

Cassie's face scrunches up. "How?"

"Because, it shows that no matter what happened, no matter the setbacks, you persevered. Instead of crumbling, you faced a challenge and didn't let it defeat you. That's something to be proud of. Not everyone could do that."

***

There's a lull, the hour between presentations and awards, where parents crowd the bleachers, and kids trade compliments or critique, depending on their blood sugar. Nathan disappears briefly, returns with two cans of soda and a donut from the teacher's lounge. "Sugar rush," he says, handing them over like contraband.

Cassie breaks the donut in half, gives me the bigger piece, then perches on the edge of the chair, legs swinging, eyes locked on the judges huddled at the front of the gym with their clipboards and whispers.

At the next table, a boy demonstrates his Rube Goldberg machine, which works beautifully until the final step, when the balloon pops prematurely, and the dominoes scatter sideways.

All the while, Cassie's project stands, imperfect but proud, the new ocean horizon sketched by Nathan catching the overhead lights in shifting shades of blue. I wonder if it will ever come home, or if it will wind up on some forgotten shelf in the school, an artifact of this day.

Finally, the judges step up to the microphone, their faces composed into neutral optimism. The science teacher, a man with a mustache so assertive it could anchor a bridge, does the introductions. First, there are the Honorable Mentions, which go to a potato battery and a surprisingly accurate model of a tornado alley trailer park. Then, the ribbons, which are distributed with fairness. Everyone gets one, color-coded to soften the blow.

When they announce the Grand Prize, I feel my heart stutter. They say her name, full and clear: "Cassandra Jade Montgomery." Cassie doesn't react at first. Maybe she's waiting for the universe to correct itself, but then she looks at me, wild-eyed, and for a second I see her as she was at five, legs too short, teeth too new, the entire world a miracle waiting to happen.

She walks up to the front, the gym floor echoing her footsteps, and the teacher hands her a shiny trophy. She holds it above her head, not in triumph but as if testing whether it might float away.

From the bleachers, I want to scream, to embarrass her with a howl of pride, but all I manage is a sharp intake of breath that leaves me lightheaded. Next to me, Nathan claps, steady and deliberate, and I realize I'm gripping his arm so tightly he may have bruises tomorrow.

When Cassie comes back to us, she sets the trophy on the table, then pulls me down to her level and hugs me, hard. She smells like donut glaze and dry-erase marker.

"You did it," I say, voice thick.

She nods, a single solemn bob, then, before I can even process, she throws her arms around Nathan. For a second he freezes, as if uncertain of the rules, then hugs her back, gentle but real.

Cassie is the first to break away. She sits, cradling the trophy in her lap, then looks up with the gravity of a Nobel laureate. "Can we get pizza?"

I laugh, the sound more relief than amusement. "Of course. You can have whatever you want tonight."

"Even soda?"

"Even soda."

"What about Nathan?" she asks, her gaze darting between us. "Can he come too?"

Nathan raises an eyebrow in mock surprise. "You think I can be bought with pizza?"

Cassie's lips curl. "Maybe."

"Well," he says, looking at me, "I do know a place, right on the boardwalk. They have the best pepperoni in town. Arcade games, too."

Cassie's face is a sunbeam.

I glance at Nathan and our eyes meet, a silent exchange that binds us to this new reality of ours. At his nod, I turn back to Cassie. "All right then. Pizza it is."

Her cheer bounces off the gym walls and confirms our victory as more than just a trophy on a table. As we walk out, the other parents stare, some with envy, some with that soft-eyed look reserved for families who seem to have everything under control. I know better, but I let myself pretend, let the feeling settle in my chest like the aftermath of a storm, fragile and dazzling and improbably whole.

Nathan holds the door, and for once I don't hurry to step through. I stand in the gym doorway, watching Cassie parade ahead, trophy in hand, her silhouette sharp against the parking lot sun.

"Thank you," I say, low, to Nathan.

He shrugs. "Wasn't much."

"No," I say, and I hear the tremble in my voice, the reverb of everything he'd managed to salvage. Not just the cardboard ocean but the morning itself. "It was everything."

CHAPTER 16

DIANE

The pizza parlor is neon-lit and unapologetically loud, the kind of place where a quarter buys you sixty seconds of glory, and the only salad is iceberg lettuce beneath a snowdrift of ranch. Booths line the windows in red vinyl, sticky and cratered with the scars of a thousand Friday nights. In the corner, a pair of plastic dinosaurs battle for dominance atop a faux-volcano, and the air smells of dough, sugar, and deep-fried mozzarella sticks.

Cassie makes a beeline for the trophy display. There's a local Little League Hall of Fame on one wall, the rest crammed with bobbleheads and Polaroids of past pizza-eating champions. She holds her own trophy next to a gold-plated soccer ball, comparing their weights with scientific rigor.

We crowd into a booth near the arcade entrance, the pizza menu laminated and curling at the corners. Nathan slides in beside me, and Cassie takes the outside seat so she can keep an eye on the Skee-Ball machine.

"I want pepperoni and black olives," she announces.

Nathan raises an eyebrow at me. "Objections?"

"None," I say. "Just no pineapple."

"We can all agree on that," he says.

The server comes by, hair in a cloud of scrunchie and

flyaways, and takes our order. She doesn't blink at the odd geometry of our trio, just asks if we want pitchers of soda or water for the table.

"Root beer, please," Cassie says, with all the authority of a CEO.

When the server leaves, Cassie produces her trophy again, polishing it with a napkin. "Do you think they'll let me put this in the school office?" she asks.

"I think they'd be fools not to," Nathan says. "That's a seriously competitive trophy."

Cassie beams, then leans into the table conspiratorially. "I heard they used to have an 'insect of the year' trophy, but the last principal was scared of them. So, they stopped giving it out after someone brought a praying mantis to the awards ceremony, and it got loose."

Nathan looks at me, mock-serious. "This is why I love science. The surprises never end."

The root beer arrives, sloshing in a heavy plastic pitcher. We toast, clinking our glasses over the table, and I let myself dissolve into the noise and the sugar high, the small miracle of a good night after a bad day.

Cassie is full of postmortems. "Did you see the Rube Goldberg machine? It used a real hamster. He was supposed to run on the wheel, but he just fell asleep. The whole thing was a disaster."

"Hamsters are notoriously unreliable," Nathan points out, a half-smile creeping up his face. "Should've used a gerbil instead."

Cassie snorts so hard she almost spills her drink, then wipes her chin with the back of her hand. "What was your science fair project when you were a kid?" she asks Nathan.

He leans back, hands behind his head. "I tried to make a robot shark. I glued a tin can to a remote-control car and used tinfoil for fins. It barely moved, and the paint smelled like old cheese, but I was very proud."

"Cool," says Cassie, impressed.

The pizza arrives, still volcanically hot, cheese stretching in long, sticky filaments. We each grab a slice, and for several minutes the only sounds are chewing and the distant ringing of an arcade jackpot. I watch Cassie's face as she eats. She savors each bite, as if every new flavor is a tiny adventure.

After two slices and a refill of root beer, she wipes her hands, then asks if she can have some quarters for the games?

I check my purse. There's a stash of change just for this purpose, a habit carried over from the days when a handful of coins could buy ten minutes of quiet. I hand her a few dollars in quarters.

Nathan adds his own. "Go wild. Just not actual wild. The manager hates it when kids climb inside the claw machine."

Cassie grins, pocketing the loot. "I'll come back when I run out."

She's gone in a blink, sneakers squeaking over the linoleum, and we both watch her weave through the crowd of birthday parties and baseball teams.

Suddenly, it's just Nathan and me, the stretch of red vinyl between us charged with something electric and unfinished.

He takes a long drink, sets the mug down. "She's really something."

"Yeah." I pick at the edge of a pepperoni, unsure if he means the project or the person. "She's tougher than she lets on."

"I noticed," he says. His eyes are on Cassie, but he's clearly working up to something else.

The conversation stalls, and in the pause, I feel the weight of the day press into my shoulders. I glance sideways, catching Nathan's reflection in the chrome napkin dispenser. He's nervous, which is new.

"What?" I say, half-laugh.

"Nothing. Just... You're a good mom."

I blink, caught off guard by the directness. "Most days I don't feel like one."

He shrugs. "She wouldn't be the person she is if you weren't."

It's a simple statement, but it hits deep. I look down at my hands, tracing the line of my lifeline, and try not to cry in a pizza parlor. "Thank you."

He clears his throat, eyes fixed on a slice he's not eating. "Listen, I was wondering if you'd like to go out sometime."

"We are out," I say, teasing, trying to lighten the suddenly heavy atmosphere.

"I mean, on a real date. No science fairs or pizza trophies. Just you and me and perhaps, dinner."

The words hang, suddenly enormous. I watch Cassie at the Skee-Ball, winding up for a perfect score, the tiny orange balls blurring through the air. She's focused, determined, and absolutely alive.

A real date.

"Sure," I say, surprising myself with the speed of my response. "That might be nice."

He beams, wide and sudden, then does a victory gesture so dorky I burst out laughing.

Cassie returns, breathless and sweaty, clutching a plastic ring she's won at the prize counter. She looks from me to Nathan and back, antennae up. "Why are you guys being weird?"

"We're not," I say, maybe too quickly. "Are you having fun?"

She shrugs, then sits down, sliding the ring onto her pinkie. "It glows in the dark. They said you can see it from space."

"You'll have to let us know if any satellites call," says Nathan.

She rolls her eyes, then leans against my arm, content and tired.

We finish the pizza, then gather our leftovers and walk out into the wet-blue dusk. The air is thick with the promise of summer storms, and as we cross the parking lot, I catch our reflection in the restaurant window—three shapes, two grown and one growing, huddled under a single, unreliable umbrella.

Nathan offers to drive us home, and Cassie, half-asleep in the back seat, hums along to the radio. The roads are dark and empty, and when we pull up to the cottage, Nathan gets out and walks us to the door.

I hesitate there, hand on the knob, searching for the right words. There's no script for this part.

"Thank you," I say, "for today."

"You're welcome." He leans in, slow, a question asked and answered before it's finished. The kiss on my cheek is soft, so brief I barely have time to register it, but when he pulls away, I feel it for hours after.

He waves goodnight and heads back to his car. I watch until the taillights disappear, then go inside, where Cassie is already curled up on the couch with Rolo, the trophy on the coffee table like a beacon.

I sit beside her, take her hand, and let myself believe that maybe, just maybe, the world is ready to give us another chance.

CHAPTER 17

DIANE

June

The door slams with the exuberance of a small bomb, and Cassie's voice ricochets down the hall ahead of her. "I'm home!" The backpack lands, as always, a foot short of the coat rack, scattering pens and a year's worth of loose homework assignments across the mat. I hear the frantic shuck of her sneakers, then the rapid-fire slap of socks on linoleum as she hunts for food. Rolo is already at her heels, his tail whipping back and forth in excited anticipation of the crumbs she'll inevitably drop.

I meet her in the kitchen, leaning against the counter in a show of nonchalance I do not feel. She's already at the fridge, rooting for leftover lasagna or cold cuts or whatever her food-obsessed teenage appetite deems acceptable. There's windburn on her cheeks, and a new spray of freckles across her nose that wasn't there last week. I make a mental note to add sunscreen to the grocery list.

"Hey, bug," I say, and she answers with a mouth full of cold pepperoni. "How was the last day of school?"

"Hey, Mom." She swallows a mouthful of food before answering. "Absolute chaos. Everyone's already in summer mode. Even Mr. Enfield gave up trying to teach us anything new." She tosses the cheese wrapper at the trash can, missing by a mile. "So, did you write anything today?"

The question is so direct I almost laugh. Instead, I slide a sleeve of cookies across the counter toward her and say, "A little. Mostly just staring at the screen, but I think I'm getting closer."

She raises an eyebrow, unconvinced. "You used to write, like, thousands of words every day. When are you going to write something cool again?"

I frown at her, mock-offended. "What makes you think what I'm writing isn't cool?"

She shrugs, snagging a cookie. "It's about the lighthouse, isn't it? Everyone writes about the lighthouse. You should write about pirates or sea monsters instead. Or, like, a haunted house."

"Maybe I will."

She leans against the opposite counter, chewing. "Saw Nathan at the lighthouse just now."

My heart gives a weird double-thump, but I keep my voice steady. "Oh yeah? Is he painting?"

She nods. "Mostly just staring at it. I think he's waiting for inspiration or something."

"Maybe he's just stuck, like me," I say, which is a little too honest, but Cassie doesn't seem to notice.

She finishes her cookie, wipes her hands on her jeans, and asks, "Do you ever think about dating him?"

I blink. "Where did that come from?"

"I dunno. Sara says he's handsome. So do my teachers."

I want to tell her that Nathan is more than handsome, that he is complicated and kind and slightly broken in a way that feels familiar. I want to tell her I think about him more than I should, that I see him everywhere—in the way the light hits the lighthouse at dawn, in the sound of gulls bickering over a crust in the shape of her own uncertain smile. But I can't say any of that. Instead, I say, "I'm not sure I'm ready for dating, Cass."

She studies me, head cocked. "Maybe you don't have to be ready. Maybe you just have to try."

The wisdom lands like a stone at the bottom of a well, sending up a small, bright splash. I ruffle her hair as she passes, and she bats me away, giggling, before heading up to her room.

I stand in the kitchen, shell-shocked. I pour myself another mug of coffee, ignore the fact that it's nearly dinnertime, and return to my desk. The laptop waits, open and impassive. The words I typed that morning are still there, but now, with Cassie's voice ringing in my ears, I feel a new, nervous energy.

I start to write. Not about the lighthouse, not about pirates or sea monsters or the haunted house. I write about a woman who has lost everything she thought she needed, and a girl who is teaching her how to build something new from the pieces. I write about the way salt air gets into your skin, the way light bends around the edges of heartbreak, the way laughter can be both a shield and a bridge.

I don't stop to edit or second-guess. I just type, and the words come faster, clumsier, but more alive than anything I've written in years. My fingers cramp, my shoulders ache, but I keep going. Cassie's wisdom echoes. Maybe you don't have to be ready. Maybe you just have to try.

When I finally look up, the sky is dreamsicle-orange and dusty pink. There's a golden hour that belongs to the guest cottage alone, when the sun, tumbling westward, sneaks through the warped windowpanes and turns the floorboards into a melting river of light. I'm halfway up the stairs when I hear it, Cassie's voice, thin and bright, threading through the space between her door and the jamb. I freeze, one foot hovering above a groaning step, my fingers gone white on the banister.

She's on the phone. I can tell by the cadence, the lift and drop of her sentences, how her laughter comes in sudden, tidal rushes before cutting off. I know I shouldn't listen. I know, I know. But there's something in her voice that stops me, a waver I haven't heard since the night the pediatrician called with her allergy test results, and I spent an hour holding her in the bathroom while she sobbed for her forbidden peanut butter.

She says, "No, he's not my stepdad, dummy. It's not like that." The bed frame squeaks as she shifts, and I picture her sitting cross-legged, picking at a fraying edge of the duvet, phone balanced between ear and shoulder. "He's just...around a lot. Mom says he's just a friend, but I think she likes him. Maybe more than just likes him."

My pulse does a strange thing, skipping out of rhythm and then resuming, slightly off-beat. I lean against the wall and press my thumb into the place above my heart where the ache has been growing all spring. I can see her room from here—door ajar, posters curling at the corners, a constellation of shells and bottle caps arrayed on the windowsill. Her sneakers are abandoned just outside, one tipped over, as if she'd kicked them free mid-sentence.

She's silent for a second, then, "Yeah, he's nice. And smart. But it's still weird." Her voice drops, and I have to strain to catch it. "Like, when she laughs at his jokes, it's a different laugh. Not the way she used to laugh with Dad." There's a creak as she stands, and her shadow flickers on the wall through the crack in the door. "I want to be happy for her. But sometimes I just want things to go back to the way they were before, you know?"

I want to knock, to interrupt, to tell her that nothing is

ever "before" again, that the best we can do is swim through the present without drowning. But I remember Sara's words on the porch—watch, record, react—and I force myself to stay, to let Cassie unspool this ache without rushing to tie it up.

The phone conversation picks up again, a low murmur from the other end, the words lost to distance and drywall. Cassie's reply is soft and uncertain, not the bravado she wears like a shield. "Yeah. I mean, he's cool. He showed me how to draw properly, and he knew all these names for shells. But sometimes I look at Mom, and it's like she's trying really hard not to mess up." A pause, then, "I guess I'm doing that too."

The words land harder than I expect. I slide down the wall until I'm crouched on the bottom stair, forehead pressed to my knees, trying not to inhale too loudly. The air in the hallway is thick with dust and the citrus-salt of laundry detergent, and I remember a thousand scenes like this. Cassie at six, screaming about a lost tooth; her at eight, shutting herself in her room after her first fight with a friend; her three years ago, standing at the edge of the driveway, eyes brimming as the hearse pulled away.

"But you still miss him, right?" Amaya asks, and it comes through so clearly I wonder if the phone is on speaker.

"Every day," Cassie says. There's no hesitation. "But I don't want Mom to be lonely, either. I just... I don't know how to do both."

There's a shuffle on the line, the intimate sound of two kids doing their best not to cry, and I realize I'm doing the same. My hands are shaking, and the rawness of the moment is so exposed, so unvarnished, that I want to gather it up and keep it safe, never let anyone, least of all Cassie, see how deeply it hurts.

She laughs, brittle but real. "Anyway, I have to go. Mom

gets weird if I'm on the phone too long. She says my brain will turn to oatmeal." She hangs up, and I hear her flop back onto the bed, the mattress sighing under her.

I wait, counting out thirty slow breaths. On the other side of the door, silence pools. I hear the lazy whir of her ceiling fan, the soft thud of her sketchbook falling to the floor, and then, finally, her voice.

"Miss you, Dad," she says, and the words pierce straight through the wall, straight through me.

I stay there for a long time, letting the sadness roll through me, letting the light from the window fade into dusk. I want to be the kind of mother who knows what to say, who can stitch the edges of grief into something less jagged. But tonight, all I can do is listen.

When the house is dark and the only sound is the hiss of the ocean beyond the glass, I tiptoe to Cassie's room. The door is still ajar, and she's already asleep, hair tangled across her cheek, one arm curled around the stuffed turtle she's had since she was three. I watch her breathe, the slow, even rise and fall, and promise myself that tomorrow, I'll try to do better.

But for now, I let her be. I back down the hallway, the stairs cool under my feet, and find the notebook on the kitchen table where I left it. I open to a blank page, hand trembling only a little, and write:

Cassie is learning to let go. I am learning to watch. I close the book, press my palm to its cover, and try to believe it.

CHAPTER 18

Diane

After a night of restless sleep, I'm awake early. Dawn paints the horizon, the promise of a new day. The house is still in slumber, but I cannot keep the thoughts at bay. I make my way toward the kitchen, moving as quietly as possible to avoid disturbing Cassie, but as I round the corner, I find her already there. She's sitting at the table, a sketchpad in front of her, lost in the maze of her fingers. Her hair is a chaotic nest of waves and knots, backlit by the light filtering in through the window.

"Do you always wake up this early?" I ask, trying to keep my voice light and casual.

"Oh, hi, Mom," she says, resting her pencil on the sketchpad. She rubs her eyes with the back of her hand, stifling a yawn. "I couldn't sleep."

"No dreams?" I ask, reaching out to gently ruffle her wild hair.

"No. Just...thoughts."

I pull out the chair opposite her and settle into it. "Thoughts can be tricky that way."

She tries to give me a look that says everything is fine. It's not even close. "I think... I think I'm okay with Nathan," she says finally. Her voice is small, hesitant. She turns her gaze back to the sketchpad, picking up her pencil. But she doesn't move it. Just holds it, poised over the paper. "If you want to go out with him, I mean."

I stare at her, surprised by her words. Nathan and I have been dancing around each other for weeks now, never defining our relationship but always somehow gravitating toward one another. "That's very mature of you, sweetie," I say, carefully treading the thin line between motherly gratitude and an overall enthusiastic response that might scare her off. "But remember, it's important that you're okay with it because you really are okay, not just because you think that's what would make me happy."

She nods, her fingers tapping nervously against the sketchpad. "I know, Mom."

"Listen, I heard you on the phone last night...talking to Amaya. Not all of it, but enough."

Cassie's face goes tight, but she doesn't try to deny it. For a second, I think she'll clam up, turn away and shut me out like she did when she was little and the world was too big to face. Instead, she says, "I'm glad you heard. I didn't really know how to start talking about it."

I swallow against a sudden tightness in my throat. "Cassie, you can always talk to me. About anything. I don't have all the answers, but I'm here to listen. And try to understand."

She nods, staring at the wall. There's a photo of the three of us tacked up by her desk—me, hair sun-bleached and wild, grinning at the camera; Cassie, maybe eight, her cheeks flushed and her mouth open in mid-laugh; and Kyle, the gravity at the center, his arm around both of us, his smile so easy you could mistake it for ordinary happiness.

"Do you ever think about him?" she asks, voice wobbly.

"All the time," I say, and it's the only honest answer.

She presses her palms together, fidgeting with the cuticle of her thumb. "It's just...if you start dating Nathan, does that mean you don't miss Dad anymore?"

My first instinct is to recoil, to tell her no, that's not how it works, that love is not subtraction or division; but I force myself to hold still. She needs to say the words out loud, to make them real before I can try to answer.

After a minute, she adds, "I like Nathan. I really do. But when you talk about him, it's like there's a part of you that's already gone somewhere else. And I feel like if you let him in, you'll have to let Dad go."

I reach for her hand. She lets me, and her fingers are cold, the nails bitten ragged. I want to smooth every rough edge, but I know better. "Cass," I say, "no one could ever replace your dad. Not for me, and definitely not for you. What we had... It doesn't go away just because something new comes along."

She glances at me, skeptical but not unkind. "Is that really true?"

I wish I could make her believe it with just the force of wanting. "It's like—" I fumble, searching for the right analogy. "You remember when you were obsessed with that series about the girl and the magic horse?"

Her lips twitch. "Starlight Academy."

"Right. When you finished the last book, you cried for a week. I thought you'd never pick up anything else. But then you found the turtle books, and it didn't mean you loved the horse books any less. You just...made more room."

She lets this percolate. "It's not the same."

"No, it's not. But I think people are like that, too. We don't run out of love, Cass. Sometimes we just...make more room."

She tucks her knees up, chin resting between them, and I see the child she was and the grown woman she's hurtling toward, all in the same shivering bundle. "Are you sure? Because sometimes I feel like there's not enough room left for me."

The admission cracks something inside me. I slide closer, wrapping an arm around her shoulders. "Oh, bug," I say. "You are my heart. You will always be my heart."

She leans in, her head heavy on my collarbone. I stroke her hair, the same way I did when she was tiny and feverish and afraid of thunderstorms. We sit like that for a long time, saying nothing.

After a while, she asks, "Are you going to marry him?"

The question catches me off guard, and I laugh. "I don't know, Cass. I don't even know if he likes me like that. I'm still figuring it out. But I promise you, no one is marrying anyone until you and I have had about a hundred more talks like this one."

She laughs, a hiccup through her tears, and it's the most beautiful sound I've heard in ages.

"Okay," she says, sniffling. "Just...let me know before you do anything crazy, all right?"

I cross my heart. "You'll be the first to know."

We stay tangled together, her head under my chin, my arms around her. The radiator clanks, the wind howls, and the world shrinks down to the blue-lit cocoon of this room. I think of all the ways I've tried to protect her from sadness, all the stories I've told to keep her safe, and realize that the most important thing I can do is let her see me try, even if it means showing her my own fear.

Eventually, she raises her head. "Can I ask you something else?"

"Of course," I say, bracing myself for the next question.

"Do you think Dad would be okay with this? With you and Nathan?"

I find myself searching for a quiet place, where all the echoes of Kyle still reside. The way his eyes sparkled when he laughed, how he held me close on nights when the world felt too big and chaotic to face alone. "I think..." I start slowly, carefully, aware that this is a delicate terrain. "I think your dad would want us both to be happy, don't you?" I watch her face as I say this, searching for the flicker of belief.

"I guess," she mumbles, but there's a little less tension in her shoulders that I take as a small victory.

She rises from her perch at the table, leaving an imprint on the cushion that slowly fades away. "Okay," she says, and there's a new conviction in her voice. She heads for the stairs, but just before she ascends, she pauses and looks back at me.

"Thanks, Mom," she says, words threaded together with an understanding that feels older than her years. "For listening."

CHAPTER 19

DIANE

By late afternoon, my earlier conversation with Cassie is still lingering in my mind. Fortunately, Sara has invited me over to her place, leaving me a chance to escape from the remnants of my thoughts.

She is waiting for me on the back porch, a glass of sweet tea in her good hand. I've been so busy lately with the novel and Cassie that I haven't noticed how much Sara has changed. Her hair, once thick, now carries a wispiness that speaks of the worsening of her condition. And that's not all. Even her gait, once agile and sprightly, has slowed down to a measured shuffle.

Inside, the house carries the scent of old books and years of memories. There are photos on every wall now, some of her kids, some in caps and gowns, some clutching fish almost as big as their bodies. On the piano sits a faded wedding portrait, Sara in bell sleeves and a crown of wild daisies, Andrew standing behind her with his hand barely resting on her shoulder, both of them squinting into the sun. There are books everywhere, whole driftwood shelves of them, and a wall calendar with every square marked in her loopy script. *Doctor's appointments, bridge club, SHELL SALE!!!, Cassie's birthday* circled three times in red.

Sara lowers herself into the living room armchair, breathing a little heavier. "If you want to see the only decent picture of Andrew," she says, "it's over there." She points to the mantel, where a single five-by-seven stands alone, framed in rough slate. I cross to it and pick it up. He's older here than in the wedding photo, his hair gone white, but the eyes are the same. I imagine the voice that went with them, the clever retorts, the dry jokes. I understand immediately how a person could fall in love with a face like this and know too well how hard it must have been to let it go.

When I turn back, Sara is trying to stand. Her hands grip the armrests, knuckles white with effort. I set the photo down and hurry to her side, but she's already up, swaying a little.

"I'm fine," she insists, but I see the panic flash in her eyes, just for a second, before the mask drops back into place. She takes a halting step, then another, before her knees buckle and she sinks back into the chair, breathing hard.

I kneel in front of her, afraid to touch but unable to look away. "Should I call someone?"

Sara shakes her head, fiercely. "No. Just...give me a minute." Her voice is brittle, almost angry, but I stay where I am, feeling helpless and intrusive and terrified all at once.

We stay like that, the only sounds the whir of a distant ceiling fan and the slow, deliberate count of her breaths. After a few minutes, the color returns to her face, and her jaw unclenches.

"I'm supposed to be the wise old crone," she says, a grim smile forcing itself up. "Not the tragic hero."

"You can be both," I say, surprising myself with the steadiness in my voice.

She laughs, a thin thread of sound, but it seems to help.

"Do me a favor?" she says, gesturing vaguely toward the kitchen.

"Anything."

"Could you water the succulents on the sill? I always forget."

I do, and as the tap runs and the glass fills, I spot the evidence I've been looking for—a neat row of prescription bottles on the counter, one of them already tipped and rolling slowly against the backsplash. I right it, read the label—something I can't pronounce—but the warning stickers are all the same: *MAY CAUSE DIZZINESS, TAKE WITH FOOD, CAUTION OPERATING HEAVY MACHINERY.* I set it gently back in line, wondering if the pills are helping or just slowing her down, tamping the vital parts so she won't suffer too much on the way out.

I bring the glass to the windowsill and pour it into the crowded jungle of aloe, jade, and some spindly cactus that seems to thrive on neglect. When I return to the living room, Sara has managed to shift from chair to couch, a feat of willpower that makes me want to both applaud and cry.

She pats the cushion beside her. "Sit," she commands, and I do, folding myself in at the edge.

"There's something I need to ask you," she says. "I've been putting it off because I hate the idea of burdening anyone, but it's getting harder. The day-to-day stuff." She stares at her hands, as if they belong to someone else.

"Of course. Whatever you need."

"Thank you," she says. "I know you're dealing with your own mess. I just... If you could come by, now and then... Help with groceries, or maybe driving me to an appointment. It wouldn't be forever... Just until Judy arrives, and after that...who knows." She tries to smile, but it doesn't quite land.

I cover her hand with mine. "I'd be glad to help. It's the least I can do after all your kindness." I give her hand a slight squeeze, and she relaxes.

For a long time, we just sit there, the physical contact solid and anchoring. I can feel the tremor through her palm, the way it never quite stops, even in rest.

"Thank you," she says, and I realize how little she's used to needing anyone.

When the clock in the hallway chimes seven, I move to stand, but Sara holds my wrist for a second longer.

"One last thing." She reaches down beside the couch and produces a small, well-worn paperback. It's a book of poetry, the spine cracked and the cover worn soft as cloth. "Andrew gave me this the week before he proposed. He said I should read it cover to cover, then mark the lines I thought were true, and he'd do the same. When we finished, we'd compare. If we had enough in common, we'd get married." She grins, the mischief back. "He proposed anyway, the coward, but I still have the book."

She presses it into my hands, urgent. "Maybe the marked lines will help. For the writing. Or for whatever comes next."

I turn the book over, touched by the worn fingerprints on the cover, the edges soft with years of handling. "Are you sure? This looks irreplaceable."

She shrugs. "Things aren't meant to last, dear. Neither are people. But stories, they're different. They survive. That's the only afterlife I believe in."

I help Sara to her feet, and this time she doesn't refuse, leaning into me as we cross the room, the poetry book pressed between our bodies like a shared secret.

At the door, she steadies herself, then lets go. "You're

stronger than you think," she says. "You just need practice."

"Isn't that true of everyone?" I reply, the book of poetry tucked under my arm.

Sara smiles, a little sad, a little proud. "Not everyone tries."

I leave her standing in the doorway, backlit and unbowed, the queen of her seaside kingdom. The walk home is silent except for the call of gulls and the faint, persistent ache of being seen.

In the guest cottage, I put the poetry book on the table and stare at it for a long time, afraid to open it, afraid of what I might find in the margins. Eventually I do, and the first page is covered in Andrew's handwriting, all sharp angles and unnecessary flourishes. There's a line, starred and underlined twice: *Only the present is real. Only the present can be saved.*

I sit there, the evening thick with the scent of wet grass and salt, the book open on my knees, the notebook beside it. I wait, counting the seconds, not for permission this time, but for the feeling that tells me I'm finally ready.

And when it comes, I pick up my pen, and I begin.

CHAPTER 20

DIANE

I'm not proud of how long I spend in front of the mirror. First the bathroom, then the hallway, then the cheap full-length glass tacked to the back of my closet door, which distorts everything below the waist and gives my reflection the vague proportions of a spoon. There are three dresses on the bed, all of them in safe, forgettable shades. Navy blue, white, a washed-out green that reminds me of celery left too long in the fridge. I try each one, stand with my arms limp at my sides, tilt my head, and squint to see if I look mysterious or just deeply uncomfortable.

Cassie leans in the doorway, her hair still damp from her "I-don't-need-a-shower" shower and observes. Rolo is curled at her feet, his wet nose twitching in his sleep. "The blue one," she says, not even bothering to enter the room. "You look like a librarian in the other two."

"That's...not actually the insult you think it is," I mutter, but the blue goes back on.

She smirks, then disappears, sneakers squeaking a retreat down the hall. Alone again, I sweep my hair up, then down, then up again. I dab mascara, rub it off, reapply with more conviction. In the low light, my face appears unexpectedly young and then, from another angle, not young at all. I lean in close, searching for some hint of what Nathan might see. I find only myself, layered and receding.

He is supposed to arrive at six. I finish dressing at five thirty and then spend twenty minutes pacing, picking at my cuticles, and trying not to sweat through the dress. The cottage smells faintly of last night's burnt popcorn, so I light a candle and immediately regret it. The scent is called "Seaside Escape," and it fills the room with a chemical imitation of suntan lotion and pineapple. I open the window, let in the real salt air, and sit on the edge of the bed, hands folded tight enough to blanch the knuckles.

When I'd said yes to the date with Nathan, I'd imagined it as something distant, a point on the horizon that could be safely ignored until its arrival. But time, as always, has marched with merciless precision, and now here I am, staring at the second hand of my watch, counting down the minutes until he arrives.

I pick up the photo of Cassie and me that sits on the antique dresser. In it, we are laughing, wind messing our hair, under a sky so blue it seems to vibrate. The joy in our faces is genuine, but I cannot ignore the void right next to us, the space where he should be. The absence is almost tangible, a ghostly silhouette that seems to mock my attempts at moving on. I gently put the picture down and close my eyes, trying to shake off the dwindling specter of the past.

At 6:01, Nathan's car pulls into the sandy rut that serves as a driveway. I watch from behind the curtain as he steps out, runs a hand through his hair, and stares at the cottage like he's making up his mind about something. He wears a dark shirt, sleeves rolled, and jeans that look clean but lived-in. He's shaved, and there's a nervous energy in the way he lingers beside the car.

The front door is only a few steps from the bedroom, but it takes me longer than it should to answer his knock. When I open it, he smiles, quick and lopsided, as if he's been caught at something. There's a small, crumpled bouquet of wildflowers in his left hand. Queen Anne's lace, bluebells, a few pale weeds that haven't yet decided if they're flowers or not.

"These are for you," he says, thrusting them forward with a shy confidence that makes my heart stutter.

"They're beautiful." I take the bouquet, unsure what to do with my hands, then settle for cradling them awkwardly at my hip.

Cassie materializes at my elbow, having changed into a fresh T-shirt with a cartoon whale on it. Rolo is not far behind. Cassie regards Nathan with a blend of suspicion and admiration. "You're late," she observes, "but Mom looks nice, so I forgive you."

Nathan laughs, his gaze darting between us. "I'm glad I have your approval, Cassie. And thanks for the recommendation. Dinner at the pier sounds perfect."

He says it like it's our idea, which technically it is. The Kitty Hawk pier has a restaurant attached, old as driftwood and just as knobby, famous for crab cakes and for being the only spot in town that doesn't play Jimmy Buffett on a loop. I had mentioned it once, in passing, and he remembered.

As we leave, Cassie hovers on the porch, arms folded, as if she expects a full report upon my return. For a split second, I want to call the whole thing off, to stay home and order pizza and watch her doze off to *Animal Planet* reruns while the dog snuggles between us on the couch. But then Nathan is opening the passenger door, his palm gentle at my back, and I let myself step into the unknown.

The drive is short, but the quiet inside the car feels like a second, smaller room. Nathan fiddles with the dial, finds a station playing old Motown, and leaves it there. My hand rests on my knee, gripping the fabric of the dress so tightly that the skin underneath prickles.

"You look...really nice," he says, eyes on the road.

"So do you," I say and immediately wish for a better word. Dapper? No, too performative. Handsome? Too risky, too intimate. He is both, and neither, and something else entirely.

He seems to sense my nerves and offers up small talk. I respond in kind, describing my failed attempts at baking with Cassie, the latest discovery of a local goat farm, the impossibility of keeping sand out of the bedsheets. Each exchange is a stroke, gentle and careful, until the car is filled not with silence but with something approaching comfort.

As we pull into the parking lot, the pier stretches out before us. The restaurant sits halfway down, perched over the water on a spindly network of pilings. From the lot, you can see straight through the windows, the amber glow inside contrasting with the blue dusk outside. The entrance is marked by an old bell buoy, pitted and red, hung above the doorframe like a relic of some more nautical past.

The place is half-full. There are a few tourists in crisp polos, a cluster of locals at the bar, an elderly couple eating near the window. The walls are paneled with rough cedar and adorned with vintage photographs of hurricanes, shrimp boats, and teenagers in swimsuits holding up improbable fish. Nets hang from the ceiling, dotted with glass floats and the occasional plastic starfish. The tables are old, the wood worn smooth and sticky in places, the chairs so light you feel as if you might float away at any moment.

The hostess, a girl with salt-bleached hair and forearms like taffy, leads us to a table beside the main window. The ocean is right there, just beyond the glass, restless and darkening with the evening. We sit, and for a second neither of us speaks.

I busy myself with the menu, even though I already know what I'll order. Nathan does the same, but his eyes keep darting up to meet mine, then away again, as if checking for a signal.

"Do you come here often?" he asks, and we both wince at the cliché.

"Yes, quite often," I say. "Cassie loves the hush puppies. I'm pretty sure she's angling for a job in the kitchen when she's old enough."

He laughs, shoulders relaxing. "I'd hire her. She's got the kind of ambition I respect."

The waiter arrives, a kid barely older than Cassie, nervous and eager to please. He takes our drink order (Chardonnay for me, local beer for Nathan), and when he leaves, I realize my hands are trembling just enough to make the menu shake. I set it down, folding my fingers in my lap.

Nathan sees the motion, but instead of commenting, he shares a story about the time he nearly set his apartment on fire attempting to flambé bananas, how he spent the next week trying to get the scorched smell out of his hair. I find myself laughing, not because it's the world's funniest story, but because he tells it so sincerely, unafraid to sound ridiculous.

The wine arrives, cold and bright, and I take a sip for courage. Nathan mirrors me, raising his glass.

"To first attempts," he says.

I clink his glass, feeling a tiny jolt of electricity at the sound. "And to surviving them," I add.

The ice between us starts to melt, not all at once, but enough that I can feel the warmth beneath. We talk about everything but the things that matter most. How the weather here can flip in an instant, how people in small towns remember what brand of cereal you buy, the subtle differences between North and South Carolina barbecue. It's easy, almost effortless, and I can see why people want to spend time with him.

When our food arrives, I'm so hungry I could cry. The crab cakes are perfect, crisp, and buttery, and the fries taste of malt vinegar and summer. Nathan orders the blackened fish, and when he takes the first bite, his eyes close in bliss.

"This is," he says after swallowing, "maybe the best meal I've had since moving here."

"I'm glad."

As we eat, the conversation edges closer to the things we're both avoiding. He asks about my writing, why I left journalism, how it feels to have so much time alone with my thoughts. I answer honestly, even when the truth feels jagged. I tell him about the memoir I wrote for Sara that started all this, about the pressure to produce, about how sometimes I worry I've already written the best thing I'll ever write.

He listens, really listens, the way Cassie does when she's learning a new word. When it's his turn, he admits to days when painting feels like a punishment, when the prospect of an empty canvas makes him want to sleep for a week. He confesses to falling in love with the coast when he was a child, how he used to dream of becoming a marine biologist before discovering his talent for art.

Between courses, I excuse myself to the restroom, where I stare at my reflection in the harsh fluorescent light. The wine has brought a flush to my cheeks, and my hair has collapsed from its earlier effort. I smooth it, dab at the smudged eyeliner, and practice a smile that doesn't look forced. When I return, Nathan is watching the ocean, his fingers drumming a slow, absent rhythm on the tabletop.

"I could get used to this view," he says when I sit. He's not looking at the water anymore. He's looking at me.

I blush, grateful for the restaurant's low lighting. He shifts in his seat, and our knees touch beneath the table.

The restaurant begins to empty, the tourists trickling back to their rental houses and the regulars retreating to the bar. The hush of voices fades, leaving only the murmur of the waves and the soft clink of dishes from the kitchen. The candles on each table burn lower, and the light in the room shifts from golden to something softer, more forgiving.

We order dessert. Key lime pie, tart enough to make the corners of my mouth ache, and split it, each bite a negotiation of forkfuls and glances. I find myself wanting to linger, to stretch the moment into something infinite.

Nathan leans in, his arms folded on the table. "Can I ask you something personal?"

I nod, the fork paused midway to my lips.

"Were you nervous about tonight?"

I almost laugh. "I spent an hour deciding whether to wear mascara. I changed my dress three times. I even considered calling to cancel, just to get out of my own head."

"Me too. Not the mascara, obviously. But the rest of it." He raises his bottle, catching my eye. "To surviving the dreaded first date."

I clink my glass against his. "And to not being as dreadful as we feared."

The candlelight dances in his eyes as he smiles, genuine and unguarded, and something in my chest unclenches. We sit, letting the laughter die down, letting the world around us recede into the background. Eventually, he asks about my family, and rather than evade the question, I embark on a journey of the past.

"My family isn't exactly...standard," I tell him as I scrape the last of the lime filling from the plate.

"Is anyone's?"

"Mine is less so, maybe." I exhale, surprised by how much I want to tell him. "I was adopted. Henry and Mary Anne Montgomery. They raised me from when I was about three months old. I never met my biological parents. Didn't know anything about them, actually, until I came here to interview Sara."

He listens with his whole body, arms folded, leaning slightly forward.

"My mother... My biological mother... Her name was Rosalie, and she lived right here in Kitty Hawk. In fact, she worked here, in this very restaurant. She was best friends with Sara and another woman named Judy. She died shortly after I was born, so I never had a chance to know her."

Nathan's hands still on the table, fingertips touching. "What about your father? Where was he?"

"His name was Hank. He was killed in Vietnam, just a few weeks before I was born." Nathan's gaze is steady, his expression unreadable, but he makes no move to interrupt. The memory of my father, as told by Sara and Judy, is a hazy collage of stories and pictures. They painted him as a kind man with an easy laugh, a lover of beaches and dogs, a man who would have been a loving father.

"It must have been quite a shock, discovering all of that."

Something about his tone, his willingness to sit with me

in this moment of exposure, steadies me. I nod, swallowing around the lump in my throat. "It was. Even more so because Sara and Judy, they've welcomed me into their lives. They've given me a whole new perspective on...well, everything. And despite the circumstances, it's brought me closer to them, you know? Before, it was just empty spaces in a family tree. Now... Now there are roots and branches, filled with stories and history."

"And how does that change things for you?" he asks, his words tracing the outline of my vulnerability.

"It's bittersweet," I admit, tucking a loose hair behind my ear as I watch the flickering candle cast shadows across our table. "Learning about them, it's like having a piece of them with me. But it's also a reminder of what I've lost, what could have been."

After a momentary pause, he reaches across the table to gently squeeze my hand. "You're incredibly brave, Diane. That's a lot to carry, for anyone."

"It is," I say. "But it also isn't. My real family is the one I grew up with. They're the ones who raised me, loved me, taught me how to be the person I am today. And Rosalie and Hank...." My voice trembles, my hand slipping out of Nathan's to run through my hair. "They're like...distant stars, I guess. They've always been there, even when I couldn't see them."

He studies me for a few long seconds, then says, "Sara was right, you are a rain catcher."

"What?"

"A rain catcher. She told me that's what she calls you. Says you have this ability to take life's storms and turn them into something beautiful. Something meaningful."

I blink, surprised and oddly moved. "She said that?"

He nods. "She thinks very highly of you."

Tears sting my eyes, and I blink them away, masking the urge with a forced chuckle. "Well, she's biased. She's practically family."

There's a lull, long enough for the server to collect our plates and ask if we need anything else. I shake my head, then glance at Nathan, who surprises me by asking for two coffees, black.

"Just to buy us a few more minutes," he says when the server leaves.

The restaurant is nearly empty now. The ocean's voice comes through the glass, constant and soothing. Nathan rests his chin on his hand and studies me with an openness that is both alarming and magnetic.

"I should probably confess something, too," he says, and the words tumble out of him with a candor that stuns me. "I was engaged before I left Charlotte. For three years, to a woman named Melissa. Though we were together for almost a decade. We called it off a month before the wedding. Sometimes I think about her more than I want to admit. Not in a pining way, just... trying to figure out what I did wrong."

I swallow, both moved and relieved by this revelation. "Do you know...what you did wrong?"

"I think...I wanted more than she was able to give. In the end, I wanted a different life, a different person." His tone is devoid of bitterness, but there's an undercurrent of regret. "I think we just both got lost somewhere along the way."

I process his words, wondering what it means that he's chosen now to share this with me. "Do you regret it?"

"The relationship? No, she was the love of my life. But I regret the way it ended."

I must have looked shocked because he's quick to explain, "Not that I want her back or anything like that. I just... I wish it hadn't ended so messily. We both said things we didn't mean, and I think it made both of us feel worse. It's strange, you know? How someone can go from being the most important person in your life to a stranger you used to know."

It's raw and real and surprisingly tender. I find myself both admiring his strength in being so open and feeling a twinge of jealousy toward his ex. The feeling is childish, I realize, but it doesn't vanish entirely.

"So..." Nathan's voice cuts through my thoughts, drawing me back into the glow of the restaurant. "That's my baggage."

I give a soft laugh, the tension dissolving. "Well, it seems we both have suitcases to carry."

"Makes the journey more interesting, doesn't it?"

I reach across the table, fingers grazing the back of his hand. The touch is tentative, but he turns his palm upward, inviting. I let my hand settle there, warm and awkward, two grownups pretending not to notice how badly we both want contact.

The server brings the coffee, sets it down quietly, and disappears. For a minute, we say nothing, just let our hands rest together on the wood.

"I think everyone's afraid of starting over," I say. "Whether it's after a breakup or a personal loss, it's a chapter of life that's ending. We're conditioned to believe it's a failure, or a sign that we've somehow gone off track. But maybe it's just the universe giving us another chance to find what we're meant for."

Nathan's thumb brushes over my knuckles, slow and deliberate. "You're wiser than you give yourself credit for, Diane. And far braver."

"I'm not so sure about that," I say, but his words, the soft way he pronounces my name, sends warmth spiraling through me.

We sip our coffee, staring out at the blue-black void beyond the window, and for a rare moment, I feel at home in my own skin.

By the time we leave, the staff is stacking chairs and mopping the floor. Nathan stands, offers me his arm. I take it, more certain than before. As we walk to the car, I glance back at the restaurant. I wonder how many people have started something new in that little room, how many have risked the awkwardness and the unknown. I also think about my parents, who long ago might have sat in that same spot, staring out at the same restless ocean. Maybe we're just another pair in a long, unbroken chain.

CHAPTER 21

DIANE

We're almost to the car when Nathan stops, just shy of the curb. He hesitates, rocking on his heels. "There's a theater in Manteo," he says, voice low. "They're showing this Japanese monster movie, I think. I know it's late, but...if you're not sick of me yet?"

I'm so relieved at the prospect of not ending the night that I almost laugh. "I'd love to. Just let me call Cass to tell her where I'll be."

I find the pay phone and drop a coin into the slot. Cassie answers on the first ring, "Hello, Montgomery residence."

"Cass, it's me," I say, my words hurried. "Nathan and I are going to catch a movie in Manteo. I just wanted to let you know so you wouldn't worry."

"Oh, a movie. How romantic," she teases. "That must mean things are going well."

I blush, fighting the urge to roll my eyes. "Yeah, yeah. Just don't wait up for me, okay? We might be late."

"Fine, but you better tell me all about it tomorrow." She hangs up, leaving me to smile at the dial tone.

The drive to Manteo is longer than I remember, the road winding inland and then back out over the low causeways that stitch the islands together. The sky is all indigo, the salt marshes on either side reflecting a sullen moon. In the quiet, Nathan plays the radio, low and oldies-heavy, and we both sing along to a fragment of "Be My Baby." I haven't sung in front of another adult in years. My voice isn't pretty, but it's loud and unafraid, and Nathan beams at me like I've pulled off some impressive trick.

The theater is a relic, its neon sign flickering at intervals, the carpet worn and matted. We're the only people in the lobby, save for a teenager in a "Chill Out" hoodie manning the popcorn machine. Nathan orders two tickets, and I let him, and then he orders popcorn, and I let him do that too. The air smells like salt and synthetic butter, the kind of scent that imprints on your hair for a week.

The movie is already starting. The projector flickers, the subtitles a little out of sync, and the auditorium is cavernous and empty except for one pair of kids making out in the back row. Nathan steers us to seats near the middle, not too close, not too far. We settle in. The screen fills with images of rain-lashed cities and rubber-suited monsters, but I barely register any of it. My awareness narrows to Nathan beside me, the way his thigh presses against mine.

I sneak glances at him between scenes, noting the way he reacts to the movie—the small smiles, the furrow of concentration, the occasional soundless chuckle. When he offers me the popcorn, his hand lingers just a fraction longer than necessary, the back of his fingers grazing my wrist. I don't move away.

About halfway through, during a lull in the on-screen carnage, Nathan's hand finds mine, palm up on the armrest, hesitant and slightly clammy. He's not slick about it. He's vulnerable, almost sheepish, as if he's unsure if I'll reciprocate.

I curl my fingers into his, and the relief in his whole body is immediate.

We hold hands for the rest of the movie, sometimes tightening, sometimes slackening, but never letting go.

Afterward, Nathan drives me home., but he doesn't pull into my driveway right away. Instead, he circles the block once, then pulls over by the dunes where the glow of the porch lights can't reach us. The sound of the surf is a distant hiss, and the only light comes from the dash and the half-moon overhead.

He lets go of my hand, but only so he can turn to face me. "I had a great time tonight," he says, and it's the kind of simple truth that makes me want to cry a little.

"Me too."

He reaches for me, slow enough that I could refuse if I wanted, but I don't. His lips are soft, hesitant, and for a moment it's just the brush of skin on skin, a tentative question. I answer, and the kiss deepens, still gentle but surer now. I tangle my fingers in his hair, his hands at my waist, and we stay like that for a minute or a year. When we break, we're both breathless and a little dazed, like we've surfaced from a deep dive.

Neither of us speaks on the walk to the porch. The porch light is on, and the little cottage glows warm and inviting. Nathan stops at the steps, his hand slipping from mine, and I think he might say goodnight and leave it at that.

Instead, he reaches up, tucks a strand of hair behind my ear, and looks at me with a tenderness I can barely stand.

"I'll call you tomorrow," he says.

"I'll answer," I say, and then he's gone, walking backward down the steps, smiling like he's afraid to turn away in case I vanish.

I watch until his taillights disappear, then step inside,

pulse racing.

Cassie isn't in bed. I find her in the kitchen, sitting on the counter with her knees up, an apple in one hand and a comic book in the other.

She looks at me, then at the clock, then at me again.

"So," she says, biting into the apple, "was it the best date ever?"

I lean on the opposite counter, wondering how to translate what just happened into language a thirteen-year-old will accept. "It was...really good. We saw a monster movie. We had pie. I think we're going to see each other again."

She shrugs, too-cool. "You seem happy."

"I am," I say, and I mean it.

Cassie hops down, abandoning the apple core in the sink. "Okay, but next time you have to bring me pie. It's the rule."

"It's a deal," I say, and we bump fists.

After she's in bed, I step out onto the porch, stare at the moonlit ocean, and let the new feeling in my chest expand until it's as big as the sky. For the first time in a long time, the future doesn't scare me. It feels like something I want to run toward.

On the hill, I spot a flicker of movement in Sara's window. I can just make out her silhouette, watching, maybe waiting for me to wave. I do, and she waves back, her arm a slow arc against the lamp-lit room.

I go inside, lock the door, and sit at the desk, fingers hovering over the keys.

I write:

It's possible to be broken and still believe in mornings.

I let the words stand, then close the laptop and climb into bed, the sound of the sea and Cassie's soft snoring my lullaby.

PART II

CHAPTER 22

DIANE

July

It's just after seven when the wind begins to peel the whitecaps back from the waves, pushing them toward the shore with a newfound ferocity. We're already at Sara's place, three mugs of tea growing cold on the living room table and a board game halfway set up between us. The first bands of Hurricane Bertha's leftovers have been lashing the coast since noon, but the sun is only now sinking behind a wall of green-black clouds, the sky thick with a static that makes the air taste like metal.

Cassie is on the floor, legs crossed, sorting the colored plastic chips into neat stacks. While Rolo is asleep, curled up against her leg. My attention keeps circling the window, as if the storm will make more sense if I catch it in the act. Each gust bends the pines in the side yard until they almost double back, and every so often a burst of rain needles the glass hard enough that I flinch.

Sara doesn't even blink. Her good hand is a blur, dealing out cards with a dexterity I wouldn't have expected from someone whose other arm refuses to cooperate. She's humming, too, low and off-key but stubborn. Every now and then she looks up at Cassie, who's gradually become like an adopted granddaughter, and smiles in a way that's more challenge than affection.

"It's just wind," Sara says, flipping the next card. "If you don't let it bully you, it loses interest."

Cassie snorts, eyeing her hand. "Tell that to my mom."

I give her a look, then turn back to the window. The sky is charcoal, the horizon lost to the sheets of rain slanting down from the heavens. I picture Nathan hunkered in his studio, windows rattling, the paint on his easel still wet. Then I force the thought away, embarrassed by the specificity of my concern.

Sara's house smells like old books and oranges and, faintly, the must of rain seeping into decades of wood. She's set out candles, dozens, scavenged from every closet and drawer, the majority of them shaped like seashells or, in one case, a banana slug. The overhead lights flicker every few minutes, and Sara just winks at us as if to say, *Let it try.* She's told me twice now that the power lines out here are more suggestion than infrastructure, and if the wind keeps up, we'll be on full *Little House on the Prairie* mode by nightfall.

It's cozy but also precarious. Cassie's been bouncing between excitement and thinly masked anxiety all day, and every time thunder mutters in the distance, she stares at the ceiling, as if expecting it to collapse. I'd considered evacuating to the mainland, but Sara had scoffed at the notion. "We'll be fine," she assured us. "This old house has weathered far worse than a tropical storm."

Sara makes a production of lighting another candle, her left hand steadying the match while the right fumbles the striker, and I have to fight the urge to jump in and help.

"I'll get that," I say, rising too fast from the couch. My knees bang the table and a mug sloshes, but Sara shakes her head, her mouth set in a line.

"I've been lighting my own candles since the Roosevelt administration," she says, but she lets me take the box anyway.

I lean over, smell the paraffin and salt, and realize how tired she looks. There are purple circles under her eyes, and her cheeks are hollowed out more than usual. The frailty is new. Last week she climbed three flights of stairs at the museum, albeit slowly and with a grimace, but today, even the act of standing to fetch her cardigan left her winded. I force myself not to hover, just hand her the matches and return to my seat.

Cassie eyes us both with theatrical suspicion. "You two need a referee."

Sara arches an eyebrow. "What we need is for someone to shuffle without cheating."

Before Cassie can object, a sound like the world's biggest bass drum thunders overhead. All three of us freeze, waiting. The windows rattle, the lights pulse once, twice, then die, leaving only the orange globes of candlelight and the thin, wavering music of the wind.

A few seconds of total silence. Then, with a decisive motion, Sara pulls the table lamp's chain and says, "Showtime." Cassie laughs, the fear bled out by the absurdity of the moment.

We settle in, the only light now the candles Sara lined along every horizontal surface. The flicker throws moving shadows on the walls, exaggerating the wild angle of her bookshelves and making the old ship's wheel above the mantel seem to turn slowly, as if steering the house into open water.

Cassie huddles closer to me, the board game forgotten. "Is it going to get worse?" she asks, voice pitched low.

"Probably," Sara says, too honest to hedge. "But this house has stood through six hurricanes and at least two direct hits. You'd need a nuke to move it."

I laugh, and the sound comes out too loud in the hush. But it helps. Cassie relaxes, curling her legs up under her, and I can see the tension smoothing from her shoulders.

Sara stands, steadier now, and starts lighting the backup candles. The matches catch on the first try, but her hands are trembling just a little, and I realize she's not immune to the nerves, just practiced at hiding them.

"I'll help," Cassie offers, springing to her feet. Together, they circle the room, bringing each wick to life in turn. The effect is dramatic. The whole room shifts from cavern to theater, every book spine and trinket thrown into shifting relief.

There's something old-fashioned about the dark and the candles and the way we're drawn in together, the storm outside shrieking but us stubbornly human in our defiance.

A sudden, sharp knock at the front door nearly upends the mood. Cassie lets out a tiny yelp and clutches my sleeve. Sara moves to the door, pausing only to straighten her collar, and I follow, suddenly aware of every creak in the floorboards and the way the rain now pelts the windows.

Another knock, this one more urgent. Through the rippled glass, I see a shadow, tall and hunched, water streaming from every surface. I open the door, and Nathan stumbles in, trailing water and the smell of sea air.

He's soaked through, hair plastered flat and jacket dark as spilled ink. His cheeks are raw from the wind, and he blinks, disoriented, as if the sudden transition to candlelit warmth has blinded him. When he sees us, his posture relaxes a fraction, but his hands are balled tight in the hem of his shirt, wringing water onto the floor.

"Nathan, what are you doing here?" I ask. "I thought you were going to ride out the storm in your studio."

"I—well, I changed my mind," he says, shrugging out of his jacket. "I tried to call, but nothing's working. Thought I should check on you." His gaze skips from Sara to me, then lingers, and the current between us is enough that I have to look away.

Sara clucks her tongue. "Sit down, you fool, before you ruin the floors." But she's smiling, and I catch the fleeting glimmer of satisfaction in her eyes as she steers Nathan to the couch. Cassie hangs back, half-hiding behind the door, but her expression is pure delight.

Nathan sits, dripping, and I hesitate, unsure whether to offer a towel or a change of clothes or just let him dry out by proximity. The quiet stretches, punctuated by the ticking of rain on the roof and the distant groan of thunder.

Finally, he asks, "You okay?" The question is so direct, so without preamble, that I feel myself flush.

"Yeah. We're fine. Just"—I wave a hand at the darkness—"riding out the storm."

"They're saying the worst will pass by midnight. We'll probably get a lull in a couple hours." He speaks with the authority of someone who's been reading the radar like a script.

Sara hovers for a minute, then gestures to Cassie. "Let's get some towels, sweetheart." They leave the room together, and then it's just Nathan and me, the low flame of a single candle between us.

His eyes don't leave mine. "I should've stayed at the gallery," he says. "Didn't mean to worry you."

"You didn't," I lie, and we both know it.

He runs a hand through his hair, scattering droplets onto the arm of the sofa. "It's wild out there," he says, almost to himself. "Like being inside a painting before it's finished."

I laugh, but it comes out shaky. "That's one way to look at

it."

He gives a crooked smile, and I'm struck by how young he seems in this light. "Sara says you're the only one who ever beats her at Scrabble," he says, changing the subject with a finesse that's almost surgical.

"I think she lets me win," I reply, grateful for the escape route.

The conversation could spiral, but before it does, Cassie and Sara return, arms loaded with towels. Cassie hands one to Nathan, who mumbles thanks and buries his face in it, emerging with his hair standing on end. Sara just watches us, her eyes narrowed and her mouth curved in that sly, Mona Lisa way she has.

"That's better," she says. "Now, where were we?"

We gather around the coffee table, which is a slab of driftwood sanded to near-translucence. Sara claims her throne, an ancient recliner with a quilt draped over the arms. Before she sits, I gently tuck a pillow behind her back. She scowls at me but lets it happen. I catch the flicker of a smile, quickly stifled, and make a mental note of how little resistance she actually puts up.

Cassie selects the next game, an old-school version of Parcheesi, half the pieces missing and the board soft at the creases. "House rules," she says, setting it up, "are that you have to tell a secret every time you get bumped back to start."

Sara laughs. "You little shark."

We play, the pieces sliding around the board, the dice rattling hollowly in the upturned lid of a tea tin. The candlelight is uneven, tall and guttering on the table, low and golden at the periphery. It makes the whole scene feel like something painted from memory, an image that will grow more beautiful and less precise with every telling.

It takes two turns for Sara to land on Nathan and bump him back to the start. "You first, Nathan," she says, pointing an imperious finger.

Nathan considers. "When I was eight, I buried a time capsule in my backyard. It was supposed to be for the future, but I dug it up every week to check on it and add more stuff." He shrugs. "I think it's still there, full of dead bugs and baseball cards."

Cassie raises an eyebrow. "That's not a real secret."

"Sure it is," Nathan says. "You're just not old enough to realize how embarrassing nostalgia can be."

On the next round, Cassie is forced back to start by a ruthless move on my part. "Truth time," I say, expecting a minor confession about failing a math test or stealing a cookie.

Instead, she leans in, the candlelight catching the shine in her hair. "Sometimes, when I can't sleep, I pretend I'm someone else. Not because I don't like being me. I just want to know what it would feel like." She glances sideways at Sara, then Nathan. "Just for one night."

My heart lurches in my chest, but I keep my face neutral. Sara's expression softens into something approaching reverence. "We all imagine other lives, Cassie. That's how we survive our own."

The game goes on. At every setback, another secret. Sara admits to cheating at crossword puzzles by looking up the answers; Nathan confesses that he once lied about his age to get a summer job; Cassie reveals she's never actually finished a single book assigned in English class, but always reads the ending first and then works backward. My own confession, when it's finally my turn, is that I used to write poetry but stopped when I realized I'd never be as good as my college roommate. The admission makes Sara cackle.

"Who cares about good?" she says. "Everything worth doing is better for being a little bad."

As the storm ratchets down, the games shift to Checkers, then a round of Uno played by dubious rules. Cassie nestles closer to Sara, their heads almost touching. Nathan and I sit opposite, our knees brushing under the table every time we reach for snacks or cards. With each accidental contact, a current passes up my leg, warm and a little illicit.

Sara bows, but it's Nathan who puts on a show of mock outrage, challenging Cassie to a rematch. As they argue, I find myself watching not just the way his hands move, quick and sure, but the way he pays attention. He listens to Cassie's questions, answers them without condescension, and when Sara looks tired, he's the first to suggest a break. He fits into the rhythm of us like he's always been here.

At some point, the four of us fall silent, the only sound the hiss of rain and the rare, distant boom of thunder. I study the faces around me. Sara, regal even when slumping in her chair; Cassie, eyes heavy, smiling at something only she can see; Nathan, head bowed, the curve of his neck lit gold by the dying flame. My own heart is full, bursting with something new—not quite love, but the shape it will take if I let it.

I think about what Cassie said, about wanting to know what it feels like to belong somewhere else, even for just a night. Maybe that's what we're all doing here, testing out new configurations, hoping something fits.

For the next hour, we ride out the worst of the storm together, playing games by candlelight, eating too many cookies, listening to the wind try and fail to scare us. Sometimes the thunder is close enough to rattle the glasses, and sometimes the rain softens, and we all pretend not to be waiting for it to start again.

Every so often, I catch Sara watching us, as if she's seeing something that the rest of us can only feel. I wonder what she thinks, if she remembers what it was like to sit in the dark with someone you wanted to know better while the world around you tried its best to come undone.

Eventually, the candles start to burn out, dwindling down into tiny blue flames that battle against the encroaching darkness.

Sara notices the diminishing light first. "I keep emergency candles in the hallway closet," she says, her voice softer now, tired in a way that makes my chest go hollow. "Diane, would you mind?"

"I'll go," I say, standing too quickly and setting the game pieces rattling.

Nathan unfolds from the chair beside me. "I'll help."

The hallway is a tunnel of shadow, narrow and lined with the old, heavy kind of wallpaper that absorbs noise and time. I lead with a tea light, its flame feeble but determined. Nathan walks just behind, close enough that I can feel the heat of him, which is animal, electric.

We reach the closet, and I balance the candle on a shoebox while I kneel to rummage through the bottom shelf. Nathan crouches beside me, and in the tiny pool of light our faces are inches apart. He smells like rain and the faint, honest sweat of someone who's been physically afraid.

The shelves are cluttered with old batteries, more board games, a half-deflated beach ball. We're both reaching for the back when our hands collide, and for a heartbeat neither of us moves. The air is thick, oxygen-poor, and my pulse is so loud I'm sure he can hear it.

He looks at me, not smiling but not backing away, and the light from the candle turns his irises a color I don't have words for. His voice is a whisper, like the end of a secret. "Can I...?"

Before he finishes the sentence, the candle gutters and plunges us into darkness.

I gasp, a small sound absorbed by the encroaching shadows. My fingers tighten around his, my first instinct to hold onto something real in the suffocating blackness. I feel him stiffen, then relax, his warmer hand enveloping mine.

"Yes," I whisper back, even though I am not sure what he was asking. My heart hammers against my chest, each thump a question mark. I hear him shift, then feel his fingers trace a path from my wrist up to the curve of my elbow. A sudden flash of lightning illuminates the hallway for a split second, revealing his face inches from mine. The sight sends my heart into overdrive, and I realize how close we are. Too close.

The walls of the house shrink around us, and all our pasts, all our futures, are crowded into this tiny closet space. Time seems to still, stretching out and collapsing into the span of a heartbeat. I am aware of everything—the whisper of his breath against my cheek, the faint scent of earth and sea on his shirt, the way our fingers interlace so perfectly.

Then suddenly, he's pulling me closer, his hand firm around my waist. My heart leaps into my throat as he leans in, his lips brushing against my ear. The words he whispers are lost in the rush of blood pulsing through my veins, but the tone sends a shiver cascading down my spine. It's not fear, but an awareness of the distance we've crossed, the line we're about to blur even further.

His lips, warm and slightly damp against my skin, pull away, leaving a trail of heat that dissipates almost instantly. And then, he's standing. He doesn't let go of my hand. Instead, his grip tightens subtly as he helps me to my feet.

I find the candle box, thrust it between us like a peace offering. "Found it," I say, and my voice is shaky, too bright.

He takes it, fingers lingering just a second too long, and then we're walking, our shoulders bumping as we make our way back down the hall.

At the threshold of the living room, the light from the remaining candles casts our shadows huge and awkward on the wall. Cassie's voice calls out, "Did you get lost?" and Sara, from the depths of her chair, just smiles.

We set the new candles in every dish and empty mug we can find, and when they flare to life, the room is just as before. Except, of course, it isn't.

Nathan sits farther away from me this time, but every movement he makes feels charged with the memory of our moment in the dark.

I look at Sara, and for a second her eyes meet mine. There's amusement there, but also a quiet understanding, as if she remembers what it's like to live at the edge of possibility, half-wanting and half-terrified by what comes next.

We play another round of games, the four of us, but every time I reach for the dice or move a piece across the board, I feel the echo of Nathan's hand against mine, the potential for contact humming just beneath the surface.

At some point, Cassie dozes off, her head on Sara's lap. Sara strokes her hair absently, humming that same off-key tune from earlier. Nathan glances at me, and his smile is a promise, not of anything grand, just the next morning, the next game, the next time the wind picks up.

By the time the storm gives up, the house feels even quieter than before, a kind of hush that's both earned and uneasy. I check the clock on Sara's mantelpiece. It's midnight, or thereabouts, though it's hard to tell since the power's still out, and the old pendulum sometimes loses the thread for minutes at a stretch.

Sara yawns, covering her mouth with her good hand, the other curled against her chest. "I'm calling it," she says, her voice rough at the edges. "If I don't get at least four hours, I'm no good to anyone."

I help her stand, and this time she doesn't protest. Nathan appears behind me, hovering just close enough to steady her elbow if she falters. We walk her down the hall, the shadows fatter and slower now that the storm has faded.

At her bedroom door, she leans in and whispers, "You two, don't burn the house down, okay?"

Nathan chuckles, low and private, and I feel it somewhere in my ribs. "We'll be good," he promises, and Sara vanishes into her room, shutting the door with a soft click.

Cassie is already half-asleep, splayed across the couch in a tangle of limbs and blanket. I tuck the throw under her chin and listen to her breathe, steady and rabbit-quick. The candles are mostly gone now, puddled into a single trembling flame. I sit beside her, close enough that I can feel her warmth, and wait for Nathan to reappear.

He does, silent as a thought. "I should go," he says, voice hushed so as not to wake Cassie. "Looks like the road's clear, and I need to check on the gallery... Make sure there's no damage."

I want to argue, tell him it's safer here, but the words catch behind my teeth. He stands by the door, keys in hand, raincoat hanging limp and heavy over his arm.

At the threshold, he turns. "If you need anything, just call."

I nod, because anything else would sound like begging. But the truth is, I am begging. Not for assistance or even company, but for something more elusive, the chance to lean into this new possibility, to let our paths veer closer without the fear of collision.

He hesitates, just long enough that it becomes a statement, not a pause, and then steps onto the porch. The air is shockingly sweet, the storm having scoured away all the dust and pollen, leaving only the cold smell of the ocean.

He's halfway down the walk when I hear myself say, "Nathan."

He stops, turns. The light from the last candle paints him in strokes of orange and shadow. I want to say I'm sorry for the weirdness, or for wanting him, or for being unable to do anything about it. But all I manage is, "Thank you. For... tonight."

"Anytime," he says, then he's gone, swallowed by the dark and the faint hush of receding wind.

I close the door and lean my forehead against it. For a minute, I listen to the way the house settles, the waves beating a softer rhythm on the shore. Cassie mutters something in her sleep and rolls over, her hand searching for mine.

I take it and let myself imagine what might have happened in that hallway if no one else was around. I sit in the dark, heart hammering, the ghost of a kiss pressed to my mouth, waiting for the storm inside me to subside.

Maybe, by morning, it will.

CHAPTER 23

DIANE

By morning, the storm has spun itself into memory. It leaves behind puddles that smolder with reflected sky and a beach strewn with fragments of driftwood, discarded shells, and a tangle of seaweed, as if the ocean had tried to move on land. In the aftermath, the whole town seems to exhale, the molecules rearranged by the violence of last night. Sara's house smells of smoke and wet leaves and the sweet, synthetic wax of spent candles. Every window wears a fine patina of salt, and the wooden floor, still damp in places, groans with each of my steps.

I wake on Sara's couch to the sight of Cassie curled against me, her knees drawn up, the back of her hand pressed to her nose. She's snoring lightly, breath hitching in the way it used to when she fell asleep in the car on long road trips. On the coffee table, the relics of last night's games are scattered. A single red checker, three Uno cards, a pawn from a chess set I've never seen. There's a peace to it that feels borrowed, as if the moment will snap the second anyone moves.

In the kitchen, I set water to boil, the kettle hissing against the low drone of the refrigerator. I make a mental note to check the basement for flooding. Sara said the old place was watertight, but last night's wind could have blown the river through a pinhole. I can still hear the wind in my ears, the way it howled and rattled the glass, but now it's only the slow drip of gutters and the static fizz of the radio left on overnight. Outside, the world is a palette of muted greens and pale sand, the dunes combed flat by the storm.

Sara emerges an hour later, wearing the same robe as the night before, though she's pulled her hair up in a hasty knot that makes her appear both regal and deeply unwell. She walks with a measured slowness, her good hand splayed against the wall for balance. She shuffles to the table, her lips pinched white, her whole body folded in around her chest.

"Morning," I say, trying to make it sound ordinary.

She nods, but her face has that sculpted stillness I've seen before—in hospital waiting rooms, on the faces of my own mother and her mother before her. There's an economy of motion, a deliberate conservation, as if every movement is calculated for maximum efficiency, minimal pain. Her left hand, always the traitor, hangs useless at her side. Her right is trembling in a way I've never noticed, or perhaps refused to notice, until this instant.

"Cassie's still out," Sara says, voice like crushed gravel. "How did she sleep?"

I shrug, uncertain. "She didn't seem scared. More... fascinated. Like the world's best sleepover."

Sara snorts, but it's a ghost of the sound it should be. She pours herself a mug of black coffee, ignoring the sugar, and sits at the table without looking at the food I've laid out—toast, apples, a jar of homemade preserves she gave me last week. She stares at her hands for a long time before curling her fingers, knuckles whitening, and pinching the bridge of her nose.

I watch her, trying to read the meaning in each motion. I

want to offer help, but there's a pride in her posture that repels sympathy. Still, her right hand is shaking so badly that when she lifts the cup, a crescent of liquid laps over the rim and soaks into her robe.

"Damn it," she mutters, and the cup rattles onto the tabletop.

I move without thinking, grabbing a dish towel and sopping up the spill. Up close, I can see the sheen of sweat on her upper lip, the dilation of her pupils, the way her shoulders hunch against an invisible weight.

"Sara, are you okay?" I ask, and the question sounds stupid even as I say it.

She gives a tight smile. "Bad night. I get these spells sometimes after a lot of excitement. Not a big deal."

But her left hand is trembling now, too, and the color is draining from her face. She tries to stand and sways, the chair scraping sharply against the tile. Her knees buckle, and she grabs for the counter, missing by inches.

"Jesus," I whisper, reaching out just in time to catch her before she hits the floor.

She's heavier than I expect—a sudden, uncooperative weight—and together we slide to the ground, her head thumping against my shoulder, the robe tangling around both of us. The back of her neck is slick with sweat. Her breath comes in ragged puffs, each one smaller than the last. For a second, I panic, the whole world narrowing to the frantic scramble for meaning. My hands are shaking, but I force them steady.

"Talk to me," I say, and her eyelids flicker.

"Bathroom. There's a bottle. Blue label. Need it now."

I rush to the bathroom, my heart pounding in my ears. The blue-labeled bottle is on the counter, amid a cluster of half-empty pillboxes. There's no prescription label, just a small sticker with *emergency only* scribbled in Sara's tight handwriting. I pour two pills into my hand and set off for the kitchen.

Sara is slumped against the edge of the island, head lolling. I hand her the pills and she dry-swallows them, then sits, breathing in shallow, measured sips, while I kneel beside her and try not to shake.

The lights overhead flicker, and for a heartbeat I imagine us trapped here, in this room, forever. Then the bulbs settle, and Sara's color begins to return, slowly, like water filling a bay.

"Better," she manages, after a long minute. "Sorry. It's always like this in the morning."

"Do you need to go to the hospital?" I ask, already preparing to hoist her upright.

She shakes her head. "It's fine. I'll be fine. Help me up?"

I get her back to the kitchen table, and she sags into the chair, her fingers clawing at the armrests. She tries to say something else, but the effort costs too much, and instead she just closes her eyes.

I stand behind her, hands hovering just above her shoulders. I want to touch her, to steady her, to make this all less real. Instead, I turn back to the stove, hands numb, and pour her a fresh cup of coffee. This time, I add sugar and milk, thinking of the way she took it at the bakery last week. When I set it down in front of her, she opens her eyes, the pupils tiny pinholes now, and she gives me a look that is equal parts gratitude and apology.

"Thanks, Diane," she whispers, and there's nothing left of the iron-voiced woman who commanded storm and child alike.

From the living room, Cassie's voice drifts in. "Mom?"

I go to her, my own limbs wobbly. She doesn't ask what happened; she just knows. She eases into the kitchen, silent as a ghost, and slips into the chair beside Sara, her hand resting lightly atop the older woman's. Sara doesn't flinch. She just pats Cassie's hand with her own, the two of them communicating in a series of tiny, calibrated gestures.

"I'll make you something to eat," I say, because it's all I can think to do.

I scramble eggs, burn the toast, fumble the lid on the strawberry jam. Every movement is a parody of normalcy, as if I'm acting in some amateur play where the script is missing entire pages. The tension is so thick I want to claw it from the air.

I'm still at the stove, my back to the others, when the doorbell rings. I freeze, spatula in midair, and exchange a glance with Cassie. She shrugs, but her eyes are alert, as if anything could walk through that door.

I wipe my hands and answer. On the porch, shivering in a damp windbreaker and carrying a steaming plastic tub, is Nathan.

He looks different in daylight, smaller, somehow. His jaw is unshaven, his hair is curling at the collar. His eyes, always darting, find mine and hold fast.

"Soup delivery," he says, holding out the container like an offering. "Thought you might need something warm."

For a second, I don't know what to do. There's a line in his forehead, a question that he doesn't want to ask. Behind me, the house is full of the acrid smell of burned toast and the low, animal sound of Sara's breathing.

I let him in and he hands me the tub. He stands uncertain in the hallway, dripping a slow, careful puddle onto the mat.

"What's going on?" he asks, voice low.

I shake my head, lips pressed thin. "Sara had an episode."

Nathan steps into the kitchen without waiting for invitation. He surveys the room, the scene. Sara is slumped at the table, Cassie's hand atop hers, the evidence of crisis everywhere. He moves with a confidence I envy, opening cabinets, fetching bowls, setting the soup to warm on the stove. His hands are steady, practiced. When he ladles the broth, he does so with the care of a surgeon, skimming off the sheen of oil, testing the temperature on the inside of his wrist.

He brings the first bowl to Sara, crouching beside her. He offers a spoonful, waits while she swallows. He says nothing, but his presence fills the space, drawing the anxiety out of the air and into himself.

After a while, Sara rallies enough to feed herself. She sips the soup in tiny, ceremonial mouthfuls, each swallow a visible effort.

I stand at the counter, my hands shaking so badly I have to press them flat against the granite. Nathan sidles up beside me, his voice barely above a whisper.

"Has she had these before?" he asks.

"Yes," I tell him, though for how long I'm not sure.

"Are you all right?" he asks, and the question is so unexpected that I have to blink away a fresh bloom of tears.

"I should be," I say, then, "but I'm not."

He puts a hand on my arm, light as air. "It's okay. You don't have to be."

I want to say something, anything, but the words pile up in my throat. In the space between us is all the unsaid, all the longing and confusion and grief I've been holding since the day I arrived.

Cassie watches from the kitchen table, her face pale, eyes darting between me and Nathan. She knows, somehow, what this means, what it will mean.

Sara finishes her soup and sets down the spoon. The tremor in her hands has lessened, but her face is drained, the skin around her mouth drawn taut. She wipes her lips and says, "You two—stop fussing. I'm not dead yet."

We all laugh, too loudly, and the relief is its own kind of pain.

The rest of the day passes in sips of soup, doses of medication, the careful watching of each other. Nathan stays, refusing to be shooed away. He cleans up, fixes a leak in the bathroom, distracts Cassie with stories about the ocean. I alternate between gratitude and irritation, the two emotions sparring in my chest until I'm exhausted.

In the afternoon, Sara insists on walking to the porch, and the three of us help her, supporting her weight in a lopsided, awkward procession. We settle her into a rocker, blankets tucked around her legs, and she closes her eyes, letting the breeze lift the stray wisps of her hair.

Nathan stands behind me, his hand hovering just above the small of my back. I don't lean in, but I don't pull away, either.

The sun slants low across the dunes, turning every blade of grass into a gold filament. Sara's breath is slow, measured. Cassie sits at her feet, head bowed over a book, but she isn't reading. She's listening, waiting for any sign of trouble.

I watch the horizon, the way the light fractures and bends, and think about all the things I can't say. That I'm scared. That I don't know how to do this without breaking. That, for the first time in years, I want something so badly it feels like a fever under my skin.

Nathan's hand finally finds its place. I let it stay.

The day bleeds out, the sky turning from blue to ash. Sara's head tips forward, her breathing shallow but even. She's asleep, or as close as she gets anymore.

Nathan turns to me, his eyes searching. I can see the question there, hovering on the edge.

I shake my head, just enough for him to see.

"Not now," I whisper. "She needs us."

He nods, understanding, and squeezes my hand once, then lets go.

I watch the last of the daylight fade, and suddenly, it feels like the world is holding its breath, waiting to see what will happen next.

Cassie looks up, her face an echo of my own, and I see the shape of the future.

We sit there, the three of us, braced against the coming night.

And in the hush that follows, I promise myself I won't let go.

CHAPTER 24

DIANE

The day after Sara's episode is a long, strange drift. Even the house seems to move slower, like it's adjusting to the new terms of gravity. We keep a watchful eye on Sara, tiptoe past the threshold of her bedroom with offerings of tea and toast, but mostly she just sleeps, her face slack and unguarded, hair splayed in a gray corona across the pillow. It's a shock, every time I see her like this, a reminder that the iron will she wears in public is just so much skin, so much fragile chemistry, waiting to fail.

Nathan spends most of the morning patching the fence and dragging storm debris to the curb. I watch him through the kitchen window as I clean up yesterday's disaster. He's wearing an old University of North Carolina T-shirt, hair damp from a quick rinse under the spigot. When he stoops to tie a bundle of branches, the muscles in his forearm bunch and release. I pretend not to notice. I pretend it doesn't matter.

I pretend I'm not thinking about his hand on my back, the way his lips tasted the first time he kissed me, or how easily I could let myself fall into the shape of wanting him. Lust is easier to manage than grief, even at its most inconvenient moments. But Sara is upstairs, and I am twice exiled, by guilt and by the fact that there's nothing worse than a woman who lets herself be selfish. The memory slinks off, into the nest of soap bubble I am cultivating in the sink.

Cassie is upstairs, in what's now officially her "room" at Sara's, hunched over a spiral notebook and drawing what looks like an anatomically correct pelican. Every so often, I hear her pencil snap, followed by a curse she's learned from me and thinks I can't hear. Rolo is nestled against her thigh, a solid, reassuring furry mass.

By late afternoon, Sara is resting more comfortably. Cassie camps at the foot of her bed, reading aloud from an old fantasy paperback, her voice soft and steady. I listen from the doorway for a while, just long enough to convince myself everything is under control, then slip downstairs to the kitchen, where Nathan is boiling water for pasta. He's humming, off-key and unselfconscious, and I let myself imagine this is what normal looks like. Then he turns, catching me mid-scan, and the bubble pops.

"Want some?" he asks, nodding at the saucepan. "Figured you'd be hungry."

I'm not, but I nod anyway. I set the table, folding napkins with more care than necessary, and try to ignore the way Nathan tracks my every movement as if I'm about to shatter.

We sit across from each other, the silence elastic and dangerous. I twirl pasta onto my fork, take a bite, force myself to chew.

He leans forward, elbows on the table, and says, "You did good yesterday."

I nearly choke. "What?"

"With Sara. You kept your head. I know it was rough."

I set my fork down. "I lost it. I barely knew what to do."

Nathan shakes his head. "You did what needed to be done. A lot of people would've frozen."

"I don't want to get good at this."

He sits back, exhaling. "No one does."

For a while, we just eat. The kitchen is still, the only sound the ticking of Sara's old wall clock. I try to focus on the food, the aroma of oil and garlic, but my brain is a pinball machine, every thought ricocheting off the next.

Nathan finally says, "What's going on, Diane?"

I bristle. "Nothing."

He holds my gaze, unflinching. "You don't have to be brave around me."

I want to believe him. I want it so badly, but the distance between wanting and doing is an ocean, and I'm stuck on the wrong side of the tide.

"Cassie is starting to ask a lot of questions," I say, surprising myself. "About you and me... Us."

Nathan's eyes flicker with surprise, or maybe it's concern. He sets his fork down, his attention leaning toward me like a flower to the sun.

"And what do you tell her?"

I shrug, my shoulders heavy. "I don't know. I weave around it mostly."

"She's a smart kid. She'll notice if you keep deflecting."

"I know. She doesn't miss much."

"Maybe we should tell her," Nathan offers. "Something concrete. Even if it's just that we're figuring things out."

I look up at him, struck by how earnest he seems, how willing he is to dive into this uncharted territory. "Maybe. It's just... I don't want to give her any false hopes, and then have things fall apart."

"I get it. But we're not doing any good dancing around the subject either."

Nathan is right, but my fear holds me rooted to indecision. "I know. It just seems like a lot right now," I say, gesturing vaguely at the table, the kitchen, my whole unraveling life. "My biggest fear is that the rug gets yanked out from under her again. She just got back on her feet after Kyle. And now there's Sara...and us...and it's all so uncertain."

Nathan leans in, his voice lower, urgent. "I understand. The situation with Sara is precarious, and I know you are shouldering a lot of it, Diane. But regarding us, there's certainty in my feelings for you. I promise I'm not going anywhere."

"You say that now," I shoot back. "But you don't know what it's like, having everything hinge on you. I just don't want Cassie to get hurt. Or you, for that matter."

He flinches. I can see it, the way his jaw sets, the way his hand curls into a fist on the table. "Don't worry about me, Diane. I can take care of myself. Besides, hurting is part of the bargain, isn't it? Otherwise, none of it would matter."

I want to argue, to tell him that I know from personal experience how quickly the bargain goes sideways, how even the best intentions can topple the delicate architecture of a heart. But my body is tired; my mind is tired, too, in the way it gets after sleepless nights and too much held-back wanting. So instead, I push my plate forward, cross my arms, and try to meet him where he is, even though I'd rather retreat and think it through alone.

"I didn't mean to bite your head off," I say. "I just wanted to explain how it feels. Like every step I take, I have to rehearse all the ways it could go wrong in case it does."

"That's called being a mom." There's a ghost of a grin, but

when he lifts his water glass, his hands are steady.

I stare into his eyes long enough to see my reflection swimming there and wonder what he sees in me that makes him believe I am worth the trouble. Perhaps he just wants to rescue someone, and right now I'm the nearest shipwreck. Or maybe he actually sees me as I am, stripped to scar tissue and sinew, and finds beauty in the survival. Maybe it doesn't matter why, just that he keeps showing up, even when the signals are all crossed and the landing strip is on fire.

We clear the table quietly, almost companionable now, moving in a rhythm of small negotiations. I rinse, he loads, I wipe, he sweeps. When the kitchen is squared away, I drift upstairs to check on Cassie. Nathan lingers below, his footsteps soft and then absent. I realize he's gone out again, probably to sit on the steps and think. For a second, I wonder if I should follow, but inertia holds me in place.

I disentangle from Cassie, kiss her forehead, and move down the hall to Sara's room.

She is asleep when I open the door, her mouth slightly open, breath shallow in the hush. I slip in and sit on the edge of the bed, careful not to wake her. But even in sleep, she winces, some interior pain squeezing her brow into a knot. The skin along her collarbone is almost translucent, delicate as old paper, and I realize how little time we have.

Sara's hand, under the covers, is curled around the sheet, and I want to loosen her grip, to smooth her forehead, to make promises that would sound ridiculous and childish, like "It's going to be okay," or "I won't let anything bad happen." Instead, I just sit there, silent and small, and try to imagine the next day, and the day after, and what it will mean for Cassie and myself.

When I return to the kitchen, Nathan and Cassie are at the

table, heads bent together over a crossword puzzle.

I make tea, measure out the honey, and watch as Cassie fills in answers, her tongue poking out in concentration.

Nathan catches my eye, just for a second. There's no smile, but something has shifted, a new gravity holding us in place.

We drink our tea and listen as the wind rattles the loose pane in the back window.

I don't know what comes next. I don't know if anything will ever feel easy again.

But for now, we're all here, holding fast against the undertow.

CHAPTER 25

DIANE

When the hospice nurse shows up at Sara's the next morning, the transformation is abrupt. Gone is any pretense of normalcy. The nurse, a woman named Dee, arrives with a rolling suitcase and voice pitched for reassurance, all bright vowels and cheer.

Judy is not far behind, her suitcase thumping across the porch like a warning shot. Relief and guilt twist together in my gut. She arrives with the air of a general entering a war-zone, eyes narrowed and mouth set in a determined line.

Sara is in her chair, diminished and fragile but fiercely upright. She seems to expand a little when Judy enters, as if buoyed by the prospect of being properly fussed over. I hang back in the kitchen, fingers slick with the juice from a clementine I'm peeling for Cassie, and watch the choreography as Judy orchestrates a symphony of care around Sara.

Within twenty minutes, Sara is tucked into a blanket, the morning TV tuned to a gardening show, and Cassie is dispatched to the den to build a castle out of the spare cushions and old quilts from the hall closet. Judy finds me by the sink, where I'm methodically pulling apart the fruit into a bowl, segment by segment, as if the right arrangement might make the day hold together.

"She's stable for now," Judy says. "You've done a hell of a job. You should take a break. I mean it, Diane. Go do something for yourself. I'll hold down the fort until you get back, scout's honor."

The words should make me laugh, but instead I blink hard and nod. My heart is racing for no discernible reason, a woodpecker pulse that refuses to settle. I scrape the clementine pith from my nails and set the bowl in front of Cassie, who beams as if I've delivered her a Nobel Prize.

"Maybe you should go for a swim," she tells me, cheeks sticky from the first wedge. "Or go shopping. That might cheer you up." There is a hopefulness to her voice, an eagerness for me to reclaim even the smallest piece of normal.

I ruffle her hair, trying not to show how much it costs to let go. "I'll figure something out," I say, and slip out the back door.

The air is so dense with salt and humidity that the world feels slightly underwater. I walk down to the cottage and stand there in the kitchen, hands in my pockets, as if waiting for some sign of what comes next.

The phone rings, sudden and sharp. Nathan.

"Hey," I say, voice weirdly breathless.

"Hey yourself. Did the cavalry finally arrive?"

"Yes. Judy's here now, and so is the hospice nurse. She's setting all the equipment up and getting Sara's meds sorted out. Judy insisted that I take a break."

"She's right, you know? Listen, I don't want to step on any toes, but—" There's a pause, a shuffling sound, the scratch of a pencil or a thumb across wood. "Would you want to get coffee this morning? Or, I don't know, take a walk? No pressure. You just sounded—last night, I mean—you sounded like you could use a change of scenery."

"Yeah. I'd really like that."

He names the café by the marina, the one with the blueberry scones, and says he'll meet me in half an hour. We hang up before either of us can overcomplicate the logistics, and I just stand there, letting the salt air ransack my lungs.

I trade my jeans for a skirt, the kind I haven't worn since I was with Kyle, and run a brush through my hair. Rolo peaks around the corner, bleary-eyed from his spot on the bed, and gives me an approving bark.

"Looks like you're on your own for a bit," I tell him and give him several reassuring pats. He seems undeterred by my impending absence, nestling back into the warmth of the comforter with a contented sigh.

Picking up my keys, I allow myself one final glance around the cottage, then step out into the morning, locking the door behind me.

I drive to the café. The route takes me along the edge of the harbor, where shrimpers are already double-knotting their lines, and the air is thick with diesel. I take the long way, letting the rhythm of my feet smooth out the last of my jitters. By the time I reach the café, my heart is still fluttery, but it's the hopeful kind of anxious, the kind that precedes an anticipated kiss or the opening lines of a really good novel.

Nathan is already there, perched on the back deck that overlooks the water, a mug balanced on his knee and a legal pad spread across the slats of the table. His hair is a little wilder than usual, and he's in a gray sweatshirt and khaki shorts, a look that makes him seem both adolescent and ageless. When he sees me, he stands so fast he nearly upends his coffee.

"Sorry," he says, laughing, as he rights the mug and brushes the splatter from the paper. "I forgot how small these tables are."

I wave off the apology and slide into the seat opposite him, my knees brushing the table leg, bare skin prickling where the wood is cool and rough. "Didn't take you for an early riser."

He shrugs, face open, a little sheepish. "Didn't sleep. Kept thinking about the last few days. About Sara. And you."

The candor makes me blush, though I hope he can't see it in the diffused light of the awning. "She's better today," I say. "And thank you, again. For the soup, and the company. And the candles. Cassie thinks you're a wizard."

Nathan grins, wide and boyish. "I do try." He hesitates, then says, "at the risk of reigniting our little...disagreement... I meant what I said, about not going anywhere. I don't want to crowd you, Diane. But I... I like seeing you...spending time with you."

I study him, his fingers laced around the mug, the way his right thumb taps a silent rhythm along the side. There is a vulnerability to his posture, a sense that he's bracing for something and hoping it will be kindness.

"I like seeing you, too," I confess, the words slipping out before I can overthink them. "Nathan, about yesterday, I...."

"I know," he interjects softly, his hand stretching across the table toward me. The lights reflect off his skin, casting a soft glow on his tanned arm. "Me too," he adds when I don't continue. "This thing between us... I think we're both a little scared; you because of all you've been through and me, because I'm not sure how to be what you need. But when I look at you, I see someone who's already survived the hardest part, someone who makes me want to push through whatever's left of my own fear." He laughs, short and uncertain, but his fingers remain, open and steady, on the table between us. "What I'm trying to say is we don't have to figure it all out today, or even tomorrow.

We can take our time."

He's right. Fear has been a constant companion ever since we met, ever since I stepped into this life I wasn't prepared for and found him there, an unexpected comfort.

"Yeah," I admit, my voice barely more than a whisper against the soft hum of the café. "I'd like that."

Nathan smiles gently, seeming to comprehend the weight of my confession. "All right then," he says. "Let's just...see where this goes."

We fall into an easy conversation, discussing the topics that feel safest at first: the storm, the state of the town, the ongoing repairs to the boardwalk.

When the food arrives, the conversation shifts. We start to trade stories, the kind you only tell when the world is reduced to just two people at a table and the rest of existence is on mute.

I tell him about the time I almost failed out of freshman English because I wouldn't stop arguing with my professor about the symbolism in *Moby-Dick*. He tells me about his high school prom, how he showed up in a rented tux two sizes too big and danced so badly his date abandoned him for the principal's son by the second song. We laugh, we cringe, we admit to things we wouldn't say to anyone else.

At one point, he leans forward, elbows on the table, and says, "Can I ask you something?"

"Anything."

"Why do you keep saying you're bad at starting over?"

The question floors me, not because it's unexpected but because it's so precisely aimed at the bruise I've been nursing for years.

"I don't know. Maybe because every time I try, it feels like I'm leaving someone behind. Like starting over means erasing the people who mattered most." I look away, afraid I've said too much, but Nathan absorbs the confession without flinching.

"I think you're better at it than you realize," he says. "I think the hard part isn't starting over. It's letting yourself be seen after."

The truth of it lands, solid and undeniable. I want to reach across the table and touch his hand, but I don't. Not yet. Instead, I change the subject. "Do you want to walk for a bit? I feel like I haven't seen the beach in days."

He smiles, pushes his plate aside, and stands. "I'd like that."

We pay at the counter, and as we leave, the barista waves. Outside, the air has warmed, the early fog burned off by a tentative sun. We walk side by side, not touching, but closer than before.

At the end of the block, the sidewalk gives way to a sandy footpath lined with stunted pines and wild sea oats. The wind is stronger here, threading the grains through our hair and tugging at the hem of my skirt. I tilt my face to the breeze, letting it scrub the last of the stale air from my lungs.

Nathan glances over, as if gauging my mood, then says, "Do you ever get the feeling that everything you're supposed to want is just a list someone else made for you?"

"All the time."

"I quit my job because I couldn't stand the list anymore. All those things I was supposed to want—promotions, money, the five-year plan—they felt like a suit that never quite fit."

"And now?"

"Now I just want to make things. Even if no one cares, even if it's just for me." He turns to face me, stopping at the edge of the dunes. "What about you?"

"I want Cassie to be happy, I want Sara to live forever, I want to write something that matters. But mostly I just want to feel like I belong, somewhere. And perhaps, to someone."

He reaches out and tucks a strand of hair behind my ear. "You already do."

We walk on, the path narrowing until we're shoulder to shoulder. There's a section of the beach where the windbreakers cluster, creating pockets of calm amid the gusts. Nathan leads us there, picking a spot where the sand is soft and dry.

We sit, knees drawn up, and watch the gulls wheel over the surf.

"I wish I could paint this," Nathan says, gesturing at the horizon. "But it's always moving. I'd need a whole wall to capture even a fraction of it."

"You could try words."

He shakes his head. "I'm not as brave as you."

The compliment makes me flush, and I feel as if I could float right off the sand. I risk a glance at him, and he's already looking at me, his gaze unhurried and clear.

A group of kids races past, trailing laughter. I watch them go, then turn back to Nathan.

"I don't think I'm brave," I say. "I think I'm just tired of being scared."

"Most people never even get that far."

The breeze picks up, and I shiver despite the sun. Nathan pulls off his sweatshirt and offers it to me. I slip it over my shoulders, the fabric still warm from his body, and inhale the scent of him.

"Thank you," I say, hugging my knees to my chest.

"For the record," he says, "I'm glad you're here."

We sit like that for a long time, watching the tide creep in, the line of wet sand advancing with each wave.

At one point, he leans back, propping himself on his elbows, and lets out a contented sigh. "If you still have time, I have a painting I want to show you, one I've been working on since the hurricane. I think you'd like it."

Knowing Sara and Cassie are in good hands, I say, "I still have time."

We gather ourselves, shoes in hand, and make our way up the beach to the boardwalk where the summer crowd is just beginning to trickle in.

"Welcome to the mess," he says as we step into his studio, but there's pride in the way he gestures at the explosion of canvas and color within. The space is nothing like the gallery below, which is curated and clean. Here, there are high ceilings with open air and light, the floor scattered with tarps and the walls crowded edge-to-edge with paintings. The smell hits first. Not just oil and turpentine but sweat and smoke and the unmistakable smell of the sea.

I stand just inside, uncertain where to put my hands, and let my gaze travel the room. Some of the canvases are enormous, all weather and sky, the colors so intense they seem to bleed off the fabric. Others are miniature, more intimate, little scraps of life rendered in brushstrokes so fine I want to touch them.

From the corner of my eye, I see Nathan watching me, arms crossed, chin tucked into his shoulder. "Sorry about the clutter," he says, but I can tell he loves it. There's a logic to the chaos—brushes sorted by size, palettes stacked by hue, a row of jars with paint thinner each at a different stage of opacity.

I want to say something insightful about the paintings, but all I can manage is, "They're incredible. I had no idea you could do...all this."

He laughs, soft, and moves closer. "I can't, most days. But sometimes it works."

He walks me through the room, pointing out his favorites. There's a triptych of the same inlet at dawn, noon, and dusk, each version angrier than the last, the water more choked with light, the wind more insistent. A small portrait of a dog, ears cocked and eyes knowing, that I recognize instantly as the mutt from the hardware store. "She has a better poker face than most people I know," Nathan explains, and I realize he means me, too.

We talk about process, how he primes his own canvases with rabbit-skin glue, how he can't listen to music when he paints because it crowds out the sound of his own thinking.

At some point, he offers me a beer from a tiny fridge wedged under a makeshift workbench. I accept, though I rarely drink, and he pours the bottle into a pair of glasses before handing one to me.

"To surviving the storm," he says.

"To starting over," I reply, surprising myself.

We drink, and the beer is cold and bitter and exactly what I need.

Sunset crawls up the windows, turning the ocean glassy and gold. Nathan leads me up a set of stairs to the narrow loft, where there's a futon and an old army blanket folded with military precision. There are more paintings here, smaller and more raw. Quick studies of hands, bodies, the lost profiles of people I don't recognize.

The painting of the lighthouse is here, as well, nestled among the clutter. "Is it finished?" I ask.

"No, not yet. I can't seem to find the right light for it."

"Well, you'd better hurry, or else Sara won't be around to

see it finished." The words hang heavy in the air, and I wish I could reel them back in.

"I know," he says, eyes downcast.

Before the melancholy can seize us, he leads me to a painting that's only half-finished, a woman on a windswept beach, hair whipped across her face, the horizon behind her smeared with indigo and rust. "She's not done," he says, and I can't tell if he means the painting or the woman. "Sometimes I think it's better that way."

We stand side by side, so close I can feel the heat of him along my shoulder. He smells like soap and something resinous, maybe pine. I want to touch the painting, to run my thumb along the edge, but instead I rest my hand on the frame.

Nathan turns, and I feel the movement before I see it. His face is inches from mine, his mouth slightly open. The kiss starts so tentatively it's almost an accident, just the barest brush of lips, but it blooms quickly.

He tastes of beer and adrenaline. His hands are careful, one at my waist, the other skimming up my back, fingers splayed wide as if mapping the territory of my body. I lean into him, let my own hands find his hips, the ribbed curve of his spine, the warm slope of his neck.

The rest is a blur, the kind that happens when sensation eclipses thought. Our bodies are drawn together by gravity and hunger, the space between us shrinking until there's nothing left but heat and the rasp of skin against skin.

Nathan pulls me to the futon, and the two of us collapse onto the mattress, mouths pressed together, limbs tangled in a messy geometry. He pulls off my shirt as if unwrapping a gift he's waited years to open. I shiver, nerves flaring, but he steadies me with a hand at the back of my neck, thumb tracing slow circles along my hairline.

I tug at his shirt in return, surprised by the feel of his chest—warm, solid, a dusting of hair that prickles under my palms. He laughs into my mouth, a low, rough sound, and the vibration settles somewhere between my heart and my thighs.

We break apart only long enough to catch our breath. My bra comes off with a practiced one-handed flick, and we just stare at each other. Me, breathless and half-naked. Him, lips parted, pupils blown wide.

"Are you sure?" he whispers, forehead pressed to mine.

Instead of answering, I pull him down to me, fitting our mouths together with a new certainty.

His hands are everywhere. Cupping my breasts, tracing the line of my ribs, skating down my stomach to the waistband of my skirt. He slides it down, his fingers trailing goosebumps in their wake, and I arch into the sensation, thighs parting without thought.

He hesitates, searching my face for reluctance, but I am nothing but want, and the slow-burn thrill of being wanted back.

He kisses a path down my throat, over my collarbone, pausing to worship each new inch of skin. I bury my hands in his hair, guiding him, and when his mouth closes around my nipple, I gasp, hips jerking up against him. He holds me steady, one arm curled under my back, his tongue and teeth working together in a rhythm that unties every last knot inside me.

I reach for him, eager to return the favor, and he helps me, guiding my fingers to the buckle of his belt. There is a moment of breathless anticipation as I fumble with the clasp before he's free, a sigh escaping him that reverberates through me like a promise. I trail a path downward, the rough hair against my fingertips, the softness and hardness of him that makes my breath hitch.

He runs his fingers along the inside of my thigh, teasingly slow until he reaches the top, and oh, how I've missed this.

His touch is teasing, playful, yet so very skilled. A sigh escapes me, a sound I hardly recognize as my own. His fingers trace patterns that send lightning bolts of pleasure along my spine. He watches me closely, his gaze intense and fixed, taking in every twitch of delight that crosses my face.

Eventually, he settles between my legs, lining himself up but not moving, not yet. "Still sure?" he asks again, voice shredded.

I answer by wrapping my legs around his waist and guiding him in.

He slides into me slow, slow, slow, the stretch both blissful and a little painful, the way a long-held breath aches before it's released. We move together, bodies falling into a rhythm as old as the tides. His hand brackets my hip, holding me open for him, and every thrust drives me further from the world I knew.

The room echoes with our shared breathing, punctuated by soft affirmations whispered into the hollow of each other's ear. His fingers anchor into my skin, leaving a memory of touch that I know will linger long after we've untangled ourselves. He whispers my name, the syllables broken up by ragged exhales as he moves, each stroke deeper than the last. I arch up to meet him, wrapping my arms around his shoulders, nails digging into the heat of his skin.

His eyes flutter open and lock onto mine. They're the dark blue of a stormy sea, filled with an intensity that leaves me breathless.

The world contracts around us. The canvases, the paint

splatters, the smell of salt and turpentine. All of it fades until all that exists is Nathan. His fingers find their way into my hair, gripping gently as he buries his face into the crook of my neck.

His pace quickens and I match him, stroke for stroke. A pressure builds inside me, mounting with each thrust until I can hardly hold on. I tighten my grip around him, whispering encouragement into his ear. With a final thrust and a gasp that sounds like my name, he finishes, the sensation tipping me over the edge right after him.

Afterward, we lie tangled in each other, the sweat cooling, the air thick with the smell of sex and paint and the dying sun. Nathan strokes my hair, his breath slowing as he comes down from wherever he went.

"Did I hurt you?" he asks, voice so gentle I could cry.

"No. You made it better."

We drift for a while, neither of us willing to move. I listen to his heartbeat, the heavy drum of it beneath my cheek, and wonder if I could stay here forever.

In the distance, the ocean keeps beating against the shore, a reminder that time is still moving. I close my eyes and let the sounds fill me, let the memory of his body linger on mine.

For the first time in years, I feel whole.

CHAPTER 26

DIANE

I wake with the taste of his skin still in my mouth. For a long time, I don't move. My legs are tangled in the blanket, my arm numb from the weight of Nathan's chest, his breath stirring the fine hairs at my temple. It is a rare, precious kind of quiet, the kind that doesn't demand to be broken.

Nathan stirs, pulling me closer, lips grazing the crown of my head. We stay like that, lingering in the quiet, until the sound of his phone startles us from our reverie. He reaches for it with a grunt. "Hello?" he answers, his voice still gravely from sleep. A pause and then a groan as he squints at the clock. "Yeah, I'll be there soon." He hangs up the phone. "Shit," he mutters, "forgot about a delivery."

He slides out from under me, the mattress dipping, and for a second I panic that he's leaving for good. But he just pulls on his shorts, leans down to kiss my eyelids, one, then the other, and says, "Back in five. Don't go anywhere."

I listen to the thump of his feet down the stairs, the creak of the studio door. My body is loose and heavy, every muscle blissed-out and humming. I stretch, arms above my head, savoring the afterglow, before rolling to sit on the edge of the futon.

The loft is flooded with light. My clothes are scattered across the floor: bra looped over the back of a chair, shirt trailing like a flag from the banister. The air is thick with the scent of oil paint and sweat and the deep animal smell of sex. I breathe it in, let it fill my lungs.

I wander the edge of the loft, peering down into the studio proper. Canvases are stacked in haphazard towers, some leaning precariously, others lashed tight with twine. The table is littered with brushes, the bristles stiff and stained, palettes crusted over with sun-dried color.

On a side shelf, a stack of paper catches my eye. There are letters—some opened, some still in their envelopes, all with the edges curled and creased. I go in for a closer look. I shouldn't, but I do.

The first letter is addressed to Nathan, the handwriting neat, the return address in Charlotte. I hesitate, then unfold the single page.

Dear Nathan,

I keep thinking of that night in August, how we sat on the fire escape, drinking gin and arguing about the moon. I wish I'd told you then what I was afraid to admit—how much I wanted the future you saw, even if I couldn't see it myself. You're probably painting the sunrise as you read this or fixing something I broke. It's what you do. I know I told you not to come back, but I'm not so sure now. I miss you. I miss us.

If there's any chance left, please write. Just so I know.

I'm sorry for everything.

—Melissa

I read it again. The words pinwheel behind my eyes, making it hard to focus, the letters dissolving into a blur. There's more than a half a dozen sheets, some typed, some covered in scribble, all signed by the same hand. I pull the stack closer, my breath suddenly tight in my chest.

Next to the letters is a yellow legal pad with Nathan's writing. Loopy, uncertain, begun and abandoned again and again.

Mel,

I keep fighting the urge to call you. I know I shouldn't. I don't even know what I would say. I wish I could tell you it's not your fault, or that leaving made things better, but that would be a lie. Nothing is simple anymore. Sometimes I think about driving back, just to see if you're—

The rest is crossed out in thick, angry slashes. Below it, the start of another letter:

I don't know how to let go of you. I'm trying, but the more I paint, the worse it gets. I'm scared that if I come back, we'll just end up hurting each other again. But I'm also scared of the silence. Maybe I'll write tomorrow. Maybe I'll—

Another line, aborted mid-sentence.

My hands are shaking. I can't decide if I want to scream or cry or laugh at the stupidity of it all. The whole room feels suddenly wrong. The paintings are too bright, the air too thick, the sunlight an accusation.

I am so deep in the spiral that I don't hear Nathan come back up the stairs. He's whistling, off-key.

He sees me with the letters, and for a heartbeat the entire world freezes.

"What are you doing?" he asks. The question is gentle, but his voice has gone thin and papery.

I hold up the letter. "Were you going to tell me about this?"

"Diane, it's not what you think."

"No, then what is it?" My voice is brittle, unfamiliar. "Because it looks a hell of a lot like you're still in love with her."

Nathan opens his mouth, shuts it. His jaw works, a tic pulsing at the corner. "It's complicated, Diane."

"God, don't—" I start, but the words collapse. I can't look at him. "I just... Today you made me feel like...like maybe I was the only one. The only thing that mattered." I press the heel of my hand to my eyes, furious at the sting there. "But you can't even finish a letter to her? You can't even let go?"

He takes a step toward me, then another. "It's not that simple."

I shake my head. "It never is, is it?"

For a moment, all I can hear is the blood rushing in my ears. The whole loft smells like loss, like disappointment and old paint and the heat of a body that is already slipping away.

Nathan sits on the edge of the futon, hands open and empty. "I was going to tell you about the letters," he says, voice soft. "I just—I didn't want to ruin it. I didn't want to lose you before I even had a chance."

"Too late," I say, and the words shatter in the air.

I gather my clothes, barely registering the sound of fabric as I shove my limbs through sleeves and skirt. My hands are shaking so hard I can't get the buttons right. Nathan stands, moves toward me, but I flinch away, the memory of his touch suddenly unbearable.

"Diane, please—" he tries, but I cut him off.

"I have to go," I say, but what I mean is I have to run. If I stay, I will break, and I can't afford that anymore. Not with Cassie, not with Sara, not with the part of myself I just started to get back.

I am out the door before he can finish. The stairs are steep, the boards cold against my bare feet, but I barely notice. I make it to the sand before the first sob punches out of me, so loud and guttural I have to double over to contain it.

I walk until the studio is out of sight, the boardwalk behind me, the only sound the slap of my own footsteps and the distant, indifferent caw of gulls.

When I finally stop, my face is wet, my throat raw. I wrap my arms around my ribs, hold myself together with all the force I can muster.

For a moment, I am sure I will never breathe right again.

But the air is salt and sun and the promise of rain, and eventually, I do.

One step. Then another. Then another.

CHAPTER 27

DIANE

The phone rings at 6:17 a.m., as if the universe wants to see how much static my system can handle before I short out. I stare at the caller ID, Nathan's name in brutal, black-and-white text. For a split second, I consider answering, but I let the machine pick it up instead.

"Hey, Diane." His voice fills the room, a jagged shard of morning. "I know it's early... I just thought we could talk." There's a pause, and I can almost hear him second-guessing his every word. "Please call me back when you can."

The machine beeps off, and I sit there, staring at the flashing light of a saved message. I swing my feet to the floor and get out of bed, disturbing the quiet morning with my sudden movement.

The world is still dark. Dew beads on the windowsill. The air has that pre-dawn hush, the oxygen damp and slightly metallic, a taste that coats the back of my tongue. I wait for the panic to hit, but there's nothing left this morning except a low, vibrating numbness, like I've been wrapped in a hundred layers of saran wrap and can't quite breathe right.

From down the hall comes a single cough, then the heavy sigh of an old house resettling around the ache of its inhabitants.

I slide out of bed and stretch, the muscles in my neck popping in protest, and walk barefoot into the kitchen. The house smells of last night's tea and stale bread, a comforting scent that makes my stomach growl in response. I put water on the stove, counting the seconds until it boils, and let my mind drift to yesterday afternoon's tryst with Nathan, his touch, the letters, and the horrible emptiness that came after.

I shake my head and check on Cassie. She's still asleep, curled up on the couch so tightly she's nearly a fossil, the blanket bunched around her. Rolo, ever faithful, is wedged behind her knees, his ears twitching in some canine dream. I don't want to wake her. I just stand there, watching the soft pulse of her breath, and think of all the ways I've failed her, starting with uprooting her from the only life she knew and ending, most recently, with last night's silent, shattered drive back from the boardwalk.

When the kettle screams, I jump, nearly spilling water down the front of my terrycloth robe. The noise wakes Cassie, too. She shuffles into the kitchen, hair a feral tumble.

"Morning," she says, voice small.

"Hey, bug," I manage, pouring orange juice with hands that shake a little more than I'd like, and nudge the cup her way. She stares at it, then at me, her gaze too direct for comfort.

"You okay?" she asks.

"I'm fine." I try to sound normal, but the words come out flat, the vowels bent at odd angles. I busy myself with the toaster, loading two slices of bread with the kind of mechanical precision that would have delighted Kyle and now only makes me feel vaguely ill.

Cassie sits at the table, Rolo stationed at her feet, and watches me. There's an old clock on the wall, the kind that ticks with a wet, almost living sound. The three of us form a triangle of worry, each pretending not to notice the others' discomfort.

After a few minutes, Cassie says, "What did you do yesterday?"

I flinch so hard I nearly drop the butter knife. "Not much. Just...got a coffee, sat on the beach, walked along the boardwalk for a while."

"Did you see Nathan?"

I open my mouth to lie, but I can't do it. "Yes, I ran into him at the coffee shop."

"Did he ask about me?"

"No, Cass. Not specifically."

She accepts it, or pretends to, and smears grape jelly across her toast. "I finished my drawing last night," she says. "The one of the ocean. When is Nathan coming over again? I can't wait for him to see it."

"I'm not sure, honey," I say, careful to keep my eyes on the butter, the toast, anything but that face full of hope. "He's got a lot going on right now."

Cassie chews slowly, and when she finally swallows, she says, "But you still like him, right?"

She's staring at me in a way that's all child and not child at all, some hybrid of the little girl who names her stuffed animals and the new, wary adolescent taking shape under my nose. My instinct is to insist on a version of the truth so gently it's nearly fiction, but Cassie's not buying any of it. She wipes her mouth with the back of her hand, sets the toast down, and folds her arms, an uncanny mirror of the posture I used to take with my own mother when I wanted to pick a fight but hadn't found the words yet.

"Did something happen?" she asks, her voice careful, as if

trying to tiptoe around a tripwire.

"Nothing happened, bug," I lie. "It's just...Nathan and I are... It's complicated."

"Are you mad at him?"

The truth is a mess I can't parse. "I don't know," I say, which is the closest I can get to honesty this morning. "Maybe. Maybe just sad."

She accepts it, but there's a new wariness in her face. She takes another bite of her toast, then asks, "Are we still staying here?"

"No," I say. "Not anymore. I think it's best if we return to the cottage."

She chews, thoughtful. "Good. I like it there. Feels like home." She glances toward the closed door of Sara's bedroom, where the faint hum of the oxygen machine has been running since before sunrise. "She's not going to get better, is she?"

"No, bug," I say, and at first I think my voice has disappeared into the hush, but she's listening intently. "She won't. But we're going to be okay. We're going to be with her as much as we can."

Cassie's silent for a while, picking at her toast. "Why does everyone we love go away?"

I have no answer. None that I'd want to give her, anyway. The universe just doesn't know what to do with people who love too openly, so it whittles them down, one by one, until you're left with an empty kitchen and a child who understands the math of loss better than she should.

The phone rings again, insistent. Cassie watches, waiting to see if I'll answer.

I let it ring out.

When the silence returns, thicker and more final than before, she looks at me with a kind of gentle resignation. "Done," she says and stands to take her plate to the sink.

Rolo follows, tail low.

I sip my coffee and stare at the wall, the seconds scraping by in slow, deliberate ticks. I imagine Nathan sitting in his studio, phone in hand, voice raw from repeating my name into the ether. I imagine his disappointment, his own coil of guilt and longing, and for a moment I almost give in, almost reach for the phone and let the words tumble out, broken and graceless and true.

But I don't.

Instead, I rinse the dishes, wipe down the counter, and reset the kitchen for the day ahead. Cassie disappears into the den, probably to call Amaya or play a game or just retreat into a world less complicated than mine.

It's not even 7:30 a.m., and already I'm exhausted.

When I finally summon the nerve to check on Sara, I find Judy already at her post, bent over the edge of the old cherrywood bed like a priestess at an altar. She's got a little ritual: check the lines of the oxygen mask, smooth the tangled hair back from Sara's forehead, measure out the blue pills and the pink ones into a plastic cup. Her hands are astonishingly steady, but I can see the worry lines deepening at the corners of her mouth every time Sara's breath rattles too long before the next inhale.

I stand in the doorway, arms cinched tight across my ribs. Sara appears smaller in sleep, the bones in her wrists sharp and moon-pale against the quilt. Her mouth moves, sometimes, as if tasting words she never got around to saying.

Judy looks up and gives me a small smile. "She's resting. Vitals are low but stable. The morphine helps."

I nod, like that means something to me.

Judy gestures at the cup in her hand. "She'll probably drift for a while. You should get outside, Diane. Take a walk."

I stay where I am, legs rooted to the floorboards, unwilling to leave. "I'm fine," I say. "Do you need anything?"

She studies me a moment, the way a doctor might assess a patient with a wound they refuse to show. "No, we're good here. But you should let yourself breathe, too." Her gaze flicks toward the window, where the morning is sharpening into brightness. "It's not selfish."

I don't know what to say, so I just stand there, half in and half out of the room, counting the rasp of Sara's breath.

The air is thick with the plasticky smell of hospital supplies and the sour-sweetness of whatever disinfectant Judy uses to wipe the IV pole and the bedside table. It's a smell I know too well, one that's always made my skin crawl, ever since the long winter of my mother's decline.

The house is quiet, except for the rhythmic whirr of the oxygen compressor and the distant drone of a lawnmower, somewhere down the beach. It's a silence that feels engineered, like a white-walled gallery designed to keep real noise at bay.

Cassie appears behind me, silent as a shadow. She hesitates in the hallway, then threads her way past me and into the bedroom. I watch her go, the set of her shoulders telegraphing a braveness she's faking for everyone's benefit. Rolo follows, his nails ticking gently against the wood.

Judy straightens, checks Sara's pulse with a quick, practiced touch, then gestures for Cassie to sit on the bed. "She'll like the company," Judy says, voice softer now.

Cassie perches at the edge, careful not to disturb the tubes or the blankets. She takes Sara's hand, her own so small and vital next to the translucent, trembling fingers of the woman who taught her to bake, to garden, to build the world out of words and story.

Sara's eyelids flutter. She struggles up from whatever dream she was caught in and focuses on Cassie, a slow smile carving across her face. "My sweet Cass," she whispers, the words thin as spiderweb. "You're such a good girl."

Cassie leans in, her hair falling forward, and whispers something I can't hear. Sara nods, then closes her eyes, lips parting in a sigh that barely shifts the air.

Judy kneels beside the bed, her touch so light it's almost a blessing. She looks over at me, and there's a question in her eyes—whether I want to come in, to join this tender moment, or whether I'm content to keep myself stitched together on the threshold.

I'm not sure which would hurt less.

So, I stay in the doorway, watching the tableau: Sara, her chest rising and falling like the tide's last attempt at persistence; Judy, sentinel and witness; Cassie, hand in hand with the woman who has already begun her slow departure from this world.

And in the quiet, I listen for the sound of my own heart, waiting for it to break.

CHAPTER 28

DIANE

Afternoon presses down on the house, slow and thick, the sun a pale disk behind a scrim of coastal haze. Most days I love this hour, the way light slants across the floorboards, but today it only amplifies the feeling of stasis, like time has stalled out between heartbeats.

The low whine of the oxygen machine seeps through the closed door. I linger at the threshold, not wanting to disturb what little peace Sara has left, but I hear her voice summon me in.

"Diane? Honey, you lurking, or just hoping I'll drift off for good?"

I manage a laugh, but it's more exhale than sound. I slip inside and find her propped on pillows, smiling as if she's been expecting me for hours.

"Sit," she says, patting the mattress. "If you stand there any longer, you'll wear a groove in the floor."

I perch on the edge of the bed and take her hand. The skin is parchment, the knuckles swollen, but the grip is still decisive, a little bossy.

"Tell me," she says.

"Tell you what?"

"Don't play coy. You look like someone who's eaten the last cookie and is bracing for judgment." She cracks an eye, studies my face, and then sighs. "Is it Nathan?"

I want to say no, that it's about you, it's about Cassie, it's about the impossible gravity of losing another anchor in a life already adrift. But instead I say, "I found letters. In his studio. From his ex."

Sara makes a sound, not quite a laugh. "You went digging?"

"Not really. They were right there. Like he wanted me to find them, maybe."

She lets that settle. "And?"

"And I lost it. I yelled at him, and then I just... I left."

Sara says nothing for a while, just rests her head back and lets the machine's pulse fill the silence.

"I thought you were braver than that," she says, finally, and the words hit so cleanly I flinch.

"I'm not."

She looks at me then, her gaze clear as the first cold sip of water after a fever. "You know what I learned, after Andrew died? After the casseroles stopped coming and everyone went back to their regular programming. I learned that people don't get over each other," she says. "Not the way you want them to. We drag the old loves with us, like broken shells in a pocket. Sometimes they poke through the lining. That doesn't mean there's no room for new love. It just means you have to find a bigger pocket."

"That's a terrible metaphor," I say, which is all I can manage without crying.

"But it's true."

The effort of talking has left her breathless. I fetch the water glass, hold it to her lips, then watch her swallow. Her eyes flutter closed, lashes shaking.

"You think I should call him, don't you?"

She tips her head in a yes. "But only when you're ready to have a real, adult conversation. Consequences be damned."

"I don't know if I can."

"You can," she says. "But you have to forgive him for not being perfect. And yourself, too, while you're at it."

"I'm so tired of being afraid," I say, and it comes out half plea, half confession.

"Then stop. It's not a sin to want something. Even if you lose it later. Even if it's messy."

She squeezes my hand again, and I realize she's shaking, not with cold or fear but with the effort of holding on.

"I don't want to let you go," I say, and I can't stop the tears now.

"You have to. It's the only way anything new can fit inside you."

"Nathan tells me you think I'm a rain catcher, that I gather storms and hold them in, waiting for the downpour."

"Yes, I do," she says. "You know, I was once called a rain catcher, too, many years ago."

"You?"

She nods, and I try to imagine her as she must have been, back when she was my age, hungry for every beauty and wound the world could offer. "Jack used to say I could water an entire valley with the emotions I hoarded. He was wrong, of course. I could have flooded a dessert." She manages a laugh, but it rattles in her chest. "For some reason, that always stuck with me. Judy was a rain catcher, too, and your mother..."

"My mother?"

"God, yes. She just hid it better." Sara's eyes go soft for

a second before narrowing, settling on me again. "You're so much like her it hurts to look at you sometimes. You think pain makes you real, Diane, but holding onto it is what makes you heavy. And you're not meant to be heavy. Neither was she." She coughs, the sound scraping. "Remember, rain catchers aren't just repositories for storms, they're a source of life-giving water. They're not meant to hold the rain, Diane, but to release it."

I laugh against the tears. "Maybe that's it. Maybe I'm afraid of releasing the rain. Maybe I'm afraid of what will grow in its wake."

Sara's eyes don't leave mine; they anchor me in this moment. "Then let the rain fall, Diane. Stand in it, feel it soak you to the bone. Only then can you decide whether to run for cover or dance."

I swallow hard, the words hitting me like cold wind against my face. I give her hand a squeeze, and she returns it with a comforting firmness that belies her frail state. She's still here, still fighting, and it gives me the courage to stand.

"I'll try," I whisper.

"Good."

We sit there, the two of us, tangled up in tubes and memory and the last dregs of daylight. I want to stay here forever, but I know I can't.

When she falls asleep, I stay beside her, counting the seconds between breaths, willing each one to last. I let the quiet build until it fills the whole house, then tiptoe out, closing the door behind me.

When I return to the cottage, the answering machine is blinking with new messages. I check them. There's one from Amaya, one from a neighbor, six from Nathan.

I pick up the phone and dial his number, my stomach

twisting as each ring echoes in my ears. It feels like a lifetime before he picks up, and for a moment, all I can hear is the sound of our breaths—his surprised, mine trembling.

"Diane?"

It's just my name, but it feels like an apology, like a plea.

"It's me," I say, my voice no more than a whisper. "Nathan, we need to talk."

There's a pause, then a quiet, "Of course." His voice sounds raw, as if he hasn't spoken since I left him last night.

The conversation that follows is a dance of words and silences, hesitation and confession. At first, we're both brittle. I say I shouldn't have yelled, that I was surprised by the letters but more surprised by how badly I wanted them not to exist. He confesses that he should have told me, should have trusted me with the story of her, with the version of the past that keeps intruding into his present by way of old envelopes and unsent goodbyes.

"I just didn't want you to think that I still harbored any feelings for her."

"Really? Then how do you explain what you wrote to her?"

There's a pause on the line. "Honestly, I started writing that letter a few weeks after I got here, before you and I ever met. It was my way of processing everything that had happened between us. I would have told you that, but you ran out before I could explain."

"But why did you keep it?"

"I don't know. Maybe I thought I would eventually send it. Maybe I just needed a safe somewhere for it to exist, so it wouldn't keep repeating in my head. Regardless, that was before I met you, Diane. After that, the letter felt...irrelevant."

I close my eyes, letting his words soak in.

"I know it might not be the right time to say this, but I love you, Diane," he says, rushing past the awkwardness, as if daring me to contradict him. "I know I'm lousy at showing it, but I do."

My throat closes up. I'm not sure if it's what he said or the way he said it, like a confession or a key dropped into my open palm. I clutch the receiver tighter, needing to feel something solid.

I don't say it back. Instead, I just listen. He waits, and I hear him breathing. I imagine him doodling on a pad of paper, his mind jumping ahead to what I might say next and also bracing against it. He doesn't try to force it, doesn't plead. Just waits, the way you wait for water to boil, knowing you can't hurry the process without ruining whatever comes after.

Finally, I take a breath so deep my ribs stretch, my whole chest expanding with the new air, and say, "I love you too."

CHAPTER 29

DIANE

Nathan arrives just as the tide begins its retreat, the wet sand below Sara's cliffside house gleaming like a polished wound. He stands at the threshold for a moment, blinking in the glare, both hands gripping a bulky package sheathed in brown kraft paper and blue painter's tape. He's dressed for the occasion, in new jeans, his button-down uncharacteristically pressed. Behind him, the sea breathes in and out, indifferent to all this anticipation.

I meet him on the porch. The marine layer has burned off, leaving the air sharp with salt and the faint sweetness of Sara's dying camellias. There's something careful about the way Nathan moves. His footsteps are measured, shoulders squared as if bracing for impact.

"You ready?" he says, and I nod, even though the flutter in my stomach suggests otherwise.

Sara's bedroom is flooded with afternoon, windows open to the sound of gulls and far-off surf. Sara sits up in bed, a pale blanket thrown across her lap despite the heat.

Nathan sets the painting down and slices the tape with a deft thumb. The paper peels back in crinkled layers, exposing the ornate gold frame, then the canvas. The lighthouse emerges in full, a sentinel crowned by storm light, battered but unbroken on its sandy perch.

For a second, none of us speaks.

Sara lets out a breath that is part laughter, part sob. She leans forward, eyes devouring every inch. "Oh. Oh, Nathan. It's... Well, it's exactly what I hoped. How did you...?"

"I just tried to imagine it the way you see it," he says.

Sara's lips twist—not quite a smile, not quite a grimace. She points at the sky, where slate blues and bleeding purples churn above the beacon's halo. "That's it. That's what Andrew always said. That it didn't matter how black the clouds got, the light would cut through eventually. He'd stand out there for hours, even in the worst weather, waiting for that moment." Her voice goes so soft I have to strain to catch it. "I always thought he loved the storms more than the calm."

Nathan lifts the painting with surprising ease and props it on the dresser. The lighthouse looks both proud and lonely in its new perch.

I watch Sara's face. Every line of it is an echo, every twitch a ghost of the woman she was before. "Thank you," she says, and this time it's a real smile, small but honest.

"Would you..." Nathan hesitates, scratching behind his ear. "Would you mind if I explained some of it? The choices I made?"

"You want to defend your artistic vision, don't you?"

He laughs, and the tension in the room dissolves just a little. "Something like that."

"By all means."

Nathan positions himself beside the dresser, one hand hovering near the canvas as if to usher us inside it. "I kept thinking about how lighthouses are built to be seen, but also to see. The keepers weren't just sending out signals. They were always watching for ships in trouble. So, I made the glass dome at the top extra bright, but if you look close..." He steps in, points to a tiny, almost hidden, figure in the high window. "That's the keeper. He's peering out."

Sara peers, squinting. "He's a little ragged, isn't he?"

Nathan nods, smiling. "I figured no one keeps a light like that unless they've been through storms themselves."

"You gave it a soul," she says softly. "That's not easy, you know. Most people just paint the shell."

Nathan shrugs, but I see the color creep into his cheeks. "I was just following instructions."

She shakes her head, dismissing his modesty. "You did more than that. You've made me remember things I thought I'd lost." She glances at Nathan, then at me, and for a second, the room is crowded with things unsaid—regret, longing, the kind of hope that is always tinged with grief.

"Come sit," she says, patting the bed. "Both of you. I want to stare at this awhile, and I'd rather not do it alone."

We settle in. Outside, the sea shifts from blue to gunmetal. The painting seems to change with the light, as if the storm is still roiling and the beacon still searching for something in the dark.

I wonder if that's what all of us are doing, waiting for the clouds to thin, trusting that someone is out there watching for our flicker of light.

It's a long time before anyone moves. Sara's breathing slows, becomes shallow, her eyes glazing not with fatigue but with a kind of tranquil rapture. I catch Nathan watching her, his brow furrowed, and for once he seems at peace.

After a while, Sara says, "Andrew would have liked you,

Nathan. You remind me of him, but you're...softer. In a good way."

He laughs, the sound unexpected. "I'll take that as a compliment."

She leans back, closing her eyes. "You should."

I help Nathan clean up the scraps of paper and set the room back to order, but we do it quietly, careful not to disturb the spell the painting has cast over the house.

When we're done, we stand together by the door, looking back at Sara, now dozing, her hands folded like wings across her chest, the painting keeping vigil on the dresser.

"You did good, Nathan," I tell him. "Really good. I haven't seen her this happy in a long time."

"I'm glad she likes it. I wanted to do something for her, something...memorable."

"You did. And more than that. You gave her something to hold onto, a piece of her past that's been distilled into something beautiful. That's more than memorable, Nathan. That's a gift."

***

It's nearly dusk when there is a knock at the cottage door. When I open it, I find Nathan standing in the soft glow of the porch light, a paper bag tucked under each arm.

"Hey," he says, shifting his grip so he can wave. "I come bearing food. You're not allergic to peanuts, right?"

"Only to bad manners and unripe avocados," I say, and he smiles in relief. I take the bags from him, the bottoms already greasy, and set them on the counter.

"Noted," he says, "but this place had suspiciously good reviews, so..."

We work in easy tandem, setting plates and chopsticks on

the little kitchen table, opening containers and letting the steam billow out. The food smells like ginger and soy, the sweetness of hoisin sauce, the nose-prickle of hot mustard.

I pour jasmine tea from my tin kettle, watch as Nathan inhales the scent. For a minute we just eat, heads bent, like school kids at a lunch table.

After the second helping, Nathan sets his chopsticks down, wipes his hands with a napkin, and looks at me over the rim of his tea mug. There's a heaviness in his posture, as if he's winding up for something weighty.

"I wanted to say sorry," he says. "Again. About the letters. I should have put all that behind me before—"

I hold up a hand. "You don't need to apologize again. I get it. Some things are hard to explain until you're forced to."

He turns the mug in slow circles. "I guess I thought if I ignored it, it wouldn't matter. That if I was with you, all the old stuff would just...evaporate."

"Does it work like that?"

"No. It doesn't."

We sit with that for a minute, the kettle ticking as it cools. I start to clear the table, but Nathan stops me with a light touch to my wrist.

"There's something else," he says, softer now. "Something I didn't tell you, and I think you deserve to know. About why Melissa and I really broke up."

I ease back into my chair, heart ratcheting up. "Okay."

He chews the inside of his cheek, searching for words. "We were together for so long that everyone thought we'd get married, start a family. But after her dad died, she changed. She didn't want kids. She said the world was too hard, that she didn't want to put someone through what she'd been through.

I kept hoping she'd change her mind. That if I was patient or understanding enough, she'd come around. But she never did. And eventually she told me, point blank, that she'd never want children, and that if I did, I should find someone else."

I'm frozen with a mouthful of sesame chicken, chopsticks hovering in midair. The room goes very still.

"I wanted kids," he says. "Still do, I think. I just... It felt selfish to say it, after everything she'd lost. I couldn't be the reason she was unhappy, so I told myself I could live without it. But I couldn't."

The rest of the words tumble out in a rush, as if they've been bottled for years. "When we finally ended things, it wasn't because we didn't love each other. It was because I couldn't imagine dying without ever having a family. I know that sounds corny. Maybe it is. But it's the truth."

I put my chopsticks down. For a moment, I can't think of anything to say. I study his face, searching for the cracks. They're there. The tightness around his mouth, the way his hands keep fidgeting, the faint sheen of embarrassment in his eyes. I wonder how many times he's practiced this confession and how often he's bitten it back.

"I...didn't expect that," I say finally. "When you said you wanted more than she was willing to give, I thought it was something else entirely. Commitment. Or time. Not...kids."

He laughs, but it's a tired sound. "I guess that would have been simpler. But the truth is, I tried to be the person she needed, and in the end, I couldn't."

I try to digest it all. The desire for a family is something I understand in my bones, a hunger that has shaped every choice I've ever made. For years, I told myself that my worth was in my ability to nurture, to build a safe haven for Cassie and anyone else who wandered into my orbit. The thought that Nathan shares this need cracks something open inside me.

"Thank you for telling me," I say. "That must have been hard."

He shrugs. "Easier than pretending, I guess."

"So, how do you see things playing out now? Do you think that's something you still want, with me?"

He meets my gaze, and there's something earnest and naked in his expression. "Yes. The short answer is yes. If you want that too. But I don't want to pressure you—God, that's the last thing. I just want to be honest about where I'm at. About who I am."

"What about Cassie? How does she fit into your idea of family?"

He smiles, the answer already cued up. "She's the whole point. She's this amazing, hilarious person, and as I've gotten to know her, it's been like rediscovering the world. I'd be lucky just to tag along as she grows up."

I feel my throat tighten, a swell of emotion that's as much relief as it is sorrow. I let myself imagine what it would be like to let Nathan all the way in, to trust him not just with my days, but with my future. Cassie's future, too.

There's a knock at the window, and for a second I jump, but it's just the wind rattling the loose pane.

"I should clean up," I say, standing too quickly.

Nathan rises and helps with the dishes, rinsing each one carefully before passing it to me. Our hands keep colliding in the suds, and we both laugh—soft, sheepish, but real. When we finish, we stand together at the sink, peering out at the darkness beyond the window.

The beach is invisible, swallowed by night, but I can hear

the ocean. The sound is steady, reassuring.

Nathan turns to me, hair damp from a stray splash of water. "Can we just...sit for a while?"

I nod. "I'd like that."

We move to the couch, where we fit together like two puzzle pieces. I rest my head on his shoulder, and he curls his arm around me, tentative but not unsure.

We don't talk for a long time. There's no need. The air is full of everything we've already said, and all the things we're still learning to admit.

Beyond the threshold of these four walls, the waves keep coming. But in here, I let myself believe, for a little while, at least, that new beginnings are possible, and that sometimes, even the most stubborn wounds can heal.

CHAPTER 30

DIANE

August

It's my turn to help at Sara's today, so I'm folding laundry in the den, or trying to. My hands keep losing the thread, the fabric collapsing into piles that remind me of old bones. Sara is sleeping upstairs, or so I think. Cassie is at the kitchen table, assembling a puzzle that she found in the hall closet.

Nathan's voice floats up from the porch. He's on the phone with someone from the gallery, talking about water damage and insurance adjusters.

It's almost noon, the sun a stark circle in a sky scrubbed raw by the storm. The world feels on pause, the air tense with the certainty that something is about to happen.

When it does, there's no warning. One of the monitors in Sara's room wails. A flattened shriek that echoes through the house. Nathan stops mid-sentence, and then his footsteps are pounding up the stairs.

"Call an ambulance," he yells.

I fumble for my phone, hands all thumbs, and punch in 911 with the desperation of someone trying to dial the past.

The operator's voice is calm, professional. I give the address, the symptoms, my name. She tells me to keep Sara still, to check her pulse, to stay on the line. Judy appears in the doorway. She takes one look at Sara and snaps into motion. She gets Cassie out of sight, ushering her outside with a gentleness I couldn't have managed.

I cradle Sara's head, stroke her sweat-slick hair. "Stay with me, please. Just stay."

She tries to smile, lips peeling back from her teeth. "Don't be dramatic," she whispers, but the words are drowned in a fresh surge of pain.

The paramedics arrive in a rush of boots and black jackets. They kneel, speak in shorthand, assess and act in a blur. One asks about meds, allergies, next of kin. I answer with a litany of names and numbers, as if reciting an incantation might make her stay.

They strap Sara to a stretcher, tape leads to her chest, fit an oxygen mask over her mouth. Her eyes flutter, roll back, then snap open again.

She locks onto me, fierce and lucid. "Take care of Cassie," she says, the words sharp and sudden.

I nod, tears stinging my face. "I promise," I say, but my voice is a wreck.

The paramedics move fast. Nathan holds the door, guiding the stretcher out the front door. I follow, numb, my feet moving with a mind of their own.

In the driveway, the ambulance waits with doors open, engine idling. Cassie is on the porch with Judy, fists clenched white against the railing. She doesn't cry, but her jaw is set, her entire body a refusal.

They load Sara in. One of the medics, a woman with freckles, tells Judy and me to follow in our car. I glance at Nathan and Cassie, then back to Sara, already vanishing into the machinery.

"I'll take care of Cassie," Nathan says. His hand finds my shoulder, the weight of it an anchor.

I don't argue. I get into Judy's car and we're off, the blare of sirens leading the way.

***

At the hospital, the paramedics whisk Sara away. Judy and I are left alone in plastic chairs under a light so bright it erases every shadow. The air smells of bleach, every surface wiped down to a clinical shine. I sit with my hands on my knees, afraid to move.

Judy sits beside me, her face ashen. She reaches out, placing her hand over mine. The coolness of her touch offers little comfort, but I'm grateful for the gesture. I wonder how many times she's sat like this, in hallways and waiting rooms, clinging to hope.

Nathan and Cassie arrive an eternity later. Cassie's hair is damp, cheeks flushed. She sits beside me and slips her hand into mine, fingers sticky with sugar from the vending machine.

"How is she?"

I shrug. "We're still waiting on the doctor to give us an update."

Nathan paces, his arms crossed tight. He looks at me, then away, then back again, as if searching for a horizon he can't find.

None of us speak. There's nothing left to say.

Time does strange things in a hospital. It slows and stretches, loops in on itself. At some point, Cassie leans against my arm and falls asleep, her breath warm against my skin. Nathan sits across from us, elbows on knees, his head bowed as if in prayer.

I stare at the double doors at the end of the corridor, willing them to open.

When they finally do, a doctor in blue scrubs steps out. She looks at me, then at Judy, then at Nathan, then at Cassie, as if assembling a family from the fragments in front of her.

"She's stable, for now," she says. "We're doing everything we can."

The words land like a fist, but I nod, trying to keep my composure.

Cassie wakes up, blinking in the artificial light. She doesn't ask if Sara will be okay. She just takes my hand, and Judy's too, linking us together in a chain. Nathan joins, leans forward, stretching out a hand to join ours.

And for the longest time, we sit like that, the four of us, waiting.

CHAPTER 31

DIANE

The hospital room is colder than the air outside, which seems like a design flaw until I realize it's intentional. The overhead lights are a syrupy white, the walls a colorless beige that claims to be soothing but reads as surrender. Every surface is easy-wipe, no texture for the mind to catch on, except for the ripple of blue-green blanket pulled over Sara's knees.

She lies in the bed's crook, small and receding, with her hands folded over her stomach as if she's practicing a prayer. Each finger is a different shade—knuckle yellow, palm gray, the nail beds turned a faint, almost hopeful lavender. A plastic cannula snakes into her nostrils. The oxygen hisses with a steadiness the rest of her can't muster.

I sit in the visitor's chair next to the bed. My left hand cradles hers, careful not to jostle the IV line or the tangle of hospital bracelets stacked like cheap jewelry on her wrist.

Cassie is here, too. She perches in the window-seat, knees drawn up, head bowed over the palm-sized shell she brought from Sara's porch. It's a moon shell, one of those perfect tight spirals you find by the high tide mark if you're lucky or patient. Sara gave it to her last week, pressed it into her hand with the gravity of a final gift. Cassie traces the spiral over and over, as if she might find the way out.

Nathan stands behind me, silent, his hand resting on my shoulder. He's been here for an hour and hasn't said a word. He smells like cold air and old paint, and his thumb taps an anxious rhythm where the strap of my bra crosses the blade of my shoulder. I want to reach back, to pull his hand into mine, but I can't bear to let go of Sara, not even for a moment.

Judy leans against the wall, her arms crossed over her chest. She's been Sara's friend for thirty-four years, and in that time they've weathered countless storms. But none of that seems to have prepared her for seeing Sara like this. Her eyes are red-rimmed and hollow, darting to each monitor, each machine, as though by watching she can control the outcome.

The silence in the room is heavy, pressing down on us all. It's broken only by the steady chirp of the heart monitor. Sometimes it stutters, and I find myself holding my own breath in anticipation. The nurse comes and goes, checking the numbers, adjusting the drip, then retreating into the hush of the hallway. She moves with the economy of someone who's seen too much and is saving her empathy for the really hard cases.

This should be the really hard case, but everyone seems to agree the outcome is already decided.

It's been an hour since Sara last woke, but I talk to her anyway. I narrate the weather, the beach, the state of Cassie's sneakers. I tell her about the broken mailbox and the paint that won't dry and the latest dumb thing the town council did. I even read her a paragraph from my notebook, the one she always nagged me to fill, and when I finish, I swear I see the edge of her mouth twitch. Maybe it's the nerves. Maybe it's the body's last rebellion.

Cassie looks up from the shell, her hair a static blur against the hospital glass. "Is she dreaming?" she asks, and her voice is so small I almost miss it.

"I think so," I say. "She's always liked dreaming more than being awake."

Cassie accepts this as a minor mercy. She sets the shell on the window sill, cupping it gently, then leans her forehead to the glass. Outside, the sunset is starting, but in here, time is a closed system.

Nathan squeezes my shoulder, then lets go. He drags a chair closer to the bed and sits beside me, knees barely clearing the bedrail. He folds his hands in his lap, knuckles white, and keeps his eyes on Sara's face. There's a smudge of Alizarin crimson on the back of his thumb, a relic from yesterday's unfinished canvas, and I imagine the tiny fleck of color soaking into the weave of his jeans.

For a while, none of us speak. The monitor slows, then picks up, then slows again. I rub the back of Sara's hand with my thumb, tracing the veins like tiny rivers, trying to memorize their course.

Then Sara's eyes open. Not all the way, just a sliver, but it's enough to draw us all in, gravity realigning. She scans the room, the corners of her mouth pulled into a dry smile.

"Took you long enough," she rasps, her voice nothing but gravel and air.

I lean forward, clinging to her hand. "We're here, Sara. Cassie's here, and Nathan, and Judy, and—"

She closes her eyes, then opens them again, more deliberate this time. "Promised you'd come." The words are slurred, but the shape of them is clear.

Cassie stands, shell in hand, and walks over to the bed. She lays her free hand on top of Sara's, next to mine, the three of us woven together by skin and heat and the faint metallic smell of the IV.

Sara's gaze finds Cassie, and the lines on her face soften. "My favorite mermaid," she whispers. "Don't let your mother give away my books."

"I won't," Cassie says, voice steady. "I'll keep them. Promise."

Sara turns her head, a monumental effort, and finds Nathan. "And you, young man—" She coughs, the sound thin and wet. Nathan sits up straighter, caught in the beam of her attention. "Don't let her wall herself up. You hear me?"

Nathan nods, swallowing hard. "I hear you, Sara."

She shifts her gaze to me, and I feel the weight of it, heavier than anything she's ever asked before. "Diane," she says. My name is a command, not a plea. "Promise me."

"Promise what?" My voice breaks on the word, and I hate how fragile I sound.

"That you'll write. That you'll finish the damn book. That you'll let yourself be happy." Her lips quirk. "Don't waste time grieving for an old lady. Live the life you were meant to live."

The room wobbles, horizon tilting. I nod, but it's not enough. She waits, eyes sharp as thumbtacks.

"I promise," I say, the words stuttering out of me. "I promise, Sara. I'll try."

"That's my girl."

Finally, she looks at Judy, her eyes narrowing slightly as if focusing takes a Herculean effort. Judy steps forward, her hands wringing the hem of her blouse.

"Sara," she whispers, her voice cracking like a weak branch underfoot.

"Hold onto our secrets, will you?"

"Always," says Judy, her face a mask of grief and determination.

The monitor blips faster, then evens out. Sara closes her eyes, and her breathing grows shallow, each inhale more tentative than the last. For a few minutes, the only sign of life is the rise and fall of her chest under the blanket and the damp shine on her cheeks where the tears have escaped.

Nathan takes my free hand, interlacing our fingers. Cassie leans her head against my shoulder, her hair tickling my chin, and we sit like that, a tangle of need and memory and dread, until the air in the room changes.

It's not a dramatic thing, not a rush or a gasp. It's just that one moment, Sara is here and the next, she isn't. The grip of her hand goes slack, the tremor stilled. The monitor skips a beat, then another, then draws a single, unbroken line.

The nurse comes in, silent as a shadow, and checks the chart. She touches Sara's wrist, then her neck, then straightens the blanket over her knees. She says something I don't hear, and Nathan lets go of my hand to sign a paper. Cassie presses the shell into Sara's palm, arranging her fingers around it.

When the nurse leaves, it's just us again, and the silence is so profound I feel it in the bones of my teeth.

I keep holding Sara's hand, even though it's cooling by the second, even though there's nothing left to anchor. My shoulders shake, and I try to muffle the sound against the crook of my elbow, but it escapes anyway, an ugly animal noise that I haven't made since the night Kyle died.

Judy buries her face in her hands, body shaking. Nathan wraps both arms around me, and Cassie curls into my lap, her body so small and fierce.

After a while, I lay Sara's hand gently on her chest and wipe my face with the back of my sleeve. Her mouth is open just a little, and her eyes are closed, as if she's already dreaming.

"Goodbye, Sara," I whisper, but it's not enough. I want to fill the room with words, with all the things I never said and never will. I want her to hear how much she mattered, how every kindness she gave me is stitched into my skin. But the air is too thick, and the words dissolve before I can push them out.

I let my head fall onto the bed, my hair mingling with the blanket, and for a while, I just breathe, filling my lungs with the last trace of her, holding it as long as I can.

And then, finally, I let go.

CHAPTER 32

DIANE

The corridor outside Sara's room is so quiet it feels vacuum-sealed. I stand just beyond the door, a hairline crack of glass between me and the stillness within. I'm shivering but not from cold. It's as if my body has forgotten how to regulate itself. The tremors pass through me in slow, rolling aftershocks, never quite leaving.

Cassie wraps both arms around my waist, burying her face in my sweater. She's crying the way only children can—shoulders shaking, every exhale a whimper that sinks into me and stirs up my own grief. I can't bring myself to comfort her, not yet. I just stand there, hands limp at my sides, staring at the hospital wall and waiting for someone to tell me what to do next.

Nathan disappears down the hall, his footsteps deliberate. He moves with the same purposeful energy I remember from our walks on the beach, but now it has an extra edge, like he's afraid if he slows down he'll dissolve. Judy goes with him, her fingers barely touching his elbow. I lose sight of them near the nurses' station. A moment later, they return with paper cups of water, each with a purple plastic straw sticking out at a perfect right angle. Judy hands one to Cassie, who takes it automatically, her grip still clamped around my waist. Nathan offers the other to me.

I don't realize how thirsty I am until the water is halfway gone. It tastes like nothing, but the act of swallowing makes the room a little less floaty, the floor a little more real.

A doctor approaches us. He wears the same green scrubs and tired expression as every other physician I've seen since we arrived. His hands are gentle, his voice set to low. He offers condolences, the kind I know he repeats a dozen times a day. He says Sara's name like it matters, like the syllables might preserve something of her.

There's paperwork, of course. Forms to sign, instructions about personal effects. The doctor explains the process, how the body will be moved, what will happen next. I nod at all the right times, but my mind is elsewhere, spinning around Sara's final words, the promise I made, the impossible clarity in her face as she let go.

Judy handles most of it. She listens, asks questions, signs where needed. She stands between me and the doctor, shielding me from having to make decisions, from having to speak. All the while, she keeps a hand on my arm, grounding me in the moment.

When the doctor leaves, the hallway is empty again. Nathan leans back against the wall, propping himself up.

"What do I do now?" I ask.

He shakes his head. "You don't have to know right now," he says.

"You just get through the next five minutes. Then the next," says Judy. "That's all any of us can do."

I stand between Nathan and Judy, Cassie tucked under my arm. She's quieter now, the crying reduced to an occasional hiccup. Nathan takes my free hand, his thumb tracing small circles on my knuckles.

We stand like that, the four of us, for a long time. Cassie's shell clatters to the tile and rolls into the baseboard. She scoots after it, kneeling to retrieve it. When she stands, she's looking up at me with a fierce, determined expression.

"Can we go to the beach?" she asks, her voice thin but steady. "Sara would want us to see the ocean today."

The question is so simple, so unarguable, that I almost laugh. "Yes," says Judy. "I think she would."

Nathan agrees, then pulls himself up, offering me a hand. When he lifts me, it's like pulling out of a riptide. For a second, I'm dizzy, but then the ground steadies beneath my feet. Cassie slips her hand into mine, her fingers clammy with dried tears. We follow Nathan and Judy down the corridor, past the nurses' station and out into the bright, unrepentant sunlight of the parking lot.

The world outside is unchanged. Cars shush through puddles on the street. The air has a salt edge, the promise of weather hovering in the clouds. I blink into the light, unsure how to move forward but certain that I'm not alone.

As we walk toward the car, Nathan says, "We could just sit. Or walk. Or not talk at all. Whatever you want."

I look at him, and the wall between us is thinner than it's ever been.

"Let's go," I say, voice steadier now. "Let's see the ocean."

Cassie leads the way, the shell cradled to her chest. Nathan and Judy and I follow, all of us holding on to the only things we can: the space between us, and the memory of what we've lost.

***

The wind at the shore is sharper than I expect. It catches the edge of my hospital-wrinkled shirt and flaps it against my ribs, working salt and heat into every seam. Nathan stands a few feet to my left, hands buried in his pockets, his eyes fixed on the horizon where the sky is bleeding color into the ocean. Cassie is already at the water's edge, shoes abandoned, hair streaming behind her like the pennant of a ship lost at sea. Judy is with her, feet in the water, staring out at the endless horizon.

We haven't changed, haven't showered, haven't eaten since breakfast, and even then it was a half-bagel shared in the waiting room. My notebook is tucked under my arm, not for writing but for holding onto something that feels familiar. I press it to my side with the kind of pressure that bruises, half afraid if I let go, I'll just drift out with the next set of waves.

We walk, four shadows in a world of burnt orange and mercurochrome pink, until the hospital falls away, and the only sounds are our own feet and the slow, uneven pulse of the surf.

Cassie is the first to speak. "Look," she says, crouched low, finger tracing something in the sand. She's found a line of shells, perfect and unbroken, the kind of strand that usually gets picked over by gulls or kids with buckets. She sorts them by color, then by size, then by the faint spiral ridges along their backs.

Nathan kneels beside her. "That's a good one," he says, holding up a translucent sliver of olive shell. His voice is gentle, thin-edged.

Cassie nods, her eyes puffy but bright. "I'm making a memorial," she announces. "For Sara."

I kneel, too, the sand damp and cold through my jeans.

Cassie shows me the moon shell from the hospital, now nested in the palm of her hand. She places it at the center of the growing pile, then arranges the others in a sunburst around it.

"Do you think she can see it?" Cassie asks.

I want to lie, to give her the comfort of an easy answer, but the words won't come. Instead, I just say, "I hope so. She'd love it."

Nathan glances at me, and I see the echo of my own exhaustion in his face. He sits on the sand, cross-legged, like a kid waiting for the tide to decide what to do with him.

"She believed in me more than I believed in myself," I say, not really meaning to. The admission floats out over the water and is gone before I can call it back.

Judy plucks a shell from the pile and turns it over in her hand. "She saw something special in you," she says. "I see it too."

I study the sand at my feet, the way each grain clings to the skin, refuses to let go. "I don't know what I'm supposed to do now."

"Neither do I," says Judy. Her laugh is soft but real. "As you know, there's no manual for these sorts of things."

Cassie looks up, mouth set. "We just keep going. That's what Sara said. Even if we don't know what we're doing."

She's right, of course. She's always right.

We sit in the dying light, letting the wind work on us, until the sun is nothing but a blood-orange stain on the lip of the world. Cassie adds the final shell to her memorial, then stands and brushes the sand from her palms.

Nathan stands, too, and for a moment I think he's going to say something else, but then he just shrugs and offers me a hand up. His grip is firm, grounding. When I'm upright, he lets go, not making it awkward.

We walk the beach as a unit, a small, imperfect constellation, until the dark is complete and the first stars begin to prick the sky. I keep the notebook pressed to my ribs, the promise I made to Sara heavier now than ever.

When we reach the car, I glance back at the pile of shells—moonlit, solitary, but defiant in its smallness.

"I think she'd be proud," I say to no one in particular.

Cassie nods, and Judy smiles.

We drive home in silence, the sound of the ocean trailing behind us, the horizon waiting for what comes next.

PART III

CHAPTER 33

DIANE

The church on the corner of Bay and Lillian looks like every church I've ever seen in a beach town: weathered clapboard, stained-glass windows, roofline trimmed with faded red shingles, and the suggestion of a steeple more imagined than real. The parking lot is already overflowing, so Nathan swings onto the grass, skirting a puddle that mirrors the low, swollen sky. For a moment we just sit, watching the line of strangers snake up the front steps and into the yawning doors.

Inside the car, it's too quiet. Cassie has her chin pressed to her knees, not crying but not quite composed either. The shell from the hospital rides in her jacket pocket, a lucky charm or maybe an anchor. Nathan adjusts the collar of his shirt like it's a noose, but when he looks at me, there's only steadiness in his eyes. I want to tell him it's okay to fall apart, that I might need him to, but the words stick to my teeth and refuse to budge.

"I didn't think this many people would come," he says, voice thin and full of apology. "Maybe we should've picked a bigger place."

"I think Sara would hate that," I manage. My mouth tastes like dust and panic. "She liked things small. Manageable."

Cassie reaches for my hand. Her grip is dry and certain. I

squeeze back, careful not to let her see how much I'm shaking.

The three of us make our way across the parking lot, wind clawing at the hem of my skirt, the air tinged with the same ocean salt that clung to Sara's hair in summer. There are faces at the door already, some familiar, others not, but all etched with the identical mask of bereavement, as if grief were a dress code.

Just inside, the vestibule is crowded and overheated, the walls papered with community flyers and the leftovers of last Sunday's bake sale. A teenager with a stack of programs stands by the guest book, eyes flicking from my face to Cassie's and back again, unsure whether to offer condolences or just a polite smile. I take a program anyway. The cover is cheap white card stock, the kind that wilts if you hold it too long. Sara's name is printed in block letters above a watercolor of the sound. I have to blink twice before the letters stop swimming.

We find seats halfway down, wedged between a family I vaguely remember from the marina and a pair of men in dark suits who seem allergic to sunlight. The sanctuary is filled beyond capacity, every pew jammed with people and stories and the unbearable hush of collective waiting. Cassie clings to my hand; Nathan sits on my other side, his jaw clenched so tightly it looks carved.

The air in the church is thick with lilies, their sweetness so aggressive it borders on offensive. The altar is drowning in white and yellow arrangements, and somewhere beneath their shadow sits the casket. It's made of plain, pale wood, almost humble, like a piece of driftwood the sea spat out. There is no photo, no video montage, just the casket and the lilies and the hush.

At the front, Judy is already crying. Her shoulders hitch in silent spasms, the tissue in her hand shredded to confetti. The woman beside her rubs circles on her back, but Judy doesn't seem to notice.

People keep arriving, crowding in wherever there's room. I spot a couple from the bait shop, a girl from Cassie's old swim team, the mail carrier with the perpetually sunburned forehead. There's even a group from Andrew's old law firm in Atlanta, according to the guest book, though I can't tell who they are by sight alone. For a moment I'm annoyed. Some of these people barely knew Sara, or else haven't spoken to her in years, but the feeling passes as quickly as it came. The math of loss is never tidy. It multiplies, divides, carries over into strangers' lives without warning.

The service starts with a hymn. I don't know the words, but Cassie mouths them anyway. The minister is a thin, affable man who introduces himself as "Pastor Frank, but just Frank is fine." He talks about Sara's spirit, her "bright curiosity," her "generosity of love." It sounds canned, but he delivers it like a well-worn story, full of the pauses and sidelong smiles of someone who's practiced it on real pain.

There's a reading, a poem I recognize from Sara's desk drawer, and then Judy stands to speak. Her voice is jagged and wet, but she makes it all the way through. She tells a story about a road trip she and Sara and my birth mother took in their thirties, how Sara insisted on detouring two hundred miles to see the world's largest frying pan. "It was hideous," Judy says, cracking a smile through her tears. "But she made us laugh until we couldn't breathe." The congregation ripples with nervous laughter, the kind that has to escape or else turn into sobs.

The rest of the eulogies blur together. I stop hearing the words and start watching the crowd instead. There are people hugging in the aisle, clasping hands, dabbing at their eyes with whatever's handy. The rawness of it is overwhelming. I wonder if Sara would be touched, or if she'd just make a face and say, "Jesus, you'd think I cured cancer or something."

It's during the last hymn that I notice him.

He's standing at the very back, one shoulder braced against the wall like it's holding him upright. Younger than I expected, but with a shock of silver hair that gives away his age. His suit fits like it's borrowed, but his posture is unyielding. He watches the service with a surgeon's detachment, eyes fixed and unblinking. I know him instantly. Not from any prior meeting, but from the photograph Sara kept in her library. Jack. The Jack. The one who lived in Tennessee, who taught her how to fish, how to love, and how to rise from the ashes of a broken heart.

I glance at Nathan, then Cassie, but they are singing, too, eyes straight ahead and hearts somewhere near their shoes. Nobody notices my distraction.

Jack doesn't sit, doesn't fidget, just stands with his hands folded and waits for the service to end. When the final prayer is said and the crowd rises, Jack moves down the aisle with the slow, careful precision of someone recovering from a wound. He doesn't look at anyone. He doesn't need to.

The receiving line forms at the front. They press in, offering condolences, then trailing off into the reception room for coffee and Ladyfingers and the ceremonial sharing of stories.

I don't move. I can't. My legs have turned to seawater, or maybe I'm just afraid that if I stand, the fragile equilibrium I've found will disappear. Cassie slips her hand from mine and stands, brushing crumbs from her dress. "Do you want to go up?" she asks, so matter-of-fact that I almost laugh.

"I'm not sure I can," I say.

Nathan rises, stretching the stiffness from his back. "You

don't have to do anything you don't want to."

But I do. I have to. The feeling grows in my chest, insistent and hot. I need to see the casket, to touch it, to pay tribute the way Sara would have wanted. I nod, and Nathan takes my elbow, not guiding, just supporting as I pick my way down the aisle.

The lilies are so close now I can taste them. The casket is even smaller than I thought. I rest my fingers on the lid, tracing the grain of the wood, and think of Sara's hands. My eyes sting, but I force the tears down, unwilling to lose my composure in front of a hundred strangers. I lean in, just close enough that no one else can hear.

"Thank you," I whisper. "For everything."

I step back, nearly colliding with Jack. He stands a respectful distance away, head bowed, lips moving in what might be prayer or just private thought. There's something about the tilt of his shoulders, the careful way he holds himself, that reminds me so much of Sara I almost say her name out loud. Instead, I just watch as he presses one palm to the casket—brief, reverent, final—and then retreats before the next mourner can move in.

***

The sanctuary is emptying now, the crowd herding toward coffee urns and folding tables in the fellowship hall. I follow, trailing Nathan and Cassie, but my mind keeps circling back to Jack. He stands alone at the coffee station, swirling cream into a Styrofoam cup. I want to talk to him, to ask about Sara as a girl, to fill in the blanks she always kept private, even when I was writing her memoir. But I don't know where to start, or if he'd even welcome it.

Cassie is surrounded by a gaggle of teenagers, all bearing

the raw, unfiltered curiosity of the young. They talk about school and video games and the upcoming homecoming dance, as if nothing at all has changed. Nathan hovers nearby, fielding grown-up condolences and steering the conversation away from anything too direct. I watch them, grateful and a little ashamed for how normal it all seems.

Judy finds me by the cookies. Her makeup is a disaster, but her expression is steady.

"She would've hated this," she says, popping a piece of crust into her mouth. "Too many people, not enough wine."

"She'd probably fake her own death to get out of it," I say, and it feels good to laugh, even if it's hollow.

Judy leans in, lowering her voice. "Did you see him?"

"Yes. I recognized him from the photo."

Judy looks over her shoulder. Jack is talking to the pastor now, hands clenched around the coffee cup like it might float away. "He drove all night," she says. "Didn't even stop in Raleigh. Said he just got in the car and kept going."

"Do you think she wanted him here?" I ask.

Judy shrugs. "I think she wanted closure. For both of them."

We stand, picking at the cookies, watching the sea of mourners ebb and flow. Cassie weaves through the crowd, snagging another cup of juice. She moves with a kind of purpose, as if she's decided the best way to honor her mother is simply to keep moving.

I keep one eye on Jack. He finishes his coffee, then slips out the side door, unnoticed by most. I watch the door swing shut behind him, and with it a wave of panic rises in me. If I don't go after him now, I never will.

"I'll be right back," I tell Judy, abandoning my plate.

The air outside is cooler, rinsed clean by the wind. I spot Jack at the edge of the churchyard, back turned, staring down the length of Lillian Avenue. For a long time I just watch him, memorizing the slope of his shoulders, the way his hands disappear into his coat pockets. He stands there for what feels like hours, unmoving, until I finally gather the nerve to cross the grass.

"Jack?" I say, not too loud. "Jack Bennett?"

He turns, and for a split second I see the same blue eyes as Sara's—sharp, observant, not missing a thing. He takes me in, gaze flicking from my face to my shoes and back again, before a small, surprised smile tugs at the corner of his mouth.

"You must be..." He hesitates, as if afraid to get it wrong.

"Diane. I was with Sara. Until the end."

"She was my best friend growing up," he says. "Even when we were older, we—well...I just—"

"I know," I say, cutting him off gently, folding my arms against the wind. "She told me all about you. About your... friendship."

"Did she... Did she suffer?"

I want to cry, but I can't. Not here, not yet. "No," I tell him. "She didn't." It's the truth, or close enough. He doesn't need to know about the pain she hid or the times she was too weak to move.

Relief, or something like it, seems to wash over him. "Good," he says softly. "That's good." He doesn't say anything else. He just stands there, hands deep in his pockets.

"She missed you," I say.

Jack shakes his head, the motion loose and wounded. "I doubt that."

"She did. She told me about you, about how you two would

fish and camp, about the life you two had together. She never forgot."

He looks away as if unable to bear the reflection of his own past in my eyes. "I should have come sooner. I didn't know it was... I thought there was more time." He rubs the back of his neck, a gesture so human it makes me ache.

"None of us did. She was... She was so strong. So—"

"Stubborn?" Jack nods, a tight, almost imperceptible movement. "She always was. All her life. Even as a kid, she'd never take no for an answer. Drove her mama crazy." He huffs a short laugh, shaking his head.

"She never liked being told what to do," I say, and the relief in my voice is embarrassingly obvious.

We share a smile, the kind that's half apology, half gratitude. The awkwardness drops away, replaced by a warmth I didn't expect.

"I'm glad you came," I tell him. "I wasn't sure you would."

"I wasn't sure, either. But Ellie said I needed to be here. That I'd regret it if I wasn't."

"I'm glad you listened to her. She's right, you know."

"Ellie usually is," Jack admits. He takes a deep breath, letting it out slowly. He picks at a splinter on the bench, the skin at his knuckles gone white. "You know, not a day goes by that I don't think about her. About the times we spent together. The good. The bad. And the ugly. They're all with me, every day."

The wind rustles the leaves overhead, scattering acorns on the mossy ground. I think of Sara at sixteen, perched on a similar bench, legs too long for her frame, eyes already set on the horizon.

"She forgave you," I say, hoping it's true.

Jack blinks, startled. "How do you know?"

"Because she forgave everyone."

We sit there, strangers joined by the ghost of a woman neither of us can let go of. The wind sharpens, lifting the scent of lilies from the sanctuary and scattering it across the lawn. We stay like that for a long time, two silhouettes tangled in the roots of an old oak, neither of us needing to say goodbye just yet.

When I finally stand to leave, Jack looks up with the tired dignity of someone who's survived his own worst day.

"Thank you," he says. The words are simple, almost weightless. But in them I hear all the things we'll never get to say.

"No, thank you," I echo, and we share a final nod before I step back inside.

CHAPTER 34

DIANE

The cemetery sits in the shadow of the lighthouse, its perimeter staked by a weather-beaten fence that leans away, as if startled by the view. The sky is the washed-out blue of a faded photograph, and the wind combs the grass flat, leaving little eddies of sand to curl around the marble headstones. In the distance, the sea is a continuous pulse, rolling and receding, without fail.

The funeral procession is reverent. There are dozens of cars following the hearse, gliding like black swans. Nathan parks at the edge of the drive, then circles around to help Cassie out. She's wearing Sara's old navy blue sweater, the sleeves bunched at her wrists, and I can't decide if the gesture is heartbreakingly sweet or just heartbreaking. I climb out slowly, giving myself time to adjust to the quiet, the sudden absence of structure that comes after a ceremony.

The casket is already in place, balanced on the hydraulic frame above an open rectangle of earth. The hole itself is too neat, its corners knife-sharp, as if the world is refusing to accept what's about to be taken from it. A scattering of mourners clusters in a loose, uneasy circle.

Jack stands at the back of the crowd, hands clasped in front of him. He holds a single white rose, its stem wrapped in green tape. The flower looks impossibly delicate, a dare against the wind.

Pastor Frank waits for everyone to assemble before starting. He keeps it brief—Sara would have wanted it that way. He speaks of journeys, of salt and sand and the promise of homecomings. He reads a passage from Ecclesiastes, the one about seasons and purposes, and then invites us all to say our private goodbyes. People step forward in ones and twos, placing their hands on the casket or dropping flowers onto the lid. Cassie goes first, rolling the moon shell between her palms before laying it at the head of the coffin. She presses her cheek to the wood, lips moving in a silent promise, then steps aside with a resolve I wish I could borrow.

Nathan follows, silent as ever. He places a single yellow wildflower, plucked from the lot behind the church, and stands at attention before moving away. Judy, sniffling, leaves a note folded in half and weighted with a pebble.

I amble up last, palms empty, pockets empty, the only thing I have to offer already buried somewhere deep inside me. I rest my fingertips on the wood, feeling the chill through the lacquer. I picture Sara's hands, the stories they told, the secrets they held. I want to say something profound, but all that comes is "Thank you. For making me brave. For making me honest."

By the time I step back, the crowd has thinned. Some people are drifting to their cars, others forming huddles at the edge of the grass, as if waiting for instructions that never arrive. Only Jack remains by the casket, shoulders squared, the rose trembling in his grip.

He waits until the last stragglers are gone, then steps forward with the deliberation of someone carrying a precious artifact. He lays the rose on the center of the lid, his hand lingering on the petals, thumb stroking the curve of the bloom. He bows his head, not in prayer but in surrender.

I watch from a respectful distance, unwilling to intrude. The wind picks up, and Jack straightens. For a moment, he appears twenty years younger. He turns, catching my eye, and nods. There's no need for more words. The gesture says everything.

He passes by me on his way out, hands jammed into his pockets. "Take care of yourself," he says, voice low.

"You too. And safe travels."

He disappears down the gravel path, his silhouette shrinking against the endless sky.

The groundskeepers arrive, ready to finish the job. I don't move, not yet. I stand at the edge of the grave as the casket begins its slow descent. The rose bounces once, twice, then settles atop the lid, its white petals stark against the pale wood.

Cassie appears at my elbow, her hand slipping into mine. She doesn't speak, but I can feel the thrum of her grief, steady and strong. Together, we watch as the earth swallows the casket, as the world heals itself around the wound.

When it's done, we walk to the bluff and look out over the ocean. The wind is fierce here, blowing salt into our eyes, stinging away the last of the tears. In the distance, the horizon is a razor line, dividing what was from what will be.

"I think she'd like it here," Cassie says.

"Me too," I tell her.

We stand for a while, saying nothing, letting the sound of the waves fill the spaces where words used to live. After a time, the sun sinks low, painting the water with streaks of fire. I breathe in the briny air, feeling the weight in my chest begin, finally, to lift.

When we walk back to the car, I look over my shoulder. The grave is just another patch of earth now, the headstone a clean, blank promise awaiting the chisel. I picture Sara's smile, her stubborn spirit, the wild love that refused to be measured by any rule of reason.

In the hush of that twilight, I sense her everywhere: in the wind, in the restless surf, in the steady heartbeat of the girl at my side. And I am reminded that life goes on. But it never goes back.

CHAPTER 35

DIANE

The lawyer's office is colder than any hospital, which is saying something. It's a formal chill, the kind that has nothing to do with HVAC and everything to do with power and polished wood. The chairs are dense mahogany, overstuffed with a firmness that makes you sit up straight whether you want to or not. The art on the walls is all tide pools and salt marshes, muted seascapes rendered in the careful, bloodless style of a hotel lobby.

Nathan is at his studio, working on his first commission since the funeral, and Cassie is with her friend at the aquarium for the day. I insisted she go. I wanted to spare her this next layer of finality, but mostly I wanted to spare myself the spectacle of watching my daughter's heart fracture again. But I am not alone. Judy is with me, sitting to my left, hunched into her blazer like a turtle, her arms crossed so tight they might fuse at the wrists.

Mr. Harrington, the lawyer, sits behind a slab of desk that could double as a municipal monument. He's the kind of man whose suit fits so perfectly you almost forget it's a suit, whose shoes shine like black holes. He steeples his fingers and glances between us with the cautious anticipation of a surgeon about to announce a tumor.

"Thank you both for coming in on such short notice." He doesn't smile, but his voice is soft at the edges, practiced for delivering bad news in palatable slices. "I wish we were meeting under...better circumstances."

I manage a nod. Judy does the same, and though she seems about as comfortable as a heron in a parking garage, I'm thankful she's here with me.

Harrington lifts a folder, unties the silk ribbon with a small, deliberate flourish, and slides out the papers. He adjusts his reading glasses. "The late Mrs. Sara Hastings prepared her will with exceptional clarity," he says. "She was a woman who anticipated every contingency."

"That sounds like her," Judy says.

"She left very little to chance," Harrington agrees, then proceeds to read. He does not ask if we'd like him to skip the legalese, and so we are treated to the full aria: being of sound mind and body, debts and bequests, a donation to the Historical Society, a modest endowment for the preservation of the maritime museum. I listen, unmoored, half-expecting him to drop some last-minute bomb about a secret lover or a hidden family in Florida. Instead, it is all methodical, careful, rational.

"And lastly," Harrington says, his voice shifting to a minor key, "I, Sara Anne Hastings, bequeath my residence at 117 Drift Lane, together with all personal effects contained therein, to Judy Marie Norris and Diane Gail Montgomery, in gratitude for their steadfast companionship and in the hope they will find courage in unexpected places."

I don't know how to react. My first thought is that it's a mistake, or a setup for a punchline. My mouth goes dry. The room tilts, then rights itself, the walls pressing in at the corners of my vision. I feel Judy's hand reach for mine, slow and cautious, as if she's afraid I might break. I let her. Her fingers are warm, alive, a lifeline thrown from three inches away.

Mr. Harrington continues, "In addition, Mrs. Hastings left this." He opens a desk drawer with surgical precision and extracts a cream-colored envelope, wax-sealed, as if it's been holding its breath since the moment Sara signed it. Judy's and my names are written in her small, angular print.

He passes the envelope across the desk. My hand is shaking as I take it, thumb running over the bump of the seal, the roughness of the paper. I hesitate, unwilling to break the last physical trace of Sara's intention. Then I slip a finger under the flap and crack it open. The sound is soft, final.

Inside, there is a single sheet of heavy stationery, lined with ink in a hand I know better than my own. The letter smells faintly of verbena, the scent Sara dabbed on her wrists in the morning, claiming it made her feel awake and immortal. I brace myself, then read.

Dearest Friends,

If you are reading this, I have either made a terrible miscalculation in my prescription schedule or, more likely, you are sitting in that dreadful lawyer's office enduring the world's most awkward formality. My apologies. I always did enjoy a little drama.

I wanted to leave you something more than just dust and sea air and the myth of my own stubbornness. The house on Drift Lane is yours, both of yours, as well as the cottage, if you'll have it. I trust you to know what to do with it.

Judy, what can I say except thank you, and sorry. For every argument and every rescue, for every cake you left at my door when I wouldn't answer, and every time I made you walk on the beach in January. There's no one else I'd rather have as a co-conspirator or keep my secrets after I'm gone.

Diane, don't give it up. Don't run away. There is so much good you can do here, even if it looks like all the old anchors are gone.

You once asked me how I kept going through the worst of it. The answer is simple: I found courage in unexpected places. In the laughter of a child. In a neighbor's midnight phone call. In the taste of strong coffee at sunrise. And in the eyes of a man who saw the world differently than I ever could. Sometimes courage is just refusing to be moved, even when the world is eroding around you.

You are one of the bravest people I have ever known, though I suspect you'll roll your eyes when you read that. You'll want to retreat, to hole up and hide behind your notebook and the safe distance of other people's stories. Don't. Write your own. Build a home where stories can grow. Fill it with the laughter you think you've forgotten how to make. And if you find love, don't sabotage it, no matter how much the old griefs try to pull you back.

Cassie is lucky to have you, and you are luckier than you know to have her. The house is for both of you, and for anyone else you choose to let in. Use it as a lighthouse, or a safe harbor, or just a place to catch your breath. You've earned all of it.

You all are my family, and I love you. Try not to let my ghost annoy you too much.

Your friend, and fellow rain catcher,

Sara

The words thud through me in waves. By the time I finish, tears stream down my face. The letter is trembling in my hands, the ink blurring in places where my tears have smeared it. Judy leans against me, both of us doubled over in the strange intimacy of grief and surprise. I have no idea how long we sit there, staring at the paper.

Judy is the first to speak. Her voice is quiet, reverent. "She really loved you," she says, not as a question, but as a simple, astonishing fact.

I nod, or try to. My throat is tight, the kind of ache that feels permanent. "She always knew how to get the last word," I manage, and the effort it takes to sound flippant nearly undoes me.

Harrington clears his throat, the sound delicate. "There are, of course, some formalities." He slides a stack of forms across the desk to Judy, along with a sleek black pen that seems far too elegant for the task. "Take your time," he says and leaves us alone in the room.

The minute the door clicks shut, the air rushes out of me. I lean forward, elbows on knees, the letter still clutched in both hands. When Judy is finished signing, it is my turn. It takes three tries to sign my name on the line. The first two attempts look like a child's drawing of a signature, jagged and illegible. The third is barely better, but I hope it's good enough. I set the pen down and wipe at my eyes, embarrassed by the mess I'm making of myself.

"Are you okay with all this?" Judy asks, and the question is so raw, so sincere, that it pierces the fog of shock.

I swallow, forcing my voice back. "I—I think so," I say. "But I think Sara would be really pissed if I just sat here and cried all day."

Judy laughs, making the moment feel a little less impossible. "Yeah. Knowing her, she'd want you to go home and rearrange all her furniture, just to see if she could haunt you by moving it back."

The image makes me laugh, too, which in turn makes me cry harder. For a minute, we sit there, both of us undone, neither of us bothering to pretend we have it together.

When I finally look up, the letter is still in my lap. I read the last line again—*You are my family. I love you. Try not to let my ghost annoy you too much*—and feel something inside me begin to settle. Not heal, exactly, but reconfigure, the way sand does after the tide leaves.

After composing myself, I gather the letter and return it to its envelope. I tuck it neatly into my notebook, the edges aligning just so. When Judy inks the final document, we rise from our chairs and peer out the bay window. The world has turned a soft blue-gray. The view should be ocean, but the lawyer's office faces inland, a sprawl of manicured lawn, the squat lines of the post office, a distant bank of live oaks throwing hard shadows on the sidewalk.

I lean against the window frame, arms crossed, the keys to Sara's house pinched in my fist. They're heavier than I expected—old, with the kind of thick teeth you only find on doors that haven't been replaced since the Eisenhower administration.

Judy stands beside me, hands in her pockets, shoulders

hunched like she's expecting to be called on in class. Her face is hard to read—thoughtful, stoic, the lines of her mouth arranged in a way that suggests both resignation and relief.

We watch the cars drift by for a while, neither of us speaking.

"Do you think she knew?" I say, finally.

Judy glances at me, then at the keys in my hand. "She always knew," she says, not unkind. "Maybe not the timing, but...Sara was the kind of person who read you three moves ahead."

The words land, gentle but sure. I turn the keys over in my palm, the metal cold and bright. "It just feels—" I start, but the end of the sentence slips away.

"Big?"

"Like a life sentence, but in a good way."

She laughs, a single breath, the corners of her mouth twitching. "You get to keep a house by the ocean. There are worse punishments."

I smile, but it feels like someone else's mouth. "You know, when I was a kid, I used to dream about running away to a lighthouse. Guess I finally made good on that threat."

"You could always turn the place into a writing retreat," Judy says. "Paint the rooms weird colors. Grow herbs in the kitchen. Wear ridiculous hats and become the town eccentric."

"I think Sara would approve," I say, imagining her laughing at the idea.

We fall quiet again. I think about Sara's letter, the way she wrote about courage and home and refusing to be moved. I think about all the mornings I watched the light climb the wall in her kitchen, the taste of her coffee, the way her laugh seemed to ricochet off every surface in the house.

"I'm scared," I admit, the confession tiny in the big empty office. "I don't know if I'm brave enough to do this."

Judy's hand finds my shoulder, the weight of it as familiar as the wind. "You are," she says. "Even if you don't believe it yet."

I look at her, at the years of wisdom and experience etched into her face. "What about you?" I ask. "What are you going to do with your half?"

She shrugs. "I might take a room in the house, or I might never set foot in it again. Regardless, as far as I'm concerned, it's yours now. Sara knew that. I think she wanted it this way, wanted you to have something that kept you here." She smiles, and there's a little bit of Sara in her when she does. "You know, I see a lot of your mother in you, the way you look at the world, always half-ready to be disappointed by it, but never willing to give up the hope that something beautiful might break through if you just keep watching. Sara saw that in you, too."

There's a shudder in the air that might be the weather, or it might be me. "I don't deserve any of this," I say as fresh tears sting my eyes. "Any of you."

Judy tilts her head. "Deserve has nothing to do with it. You take what's given, and then you make it mean something. And you, my dear, are overdue."

We stand in the golden hush, the world still spinning but not as fast as before. I grip the keys a little tighter, the metal imprinting tiny crescents in my palm. The afternoon is slipping away, the light already angling toward blue, but for once, I don't feel like I'm chasing it.

Eventually, Judy turns toward me, her eyes steady. "You ready?"

"Not even close," I say, but this time it makes me laugh.

We gather the forms, the keys to the house, and the letter.

When we step outside, the sun is low over the water. The world is still spinning, but I feel like I know where I am.

"Let's go home," I say, and Judy nods. We walk out together, two survivors in the wake of someone else's perfect storm, ready to figure out what comes next.

CHAPTER 36

NATHAN

Night falls fast on the sound. In my studio, the light changes from amber to blue to the flat black of river mud, each shift making the paint on my easel look like a different idea altogether. The windows are open, and the air is thick with salt and the far-off song of tree frogs starting their shift. I don't turn on the overheads; I work in the hush, lit only by the small desk lamp and the glint of pigment on palette.

The painting in front of me is a mess—layers built up, scraped down, rebuilt. It's supposed to be a horizon, but the line between sea and sky keeps drifting, refusing to settle. Maybe that's what I like about it. Most of my life, I've craved sharp lines and clean endings, but out here, everything blurs. Edges dissolve. Even grief gets softer if you leave it out in the brine long enough.

I rinse my brush, wipe my hands on a rag, and stare at the canvas like it might offer a verdict. In the background, the old dock clock ticks, the one Sara found at a flea market the month I moved in. It's twenty minutes slow, always will be, but I keep it anyway, a small rebellion against my own need for precision.

The phone rings. I expect it to be Diane, maybe Cassie, calling to check on me the way I check on them, as if any of us could drown without warning.

I pick up, already half-smiling. "Hello?"

A pause, then a voice I haven't heard in almost a year. Clear, measured, with a trace of city in the vowels.

"Nate. It's me."

My spine goes rigid. I slide onto the nearest stool, careful not to knock over the jar of turpentine. "Melissa?" I say, and the name is a stone in my mouth.

She laughs, soft and familiar, and for a second I'm twenty-seven again, standing in the kitchen of our old apartment with the window open and her hair a storm cloud around her face.

"I didn't think you'd answer," she says.

"I always answer," I say and then want to take it back. The truth is, I'd stopped expecting to hear from her. Stopped expecting to hear from anyone, really, except the three people who make my life feel less like a waiting room.

I breathe in slowly, trying not to let her hear how fast my heart is running. "Is everything okay?" I ask, because I don't know what else to say.

She tells me about the city, about her new job at the museum, and the apartment she finally bought. Her voice is warmer than I remember, or maybe I just forgot how easy it is to get lost in it. She asks about my gallery, about the coast, about the weather. She doesn't ask if I'm seeing anyone new, and I'm grateful for that.

We talk for a while, about nothing and everything, until Melissa's voice changes, a note of intent threading through. "I've been thinking about coming down," she says. "Just for a weekend. See the gallery, maybe catch up."

There's a hollow where the words land, the kind of silence you only get from old wounds. I study the horizon on my canvas, the place where sea and sky refuse to meet.

"I don't know if that's a good idea, Mel."

"Oh?"

"It's just... I'm not sure that's what either of us need right now," I reply, and this time the words fit.

From the other end of the line, I can almost hear her deflating. "I see."

"I'm sorry, Mel," I say, and it feels inadequate, this apology that can mend neither old wound nor dashed hopes.

"No, no, it's okay. I just thought...maybe we could... I miss you, Nathan." Her voice is a whisper, a ghost of the woman I knew.

I squeeze my eyes shut, clutching the phone tighter as if I could hold onto her through the miles. I miss her too. But I've learned that missing someone isn't a good enough reason to invite them back into your life, especially when the wreckage of your past still litters the ocean floor.

"I miss you too, Mel," I admit. "At least, I did. But some bridges are better left in ruin."

There's a sharp intake of breath on the other end of the line. It's like she's been struck, and that sound, that tiny gasp of pain, it cuts through me like a scalpel, dissecting old scars. "You're right," she says. "You always were. Well, goodbye, Nate."

And then she hangs up. The line goes dead, and the room plunges back into silence. I return to the canvas, pick up the brush, and draw a new line where the old one blurred away. Not perfect, not clean, but solid enough to build on. I work in the dark, letting the sound of the water and the memory of other voices fill the space around me.

When I look up, the horizon is still shifting, but it's closer than before.

CHAPTER 37

NATHAN

September

At first, there is only the ocean and the brush in my hand. The ocean breathing beneath my windows. I'm working on a gift for Diane and Cassie, two blurred bodies running barefoot across the sand, Rolo trailing behind them. The light in the studio is all wrong for flesh, but perfect for memory.

I'm so deep in the rhythm of brushstroke, water, pigment, wipe, repeat, that I barely notice the shift at first. But then I do. A break in the quiet, the echo of footsteps on old porch planks, and then a knock. Three short, one long. My whole body goes rigid.

The brush freezes mid-stroke, balanced precariously on the lip of the easel. The sound is ridiculous, anticlimactic, almost apologetic, but it detaches something in my spine. I know this knock. I have heard it in stairwells, in city apartments, through ten years of shared doors and mornings. I know the sound like I know the back of my hand. There is a tremor in my hand and a flutter in my chest that feels less like a heartbeat and more like a bird battering itself against glass.

I set the brush down and move to the window, stepping over stacks of empty frames and boxes of dried-up tubes. The glass is wavy, old, and everything on the porch looks slightly melted around the edges. But she's there. Melissa. Her shape is unmistakable, shoulders squared, one hand clutching the strap of a leather bag, the other tucked into the pocket of her jeans. She rocks on her heels, impatient and fragile at the same time.

My mouth is so dry my tongue sticks to the roof of it. I drag my palm over my face, leaving a streak of sweat, and try to steady my breathing. I want to stay hidden behind the glass. I want to rewind the last ten seconds and pretend I never heard the knock, never saw her waiting outside my studio. But the rules of the world, even mine, don't allow that.

I descend the steps and cross to the door. I reach for the knob and realize, too late, that my fingers are still smeared with titanium white. The paint presses into the ridged brass, leaving a fingerprint that will never quite come out. I hesitate with my hand on the knob, feeling every stupid, familiar heartbeat in my veins.

When I finally open the door, I brace myself against the frame, as if the house itself might tip under the weight of whatever happens next. I don't know what to say, so I stare. Her hair is shorter than it was the last time I saw her, lopped at her shoulders, and the ends are uneven like she did it herself after a bottle of wine. Her smile, though. That part hasn't changed. It splits her face in two, reckless and honest.

"I know you told me not to come, but you know me, I've never been good at following instructions."

I want to respond, but my throat won't cooperate. I grip the doorframe with my clean hand, bracing for aftershocks. Up close, she smells like hotel soap and cheap shampoo. Her eyes search the room behind me, skimming the paintings on the walls.

"Can I come in, or are we doing this out here?"

I step back and let her pass. The gallery is cool and quiet, with windows thrown wide to the sea.

"Nice," she says with a nod at the first painting. She walks the length of the gallery, taking in the display of coastal landscapes. "I never thought you'd really do it, open up a place of your own. I thought you'd spend a few months out here, get it out of your system, and then head back to the city."

My hands start to shake again so I jam them into the pockets of my jeans. I can feel the sticky print of paint on my fingertips. "What are you doing here, Mel?"

She leans against the wall, crossing her arms. "I came to see you."

I almost laugh. "I said not to."

She shrugs, but it's a gesture thick with old ache. "You say a lot of things, Nathan."

I don't answer. There are too many things in my mouth at once, too many years of practiced silence.

Melissa's eyes drop to the floor. She tows her shoe along the hardwood, then looks up at me like she's about to confess to a murder.

"I think about you every day," she says. "The city is empty without you. So is the apartment. I quit the job. I—" She stutters, searching for the next place to land. "I know what I did. I know how I hurt you. I thought time would fix it, but...it didn't."

There's a punchline in there somewhere, but I can't bring myself to make it. "What do you want from me?"

She takes a step forward. "I want to start over. Even if it's just for a night. I want to remember what it felt like to love you without all the noise."

I take a step back, and she holds up her hands, empty. "I

just want to talk."

"Like I told you on the phone, there's nothing left to talk about."

She nods, but the edge of her smile softens, and she looks lost, the way we all are when the map runs out. "I just... I thought maybe there was something left, something that hasn't been painted over."

"You shouldn't be here," I say, thinking of Diane. "When I told you not to come, I meant it."

She holds my gaze for a second that feels longer than any winter, then nods. "Fine. I'll go." She moves toward the door and I watch her go, every step a slow-motion break. She hesitates at the threshold, then turns.

"I'm staying at the Ocean Side Inn for a couple of days," she says, almost smiling. "In case you change your mind..."

CHAPTER 38

DIANE

The trick, I have learned, is to begin before I am ready. Before the day is fully awake. Before my doubts have time to gather and conspire. So, I wake to Sara's old house clock, crawl from the folds of the guest bed, and walk down the corridor, past the sun-shocked photographs of her ancestors, all peering out, as if to judge my work ethic. I make coffee with a little stovetop pot that spits and hisses, the smell so bitter it seems to tattoo the air.

The window is open, salt in every breath, and below, the reeds lean and flatten under a fickle wind. The morning, a brilliant blue, features seagulls wheeling above the shore, their cries sharp as broken crockery. I open the laptop and watch the cursor blink at the top of a blank document. Already I can feel the pressure at my temples, the knowing that what I write will never match the thing inside my chest.

But the trick is to begin, so I do.

It's been weeks since I have managed to write anything that wasn't a to-do list or a desperate, unsent email to my agent about how I am not cut out for this. How I am squatting in the crumbling glory of Sara's house, burning through her beans and her goodwill, walking the beaches at dusk like a stray. But Sara wouldn't mind. She always said the sea was good for me.

She said all writers should be exiled to lonely coastlines with nothing but their ghosts and bad habits for company.

This morning, for the first time in months, I believe her. The story unravels faster than I can catch it.

I type until my wrists ache. I write dialogue between two people who want each other so badly that their words scrape. I write a kitchen table scene so real I can smell the burnt toast and the echo of laughter. When I pause to sip my coffee, it is already cold and thick at the bottom of the mug. I drink it anyway.

My novel is about a widow who moves to a small town and opens a secondhand bookstore. The townspeople are wary of her. They think she is running from something (they are right), but none of them can guess what. In this morning's chapter, she finds an unsigned letter in the pages of a used mystery novel, a letter that makes her shake. The handwriting is familiar; it's her own. She must have written it to herself in some forgotten, desperate moment.

The woman on the screen is not me, not exactly. She is braver. But I borrow her feelings, the way an insomniac borrows hours from tomorrow, and I make her risk what I cannot.

I type:

> *She could not name the feeling at first. It arrived like a slow leak, a drip of want that pooled and grew until it warped the floorboards of her heart. The man who made her feel it was not her late husband, not the ghost she had been faithful to for years. He was alive, infuriatingly so, and his hands could bruise a pear with tenderness.*

I stare at the sentence for a long time. The man in my book is named Calder. He wears flannel even in summer, and when he laughs it sounds like a challenge. The real man who leaks into every paragraph is Nathan, though I refuse to type his name. Maybe it would be bad luck, like saying Macbeth in a theater.

My fingers hesitate over the keys, hovering like bees over a field of clover. I know what the next scene must be. I have been avoiding it for weeks.

I write it anyway.

Calder sits at the kitchen table, peeling an orange in long, unbroken ribbons. He tells her that love is a thing that survives on attention, like a plant or a sullen child. He says it with his head down, the orange spray catching the light on the back of his hand. She wants to reach out and touch that hand, but she is afraid of what it might mean.

She is more afraid of not knowing.

The orange scent is so vivid I can almost taste it. The room fills with it, and the air in Sara's library sweetens.

I exhale, rolling my neck until it pops, and take a breath so deep it rattles in my chest.

I am still in my pajamas, my feet bare on the cool wood floor. The mug in my hand is chipped along the rim, but I run my tongue along it anyway, savoring the bitterness that lingers there. The salt in the air is everywhere, corroding, clarifying.

The words are coming easier now, so I let them.

I write:

She told herself she was content, but the lie was a garment that fit only in the dark. In daylight, it scratched and itched until she could not breathe. She wanted, she needed, she

> *could not deny it any longer. She was in love with him, and it was a kind of hunger.*

I stop, hands trembling. I am not sure if I mean her or me.

Somewhere in the house, the air kicks on with a hydraulic sigh, but I am sweating. I stand and open the window wider, even though the wind is like dragon's fire. The gulls have scattered, leaving only the distant pulse of the surf. I want to walk to the water and wade out until the cold unravels every last thought, but I have learned not to trust these impulses. Instead, I pace the small rectangle of floor between the desk and the window, counting each step.

On the third circuit, I catch a glimpse of my reflection in the glass. My hair is askew, eyes rimmed with sleepless blue, the shape of a woman who has not yet learned how to stop missing people. I laugh out loud at myself, a cracked little sound.

I go back to the desk and read over what I have written. Each sentence is a step closer to something I have been afraid to say. I delete nothing.

I write:

> *She typed and typed, afraid that if she stopped, the spell would break, and she would have to reckon with what she had written. But it was too late for that now. She had confessed herself to the page, and there was no taking it back.*

My face is hot, and my hands are cold. I am not crying, but the urge is there, lurking just under my ribs. I think of Nathan, the way he stands with his shoulders tensed, like he is bracing for an invisible blow. I think of his laugh, the rare and reckless version, the one that surfaces only when he forgets to be cautious.

I do not know what he wants from me. But I know what I want from him.

The thought is terrifying, and also—at last—clean.

I save the document, the little disk icon spinning with its false sense of security and close the laptop. I peer out the window at the water, which is the same as it ever was, but I am not. I am still afraid, but the words have made a kind of space inside me, a new room I did not know I could inhabit.

CHAPTER 39

NATHAN

I drive with the radio off, the wipers sluicing rain in a slow pulse. Every rut in the road transmits up the column of my spine and rattles my thoughts. By the time I reach the Ocean Side Inn, my teeth ache from grinding, and my hands are welded to the steering wheel. I cut the engine and sit in the quiet, the only sound the tsk-tsk of water tapping the roof.

I stare at the faded green awning of the motel. It's the kind of place that exists in every coastal town, a little too bright, a little too eager. Sand-logged rugs, plastic Adirondack chairs, a patch of hydrangeas clinging to the front walk. I could be anywhere, but I'm not. I am here. I am twenty-five and thirty-three and every age in between.

I reach for the door handle. Pull back. I roll my head against the headrest, then twist the rearview so it catches my eyes. They look like someone else's. I drag a hand through my hair, try to remember the last time I shaved, and wonder if I should turn around and drive back to the studio. Pretend I never left. Pretend I am someone who listens to his own advice.

Instead, my mind wanders to Sara. The thought of her comes so sharp it steals the breath from my lungs. She'd tell me to go in, face the thing, name the ghost.

I sit for another five minutes, mapping out possible futures in my head. None of them are good.

Eventually, I force the door open and step into the wet. The heat is immediate, a slap to the face. I walk to the lobby, nod at the guy behind the counter—he's reading a fishing magazine and hardly looks up—and take the stairs two at a time to the second floor. Room 211. I know she picked it because it's an odd number. Melissa never liked symmetry.

My hand hovers before I knock. Three short, one long, out of habit, and I hear her laugh on the other side before she even opens the door.

When she does, it's like stepping into a time warp. The room smells like her, sharp and sweet. She's in jeans and a loose T-shirt, hair wild and damp like she's just showered. She looks tired, but it suits her, carves something vulnerable into the architecture of her face.

"Nate," she says, the word almost a sigh. "You came."

I step in, keep my hands in my jacket pockets. "Melissa."

She steps back to allow me entrance, then smiles with half her mouth, and sits cross-legged on the corner of the bed. There are two coffee cups on the side table, one lipstick-stained, the other pristine. She gestures for me to sit. I hover near the dresser instead, watch the way her ankle bounces with nervous energy.

"Why did you really come?" I ask. "Why now, after all these months?"

She leans forward, her hands pressed together like she's praying. "I keep thinking... what if I made the wrong choice? What if I let something good go, and I'm too stubborn to admit it?" She shakes her head, hair swinging. "I can't get you out of my system. I thought I could. I tried. But I can't. We had ten years together, Nate. Ten incredible years. That doesn't just disappear."

I let out a slow breath. "No, but we left it behind for a reason, didn't we?"

She smiles, but it's sad, all teeth. "You remember our first apartment? The one with the leaking pipes and the neighbor who played bagpipes at 6 a.m.? We fought every day about who would get up first and make coffee. But then you'd bring me a cup in bed anyway," she says. "Even after the worst fights. You always did."

I look down at my hands, still raw from nerves. "People break habits eventually," I say.

"Not always," she says and slides up beside me. I feel the heat of her knee through my jeans. She rests a hand on my arm, feather-light, the way you'd touch a sleeping dog. "What if we tried again? What if we gave it a real shot, without all the bullshit this time? Without all the expectations?"

"No, Mel. I'm not the same man you used to know. I've changed. I've moved on. Don't you think it's time you did the same?"

She nods, lets her hand fall. "Maybe you're right. Maybe it is time I moved on. But I had to be sure. I had to see you, because I couldn't really remember what it felt like. All those years, all those fights and the love.... I guess I was just hoping that seeing you could remind me of why we let each other go."

"We? No, don't romanticize it. It was you who let me go," I say as the truth rolls off my tongue.

She winces as if I'd slapped her, her fingers fluttering to her cheek as if to stem the blow. "Yes, I suppose I did. But you didn't put up much of a fight, either."

I can't argue with that. I didn't fight because some part of me knew she was right. We were not meant for each other anymore. We had been drifting apart, and holding on tighter would only have dragged us both down.

"But what about now?" she asks. "What if things are different."

"They're not. Nothing's changed except our distance from the past."

She looks away, and I know she's disappointed. I can see the slight tremble in her lower lip, a telltale sign that she's trying not to cry. I want to reach out to comfort her, but I refrain. Some wounds need air to heal, not soothing words or tender caresses.

"What if I told you I changed my mind about everything? What if I said I wanted kids?"

That stops me, as if she's jammed a stick in the spokes of my mind. For years we fought over the shape of our future, the great divide between my longing for a family and her allergy to permanence. I thought I'd heard every permutation of this argument, but I never expected her to change her mind. "You're just saying that because you miss me. Or because you think it will change my mind, but it won't. Besides, I have someone now who wants what I want, who sees the future the way I do. I'm not going to derail that for nostalgia."

"Then why'd you come here, Nate? If it's so damn perfect, why are you here?"

"To give you these." I fish the letters from my pocket, creased and soft around the edges, and slide them across the laminate of the dresser.

She looks at them, her face tight and pale. "You kept these?"

"Didn't know what else to do with them, until now. But I no longer need them," I say.

She doesn't pick them up, just stares at the pile. Then, finally she rakes them in, holds them to her chest. Like they're a diagnosis or a prescription or maybe both. "I guess that's it, then."

"Yeah, I guess it is," I say, rising from the dresser. "I should go. I've got someone waiting on me, and I promised I wouldn't be late."

She doesn't stop me. Just nods, her chin quivering slightly as she finally meets my eyes.

"Take care of yourself, Melissa." I look at her one last time before heading toward the door. I don't look back, but I can feel the weight of her gaze on me as I leave. The hallway is colder than before. I walk out into it and hear the door click shut, softer than I expect. Down in the lot, the rain has stopped but left everything damp and shining. I get in the car, close my eyes, and let the sound of Diane's voice fills the space where Melissa's used to be.

CHAPTER 40

DIANE

When I next surface from writing, the house has gone dim and quiet. A black river of words flows behind my eyes, and my hands ache from typing too long. The light at the windows is a faint pink mush, September dusk. For a dizzy half second I'm unsure where I am, my spine pressed into the sofa's seam, my notes sliding to the carpet like scattered feathers.

I have written fifteen pages without stopping, the kind of jag that only comes once in a blue moon and leaves you both triumphant and hollowed out. I type the last line of the chapter, hands shaking from fatigue and some animal thrill, and for a long time I just stare at the words.

I want to cry but don't. Instead, I let myself feel the high and crash of it—the way a story, when it finally cracks open, can swallow you whole.

I scroll back and read the last paragraph, needing to see it as a reader would:

> *She did not know if the leap would end in flight or in the sea, but the not knowing was the point. She stepped forward, her heart loud in her ears, and decided that some risks were worth the fall.*

I read it again, slower. Some risks were worth the fall.

Outside, a branch taps the glass, a wind-shivered warning. I ignore it. The words pulse in my head.

I think of Nathan, of all the ways I have kept myself safe from wanting things I might not get. I think of the other women I have envied, those who go after what they want, who risk embarrassment, who call in the middle of the night just to say I miss you. I have never been that person, not really.

But maybe I could be.

I close the laptop and stack the loose pages of my notes, aligning the edges with unnecessary care. I brush crumbs from the desktop, then rise, stretching until my spine cracks. The room is a cave of blue shadows, my reflection barely visible in the window.

I shut the window, sliding it closed with a firmness I rarely permit myself. The house settles, the wind turns, and I breathe in the evening, letting it fill every corner. When I leave the library, I am still scared, but it is a new kind of scared, the kind that comes with wanting something you might actually get.

In the hallway, I pause and run my hands over my hair, flattening the wild strands into something almost presentable. I feel taller than I did this morning. Lighter, too, like I've been quietly refilled with helium.

Somewhere out there is Nathan, wondering, just as I am, what happens next.

I head for the door. For the first time in years, I am ready to find out.

CHAPTER 41

DIANE

The door clicks shut behind me with a sound that belongs to another life. I stand in the entryway, socked feet, heart still hurling itself at my ribs as if my body were a cage. The wind hisses around the house, and the thin glass of the storm window vibrates with a persistence I find both irritating and weirdly encouraging.

I should go. That's the point. Don't think, just do. But my legs aren't getting the message. I drift instead to the bedroom, where the ceiling is so low I can touch it if I stand on tiptoe. Cassie's glitter pens spill off her desk like a handful of candy. My own notebook, half-filled with sentences I may never let anyone see, lies open on the comforter, the ink still damp. If I leave now, it will be here when I come back. I pretend this is a metaphor for bravery, but mostly it just makes me want to never leave.

I sit on the edge of the bed, running my thumb over the grooved cover of the notebook. For weeks, I have moved through the days with the exactitude of a sleepwalker—breakfast, school drop-off, writing time, errands, dinner, bedtime, insomnia. The hours have been pale and identical, each day no more or less difficult than the one before. But tonight there is a static in the air that I can't ignore, as if the sky itself has been loaded with a charge.

I stand, pull open the closet, and stare at the contents for longer than is healthy. I try on a shirt, change my mind, swap it for a dress, lose confidence and switch again. I turn sideways in the mirror and inspect my profile. My shoulders are too round, hair refusing to lie flat no matter how much I smooth it. I catch myself sucking in my stomach and immediately let it go, ashamed of the reflex. What am I trying to prove, and to whom?

There is a comfort in rituals, even ridiculous ones. I put on the blue sweater Cassie gave me for Mother's Day, the one with the slightly lopsided collar. I swap my sweats for jeans, but in the end, I am still myself, every flaw outlined in high relief by the last fading stripe of daylight. I stand in front of the mirror, take a breath, and try out a few opening lines:

"Hey, can we talk?" Too abrupt.

"I just wanted to—" Too desperate.

"I know about Melissa." There is a flicker in my reflection's eyes, a brief suggestion of the woman I want to be.

But the mirror, of course, is a traitor. It knows I have no idea what I am doing.

On my dresser, the shell necklace sits coiled like a question mark. Cassie made it, threading white-and-amber chips onto fishing line and tying the clasp in a way that always pinches my skin. It is ugly and perfect, and Nathan was the one who showed her how to use the pliers without slicing open her thumb. I fasten the necklace at my throat, surprised at the weight of it. I let my fingers linger there, as if by pressing hard enough I could smother my nerves.

Sara would laugh at me, if she could see me now. She'd say, "It's only love, Diane. It's not a hostage situation." She'd remind me that life is a finite resource, and hoarding happiness is the fastest way to waste it. Sara was never afraid to ask for what she wanted. Even when her voice shook, she said the thing that needed to be said.

I remember her in the hospital, bone-thin and furious at the world. "Promise me you'll live," she said, "because I won't be around to make you do it."

Outside, a storm gathers itself into a low, rolling roar across the horizon. The sun has started its descent, bleeding pink into the undersides of the clouds. I step into the entryway and lace up my shoes, the act of preparation both grounding and absurd. Each knot feels like a commitment. When I stand, my knees are weak, but I force them steady.

I lock the door behind me and start down the driveway, the shells popping underfoot like distant fireworks. The air is sharp with ozone and seaweed, the smell of the coming rain. The path to the beach is familiar, but tonight it feels entirely new, as if the world has shifted five degrees off its axis, and now everything glimmers in a way it never has before.

I walk past the neighbor's house and cut through the narrow trail lined with salt-blasted dune grass. The sand is cold, almost electric against my ankles. I follow the curve of the shore, heart hammering, every muscle in my body wound tight.

Up ahead, the beach opens into a gentle arc. I see the pier and a shape that could be only one person. Nathan. His silhouette darkened against the backdrop of the sea and sky. His sketchbook lies open on the rail, and he is so focused on the page that he doesn't notice my approach. There is something unbearably tender in the way his head tilts, his brow furrowed in concentration.

I stop twenty feet away, uncertain, afraid to interrupt. I

watch him for a long minute, memorizing the slope of his shoulders, the way his hands move. The wind snatches a lock of his hair and tosses it across his forehead, and he absently tucks it behind his ear.

The sky behind him is a riot of color, a smudge of purple melting into fire, and for a second I am almost paralyzed by the beauty of it. There is no right time to do this. I take a step forward, and the board creaks beneath me. I take another, and he looks up.

Our eyes meet across the distance, and I think of all the ways this could go wrong. But then he smiles, and I remember what Sara told me, that you only get so many chances.

I close the rest of the distance, the words lining up in my chest like dominoes, waiting for the right nudge to send them tumbling out.

Nathan closes his sketchbook with a slow, careful motion, as if afraid any sudden movement will startle me back into the dark.

I stop, not quite close enough to touch. The salt wind scours my skin, goosebumps rising in its wake, and I have the sudden, unhelpful urge to laugh. I do not.

"Hey," I manage. The word cracks in the middle.

"Hey," he answers, softer than I expect. His hair is a mess, sticking to his temples in wild, wind-drawn lines. He looks tired, but not in the way that means defeat. It's more like the tiredness that comes after you finish a race and, win or lose, you're glad it's over.

The water is just beneath us, and I can hear the waves eating away at the shore, again and again and again. The ocean, it seems, is never afraid of repetition.

He glances at me, mouth opening, then closing. I beat him

to it.

"I'm sorry," I say, not because I am, but because it's easier than saying anything else. "For interrupting. You probably want to be alone."

He shakes his head, a smile flickering in the half-light. "Don't be. I'm glad you came."

I stare at the ocean, at the pale foam tracing the edge of the beach. It feels like a long drop, standing on this precipice.

He follows my gaze. "You ever feel like the whole world is just...waiting for you to jump?"

I want to tell him I do. I want to tell him the waiting is the worst part.

Instead, I twist the hem of my sweater, fabric bunching between my fingers. "I've been thinking," I say. "I can't keep pretending I don't—" My voice snags on the word. "Care. About you."

He blinks, the moment landing between us with a weight that feels like gravity. I force myself to look at him. He is so close that if I reached out I could touch the curve of his jaw, trace the lines that worry has etched around his mouth.

"I know I should be careful," I say, the words spilling now, "but I don't want to be careful. Not with you. I'm tired of living like I'm afraid of my own shadow."

His eyes never leave mine. I see the pulse in his neck, the twitch of a muscle along his jaw. "Diane—"

I barrel ahead, knowing if I stop, I might never start again. "I'm in love with you, Nathan." The confession comes out small, defiant, barely more than a breath. "I'm in love with you, and it scares the shit out of me. Because I thought—" I swallow hard. "I thought if I let myself want something this much, the universe would just...take it away. Like it always does."

I wait for him to tell me I'm wrong, or that it's too late, or that Melissa is waiting for him at the hotel.

Instead, he covers my hand with his. His fingers are warm, calloused, anchoring me to the now.

"Diane," he says. The name is careful, like he's holding it up to the light. "You don't have to be afraid of that. Not with me."

My body trembles, but it's a good kind of shaking, the kind that means the adrenaline is doing its job. I let out a ragged laugh, half sob, half exhale.

"I watched you today," I say. "With Cassie, and with the kids at the art walk, and even with strangers. You're...different. You listen, really listen. You look at me like you see something worth seeing. I haven't felt that in a long time."

He says nothing, but his hand tightens on mine. I can see his chest rising and falling, breath shallow and quick. I worry, for a split second, that I've said too much. That I've ruined the fragile truce we'd built.

"I know about Melissa," I add. "About her coming to see you. Nick, from the hotel, called and told me he saw you visiting a woman with Mecklenburg County plates. I just figured..."

"Melissa's not—" He stops himself. "Yes, she came to see me. To see if there was anything left of our relationship to salvage."

My heart seizes in my chest, fear spreading like ink through water. But he continues, his tone steady and calm.

"But I told her there wasn't. That even if there had been something, it was long gone. She's in my past, Diane. You're what's here now."

I let out a breath I've been holding since forever. My hand is still trembling in his, but I don't care if he notices. The trembling feels like permission.

Nathan turns to face me. He brings my knuckles to his lips, a gesture so old-fashioned and sincere it nearly undoes me.

"Diane," he says again, softer. "You scare the hell out of me too. But I want this. I want you. All of you. Even the parts you think aren't worth wanting."

A sob lodges in my throat, not from sadness but from relief. When I try to answer him, my voice is shredded, barely there.

He kisses me then, and it is nothing like I expected. It is awkward and urgent, a collision of teeth and nose and wet, briny lips, and I love it more than anything that came before. I grab his shirt and pull him closer. The sketchbook falls to the planks, forgotten.

When we part, our foreheads lean together, and the whole world seems to be holding us in place.

Nathan looks at the lighthouse in the distance, its beacon slicing the twilight in slow, predictable sweeps. "That's us," he says, nodding toward it. "Always a little bit lost. Always finding our way back."

I want to say something witty, or poetic, or even just coherent. But all I can do is laugh again—this time with the reckless certainty of a person who has nothing left to lose and everything left to want.

We stay until the last molecules of daylight are gone. Then he takes my hand, and together we walk up the beach, footprints erased almost as soon as they are made.

Home is not the same house I left an hour ago. It is wherever he is, and wherever Cassie waits, and wherever I let myself want something badly enough to risk falling for it.

At the front door, he wraps me in his arms, and I let the night take us. Above, the lighthouse sweeps its beam across the dark, steady and unwavering. It is the most beautiful thing I have ever seen.

CHAPTER 42

DIANE

October

I wake to the scent of salt and burnt sugar. It takes me a minute to orient myself. My mind is still half-tangled in the dream where the three of us stand at the edge of the sea, but every time I reach for Cassie, she vanishes into foam.

The kettle is already screaming on the stove by the time I stumble into the kitchen. Cassie sits at the breakfast table, arms folded, staring at the linoleum like it holds the secret to a happy life.

"Morning," I say, and it comes out like a cough.

She shrugs, which is teenager for "go away," but I take it as a win.

I pour the water, spilling a little on the counter, and the hiss reminds me that every day is just a series of tiny messes you learn to clean up. I reach for the coffee, shaking the tin over the filter, and realize my hands are trembling. Not from caffeine. From the anticipation of everything that might go wrong before 9:00 a.m.

"Cereal?" I ask, but Cassie's already poured herself a bowl of Froot Loops, the colors bleeding into milk that looks like an art project gone wrong.

"I have a math test tomorrow," she mumbles. "And a science project due Tuesday."

I want to say something reassuring, but all I manage is, "You'll do great." The words hit the table and roll away.

Through the window, I can see Sara's garden, a riot of wild violets and neglected raspberry canes, the trellis listing to one side like a shipwreck. I imagine us out there, three mismatched survivors trying to build something that floats.

Nathan is late. I check the oven clock, then the front door, as if he might materialize just by thinking hard enough. This is ridiculous. I remind myself I am a grown woman who has lived through far worse than an awkward breakfast.

Still, my fingers tap out Morse code on the Formica: anxious, anxious, anxious.

Cassie doesn't look up from her cereal. She segregates the colored rings into separate piles, picking through the loops with a calculated economy of movement. I want to reach across the table and take her hand, but I know better. The last time I tried, she pulled away like I was the one on fire. In the wake of Sara's death, Cassie has built an invisible wall around herself, one that I can't seem to penetrate.

Nathan arrives with the wind, the door slamming behind him. He's carrying a bag of bagels and two foam cups, which is so perfectly Nathan that I nearly laugh.

"Sorry I'm late," he says, his voice too bright, like he's auditioning for a sitcom dad. "Had to rescue these from the perils of the 7-Eleven bakery section."

Cassie makes a face but takes a bagel when offered. Progress.

Nathan sits across from her, unwrapping a cinnamon raisin and slathering it with the tiny packet of cream cheese. He looks at me, eyes flicking from my face to the coffee mug to the dark blue sweater I pulled from the laundry basket because it still smells faintly of last night's ocean air.

"Rough morning?" he asks.

I glance at Cassie, then back to him. "You could say that."

He smiles, and there is a genuine warmth beneath the forced cheer. "I once set an entire kitchen towel on fire trying to impress a girl with my omelet skills. This"—he gestures to the breakfast spread—"is an improvement."

Cassie snorts, and a crumb shoots from her mouth onto the table. She blushes, then immediately reverts to neutral.

Nathan turns to her, as if this is a normal family scene. "How's the science project coming? Need a hand?"

She recoils, just slightly. "I can do it myself."

"Bug," I say, my tone slipping into the careful register of post-trauma parenting, "manners."

"Please don't call me that," she mutters, "and I don't need help."

Nathan nods, unoffended. "Copy that."

My eyes drift to the far end of the kitchen, where the manuscript pages are stacked next to my laptop, binder-clipped into a lopsided sheaf. I left them out as a kind of dare to myself: Finish this or admit you never will. The top page is crumpled at one corner, stained with what might be wine or maybe just hope.

Cassie's gaze follows mine. "Did you stay up writing again?"

I nod, sheepish. "I got a little carried away."

She makes a sound, almost a laugh. "You always do."

Nathan glances at the stack, then back at me. "How's it going?"

I hesitate. I don't want to talk about it for the same reason you don't poke a sleeping bear—it might wake up. "Better," I manage to say.

He raises his mug, a salute. "To better."

Cassie eyes him, skepticism and curiosity in equal measure.

Nathan tries again, softer this time. "If you ever want a break from homework, I could show you how to make one of those baking soda volcanoes. Pure chaos. No grading involved."

The corners of her mouth twitch, the urge to smile stomped down before it can break the surface.

"We used to do those," she says, barely audible. "When I was little."

Nathan's voice is gentle. "I bet yours would put mine to shame."

Cassie shrugs. "Maybe."

I want to say something, anything, to keep the bridge from collapsing. But I'm afraid of stepping wrong and watching the whole thing fall.

It's Nathan who finally breaks the tension. He pushes back from the table, brushing the crumbs from his hands. "You know," he says, "Sara used to let me help in the garden. She always said the dirtier your hands, the better the flowers."

Cassie's face flickers, grief and loyalty in an impossible tangle.

"We could plant something today," he adds, the suggestion so tentative it barely lands. "You know, for her."

Cassie looks to me for permission.

I nod, and the smallest of smiles sneaks onto her face, gone in an instant but still there.

"Okay," she says. "I guess."

It's not forgiveness, not exactly. But it's something.

Nathan grins. "I'll get the gloves."

When he leaves the room, Cassie looks at me, her walls dropped for just a breath.

"You're really happy with him," she says. Not a question. A dare.

I want to be honest. I want to be brave, like Sara said.

"I'm trying," I say. "Some days, it's easier than others."

Cassie stares at her cereal, then stirs it with the spoon until the colors are indistinguishable.

"Okay," she says again, even softer.

Nathan's laugh echoes from the hallway. I can picture him fumbling with the garden shed, cursing under his breath, determined to win her over one awkward moment at a time.

I gather the dishes, stacking them in the sink, and watch as Cassie steps out onto the porch. Sunlight catches the edge of her hair, and she stands there, arms folded, waiting for whatever comes next.

***

I used to think the hardest part of being a mother was sleeplessness, the way it rendered you raw and brittle, an exposed nerve walking around in borrowed skin. I was wrong. The hardest part is hope. You plant it in the best dirt you can find, water it with every last molecule of wanting, and then wait—knowing the frost could come at any time, that something hungry might burrow in and hollow it out.

The garden is a testament to both: weeds and wildflowers, thriving side by side. Sara's fingerprints are everywhere, on the cracked ceramic gnome that guards the strawberry bed, the shell wind chimes strung above the rain barrel, the clusters of bluebells that only she could coax from the stubborn sand.

I kneel in the damp earth and try not to think about what it means to love something so much it hurts.

Nathan is already at work, sleeves rolled up, dirt smudged across the bridge of his nose like a battle stripe. He moves with careful efficiency, digging small holes for the flats of marigolds and morning glories we bought at the roadside stand. Every few minutes, he glances at me as if afraid I might dissolve.

Cassie trails us, carrying a bag of bulbs, but mostly she just drags her feet, leaving deep furrows in the mulch. She won't make eye contact, but I catch her staring at Nathan's back, her expression complicated and unreadable.

I try for normalcy. "Cass... I mean, Cassie, can you pass me the trowel?"

She sets it on the ground next to me, as if proximity itself might be contagious.

"Thanks," I say, and she shrugs, then busies herself picking slugs off the hostas and flicking them into the grass.

A bead of sweat slips down my temple, stinging in the open cut above my eyebrow, the remnant of an argument with the attic hatch last week. I wipe it away with the hem of my sleeve and focus on the rhythm of work.

Nathan crouches beside me, balancing a tray of pansies. "I read somewhere that these help keep bugs away," he says, nudging the edge of a joke.

I give him half a smile. "Sara would say you're full of it."

We work quietly. Above us, the clouds stack up like wet laundry, promising rain but not quite delivering. Cassie circles the periphery, every motion telegraphing her reluctance to belong.

Then it happens.

Nathan reaches for the trowel at the same time Cassie

does, their hands colliding in the dirt. Cassie jerks back as if stung, the bag of bulbs tumbling from her grip and scattering like spilled secrets. She knocks over a potted fern, the clay shattering on the flagstone.

"Shit," she says, too loud.

I start to say, "It's okay," but Cassie cuts me off, voice trembling.

"This isn't even your house!" she yells at Nathan, fists balled at her sides. "You can't just...come in and pretend like it is."

The words hang in the air, sharp as a thrown knife.

Nathan's face goes pale. He stands, brushing dirt from his palms, but doesn't move closer. "You're right," he says, his voice steady but brittle. "I'm sorry. I overstepped."

Cassie blinks, surprised by his concession. She looks at me, pleading for an ally, but I am still caught between the urge to protect and the need to let her fight her own battles.

I kneel next to her in the dirt, putting a hand on her shoulder. She doesn't pull away, but she doesn't lean in, either.

"Cassie," I say, "he's not trying to take over. He's just... trying to help."

She stares at the broken pot, breathing hard. "I don't need help."

I want to tell her that needing help doesn't make her weak, but I can see in her hunched shoulders that she's heard it all before. Instead, I just sit with her, letting the silence do what words can't.

Nathan kneels by the wreckage, gathering shards of clay with careful hands. He looks at Cassie, then at me, and I see fear on his face. Not for himself, but for us.

"She needs time," he says quietly, more to himself than to

me.

"So do I," I say

He returns to planting, doesn't force the conversation, doesn't try to fix the unfixable. He just keeps working, hands steady in the earth.

The clouds finally open, a soft mist settling over the garden. It beads on Cassie's eyelashes, turns the dirt to mud beneath our knees.

Cassie stands, wiping her hands on her jeans. She stares at the muddy smears, then at me, then at Nathan. "I'm going for a walk."

"Do you want company?" I ask.

She shakes her head. "No. I'll take Rolo with me."

I watch Cassie's retreating form, her hair wet and wild, arms swinging with a defiance that looks so much like my own.

I want to follow her, to drag her back and make her sit in the dirt and plant something that will last. But I know that isn't how anything grows.

Instead, I kneel beside Nathan and help him tamp down the soft, damp earth. For a while, we don't speak. The work is enough. When the beds are full, we sit on the edge of the porch and let the rain wash our hands clean.

The wind chimes rattle above us. Through the open window, I can hear Sara's favorite song playing faintly from the stereo, the record crackling like distant thunder.

"She'll come back," Nathan says. "She always does."

I want to believe him.

I close my eyes and listen to the rain. I can almost hear Sara laughing, mocking our crooked rows and uneven spacing, but proud anyway.

When I open them, the world is greener than it was before.

I touch Nathan's hand, let it rest there a second longer than necessary, then stand and go after my daughter, following the line of footprints she left in the wet grass. Each one an imperfect echo of my own.

CHAPTER 43

DIANE

Night comes early in this house. The old cedar beams catch the dusk and bottle it, so even the brightest lamp only grazes the darkness in patches. It feels right, somehow, privacy in every corner, as if the shadows themselves are allies.

I flick on the lamp in Sara's library, the one with the cracked base she swore she'd glue "someday, but not today." The yellow pool of light spills onto the woven rug, the battered cushions we scavenged from the attic, the stack of board games with half the pieces missing. The air smells like cinnamon and wet leaves. I open the window just enough to let in the sound of wind, the salt from the ocean.

Cassie walks in with damp socks, face flushed and hair wild from her walk. She doesn't look at me, but she doesn't look away, either. Small victories. Nathan follows, arms full of mismatched mugs and a pot of cocoa, which he deposits on the coffee table with all the ceremony of a peace treaty.

"We're out of marshmallows," he announces, feigning tragedy. "You'll have to accept my humble apologies and extra whipped cream instead."

Cassie rolls her eyes. "As if that's a punishment."

He grins, and the heaviness of the day seems to soften

around the edges.

I settle onto a cushion, the one that smells like Sara's perfume even after three washings, and pat the spot next to me. Cassie hesitates, then drops down with a sigh, curling her legs under herself in a way that reminds me of every year she's ever lived.

Nathan pours the hot chocolate, handing the first mug to Cassie, then one to me. He keeps his hands wrapped around his own, as if savoring the heat.

I count the seconds in my head, try to calculate the exact right moment to speak.

I decide there isn't one. "I was thinking," I say, "maybe we could try something tonight."

Both pairs of eyes are on me, wary but open.

I take a breath. "Let's each say one thing we're scared of, and one thing we hope for. About, you know. This." I gesture, clumsy, to the air between us.

Cassie's mouth twists. "Like therapy?"

"Kind of," I say. "But you get to hold your mug like a shield."

She stares into her cocoa, then shrugs. "Fine."

Nathan's smile is small, but it's there. "I'll go last," he says, and Cassie flashes him a look that is both challenge and gratitude.

I start. "I'm scared I won't be able to make this work. The writing, the parenting, the...everything." The confession tastes bitter, but I chase it with a gulp of chocolate. "But I hope I can do what Sara wanted. I hope I can live in every room of this house and not be afraid."

Cassie nods, her expression unreadable. "I'm scared you'll forget about Dad. Or that you'll get so busy with Nathan and your book that there won't be any room left for me." Her voice cracks just a little. "But I hope...maybe we can finally have a real home. Not just a place we crash between disasters."

She looks at Nathan, expecting—what? Judgment? Pity? He gives her neither.

He says, "I'm scared I won't measure up. That I'll say the wrong thing, or push too hard, and mess it all up for both of you. But I hope we can build something good."

No one speaks for a while. The silence isn't heavy. It's careful, like something precious you don't want to break.

Cassie wipes her nose with her sleeve. "You're both so cheesy."

Nathan lifts his mug. "Guilty as charged."

She laughs, just a little, and I want to reach out and tuck her hair behind her ear, but I know better. Instead, I pour her another mug, extra whipped cream, and she doesn't protest.

The wind picks up, whistling through the cracks in the old window. It sounds like singing, or maybe just the house reminding us it's still here, stubborn and solid.

We talk for hours. Not all at once, not about anything important, at least not on the surface. Cassie wants to dye her hair blue for the spring play. Nathan tells a story about getting locked in the art supply closet for an entire period and eating three sleeves of saltines to survive. I confess my secret love for trashy reality TV. Each admission is a pebble in the foundation, something to build on.

Eventually, I broach the subject of Nathan moving in with us, half-joking, mostly not. Cassie snorts. "Isn't he already here, like every night?" Nathan lifts his hands as though he's been caught by floodlights. I expect embarrassment, maybe even a little warfare, but instead the conversation rolls past like a slow river. We agree on pancakes in the morning, and Nathan says he makes a mean omelet, and he'll prove it if we let him handle the stove.

When the mugs are empty and the lamp is flickering, Cassie looks at Nathan. "Do you know anything about volcanoes?"

"Only that they're messy and awesome," he says, trying to play it cool.

"Okay. I might need help with my project tomorrow, if you don't mind."

He gives her a salute. "It would be my honor."

She rolls her eyes, but she's smiling when she stands to go to bed.

Nathan and I linger in the circle of lamplight, neither of us quite ready to call it a night. I look at his hands, the dirt still worked into the creases, the knuckles raw from digging.

"Feeling better?" I ask.

"Yeah," he says, "much better."

When I finally walk him to the door, I catch a glimpse of the hallway mirror, the two of us reflected side by side, no longer strangers, not quite family, but something sturdy enough to lean on.

He touches my shoulder, light as a feather. "You're doing better than you think."

I want to believe it. Maybe tomorrow I will.

When the door clicks shut, I hold Sara's keys in my palm. They're warm from my pocket, heavy with all the things I'm afraid to lose. I stand there for a long minute, listening to the house settle.

Upstairs, my desk waits. The manuscript, too—every page a piece of my heart, every sentence a risk.

I turn on another lamp, and the darkness recedes.

CHAPTER 44

DIANE

November

The light out here comes sideways, briny and bright, filling the town with a diffused, syrupy radiance that makes everything look like a painting. The gallery is only a few blocks from the ocean, so we walk, because that's what you do here, and because Cassie insists she'll explode if she has to endure another car ride with us.

I let her lead the way, and Nathan falls back, giving her room. The wind lifts Cassie's hair, and for a second I see the child she was, the one with legs too long for her body, intent on outrunning every shadow. Then Amaya materializes on the next corner, waving both arms, dark curls backlit in the haze. Her smile is all teeth and constellation freckles.

"Hey!" Amaya calls, bounding up the sidewalk. "You're late!"

"We're two minutes early," Cassie says, but she's grinning.

Amaya clutches a pamphlet, glossy and already dog-eared. "I made Mom stop by and grab a program on the way. Look, you're in it." She stabs her finger at the page.

Cassie's mouth quirks sideways, a little bashful, but she lets Amaya thread their arms together. They could be sisters instead of best friends, the kind who would share a bedroom and fight over the top bunk. I am not supposed to watch them this way, but I do. Sometimes I think it's the only way I'll ever remember what joy looks like from the outside.

We arrive at the gallery, and Nathan holds open the door. "Showtime," he says.

When I step inside, what I see takes my breath away. It's an entire chronology of this patch of coast, rendered in brushstrokes so soft they'll shatter if you touch them. There are rolling dunes in muted ochres and blue-violet shadows, a sunrise over the salt marsh, the pier at twilight, its pilings reflected in shattered mirror-water. In the back room are portraits, faces I've seen at the bakery, the post office, on the other side of a PTA table. All of them painted in Nathan's unmistakable style, alive with the subtlety of things seen in passing but remembered in full color.

And in the very center, spotlit and hung a little lower than the rest, is the painting I'd only glimpsed in progress. My breath stutters at the sight of it. It's me, Cassie, and Rolo, standing at the tide line under a sky peeled back for sunset. Cassie's hair is wind-ravaged and she's beaming, mid-laugh, her sneakers soaked through. Rolo's tongue lolls in a perfect pink curve, and I'm caught off guard by my own likeness—eyes closed, head tipped toward the horizon, wearing an expression that is pure, unmitigated peace.

I squeeze Nathan's hand so hard he laughs.

"Too much?" he asks, but the way he looks at me makes my heart gallop.

The room fills gradually, the guests trickling in. Some I know, others I've only met in passing, but every face turns toward Nathan with the same shy, proprietary pride, as if this gallery, this show, belongs to all of them.

Nathan fiddles with his tie, a deep navy color that almost matches the shadows in his paintings. It's new, and I can tell he's dying to loosen it, but he endures for the sake of the occasion. His cheeks flush whenever someone compliments the work, which is often, and the more he fidgets the more I want to grab his face and kiss him senseless, social norms be damned.

Instead, I nurse a glass of white wine and try not to spill on my new dress. The fabric is lighter than I'm used to, a soft coral that Cassie insisted would "bring out my inner beach goddess," whatever that means. I think of Sara, how she would have laughed at my discomfort and then worn something even louder, just to make me look tame by comparison.

I am drifting in a cloud of distant memory when a woman approaches, her hair coiled into a chignon and her eyes sharp as salt. She's wearing a navy blue shift dress and a single string of pearls, and she radiates the brisk authority of someone who sits on a lot of boards.

"Diane, right?" she says, extending a hand. "I'm Barbara. My husband, Chuck, used to work with Sara at the courthouse."

I accept the handshake, surprised at the strength in her grip. "Nice to meet you."

Barbara's gaze flicks to Nathan, who is deep in conversation with a pair of college-age boys gesturing at the dune paintings like they're trying to decode a secret language. "You've done something remarkable with the old Hastings house," she says, lowering her voice conspiratorially. "We worried it would go to ruin after—well. After everything."

I blink, momentarily thrown. "Thank you. We're trying."

Barbara leans in, her pearls glinting. "You're the talk of the town, you know. Some of us had bets on how long you'd last."

I laugh, genuine and startled, and I feel something old and

heavy in my chest start to dissolve. "And how are we fairing?"

She chuckles. "Remarkably well it seems," she replies, offering a small nod toward Nathan. "Enjoy yourself tonight," Barbara says, glancing meaningfully at the painting behind me. "You deserve it."

She moves on, collecting a petit four from the tray at the bar, and I watch her disappear into the crowd.

The next hour unfolds in a sequence of tiny revelations. People approach with stories about Sara, about the house, about the way Nathan's brushwork reminds them of the dunes at their own childhood cottage. The bartender pours with a generous hand, and soon the room is thick with laughter and the low hum of good gossip.

When Cassie and Amaya finally reach the family portrait, they stop dead, mouths in a perfect O.

"Mom," Cassie whispers, "is that—did Nathan—?"

"He did."

She leans in close. "It looks like it's still moving."

I want to say, *You look like you're still moving*, but I bite my tongue. Instead, I ask, "What do you think, Amaya?"

Amaya shrugs, but in the way that means she loves it and doesn't know how to say so. "It's like, really alive, you know?"

Cassie cackles. "You're such a nerd."

Amaya nudges her. "Says the girl who memorized the whole periodic table for fun."

"Not for fun," Cassie huffs, "for science club." But she's blushing, and I recognize the species of pride that blooms from genuine affection.

Nathan makes his way to us, catching the last of the exchange. He gestures to the catalog Amaya is still gripping. "Want to see the secret message?"

Amaya's eyes go wide. "There's a secret?"

He flips to the back, points to his artist statement: *In loving memory of Sara H.—and to Diane and Cassie, who kept the lights on even in the dark*. The air thins around us, then grows thick again, and suddenly I'm glad for the noise of the crowd.

"Whoa," Amaya says. "That's, like, really sweet."

Cassie doesn't say anything. She just looks at me, then at Nathan, and then away, as if embarrassed to have been the subject of a dedication. Or maybe just trying not to feel too much at once.

"You like it?" he asks Cassie, his voice almost timid.

Cassie doesn't answer, just lunges forward to wrap him in a hug, the kind that would have made me jealous a month ago but now feels like the exact right thing.

Eventually, the gallery fills up, then overflows. Guests swirl between the installations, clutching wine and cheese, making the rounds in sensible shoes.

Cassie and Amaya plant themselves in front of a smaller painting, one I hadn't seen before. It's Cassie, unmistakably, but softer around the edges, her hair loose and wild, a spiral of notes and equations scribbled in the negative space behind her head. She looks older in the painting. Or maybe just more certain.

"Dude, you look so cool," Amaya says, almost enviously.

Cassie shrugs. "He made up half the math in the background."

"Artistic license," Nathan interjects, but he's watching Cassie for her reaction.

"I like it," she says, quiet but clear. "You made me look like I'm thinking of something important."

"You are always thinking of something important," I say,

and Cassie rolls her eyes, but she's smiling.

A pair of older women shuffle closer, peering at the portrait over their glasses. One of them whispers, "Is that you, dear?" to Cassie.

Cassie straightens, shoulders back the way she does at debate tournaments. "Yeah. That's us—me, my mom, our dog, and Nathan painted it. He's really good, isn't he?"

The woman beams, her earrings bobbing. "You must be so proud."

Cassie looks at me, then at Nathan. "I am," she says. Just that. But it rings out like a bell.

I want to hug her, but I know better. Instead, I sidle next to Nathan, whose eyes are suspiciously shiny. "You did good," I whisper, and he squeezes my hand beneath the catalog.

The afternoon slides into evening, and the gallery never quite empties. People linger, hungry for beauty or maybe just company. Cassie and Amaya play docent, explaining the significance of each painting to anyone who asks. Sometimes they embellish, inventing stories about what inspired a particular piece. "This one is about the time Nathan accidentally set his sleeve on fire," Amaya tells a couple from out of town, gesturing at an abstract wash of reds and oranges. Cassie nods solemnly, and the tourists buy it completely.

By seven, Nathan calls for everyone's attention, tapping his glass with a butter knife. "Thank you, everyone, for coming out this evening. I want to remind everyone that I am available for commissions, and several pieces have already found homes tonight." He looks at me, a smile ghosting his lips. "Let's keep the creative spirit alive in Kitty Hawk!"

I catch the flash of pride on Nathan's face, but also the disbelief, as if he's still not convinced any of this is real. I get it.

Sometimes I feel like I'm living someone else's story, too.

After the crowd thins, Cassie and Amaya join us by the refreshment table, plates heaped with cheese cubes and strawberries. Amaya asks, "Do we get to do this again? Or was this a one-time thing?"

Nathan laughs. "There's another show in the spring. Different paintings, but same circus."

Amaya looks at Cassie, who for once doesn't deflect. "Yeah. I'd go again."

I reach for a strawberry, surprised at how ordinary this moment feels, and how much I want to keep it. "Next time, maybe you can curate," I suggest.

"Only if Amaya helps," says Cassie.

Amaya pumps her fist. "Dream team!"

The girls drift off, orbiting each other with a gravity I envy. Nathan and I lean against the wall, watching them move through the space. Two smart, stubborn kids in a sea of adults, perfectly themselves.

He nudges my shoulder. "You doing okay?"

"I think so."

Nathan's voice goes soft. "She's really proud of you, you know. Even if she doesn't always say it."

I swallow, suddenly aware of how long it's been since anyone's told me that. "You, too. I mean, she's proud of you, too."

He smiles. "It's mutual."

We stand, surrounded by the hush that follows applause. The last of the sunlight slants through the gallery windows, illuminating the portrait of Cassie. It's not how I would have painted her, but I think maybe that's the point. Sometimes you need someone else to show you what you look like when you're brave.

***

When it's time to go, I gather the girls and herd them into the cold. Cassie is quiet, but not in a bad way. She lets me put an arm around her shoulder, just this once. Nathan follows, hands deep in his pockets, face lit from within.

On the walk home, Amaya asks if she can sleep over, and Cassie doesn't even pretend to mind. I say yes, and Nathan offers to bring ice cream. The girls race ahead, their laughter bouncing off the empty sidewalks.

I watch them, and I don't feel like I'm chasing after my own life anymore. I feel like I'm exactly where I'm supposed to be.

CHAPTER 45

DIANE

The morning after the show, the house is quiet, except for Cassie and Amaya, who sit cross-legged in the living room, heads bent together over a faded photograph album. Nathan is in the next room, whistling off-key. There's a kind of aftermath glow in the house, a pause before the world starts up again.

The phone rings. I answer on autopilot, expecting a telemarketer or, worse, one of the school's robo-calls about midterm testing. Instead, it's my literary agent, her voice infused with West Coast vowels and caffeine.

"Diane! Got a second?"

"Sure." I step into the halo of sunlight from the front window, where the portrait of Cassie, Rolo, and me hangs. We look nothing and everything like ourselves.

My agent is all business, which is how I know it's good news. She launches right in. "You remember that publisher we sent the first fifty pages to? They're obsessed. They want to see the rest. Yesterday if possible."

My knees threaten to give out. "Seriously?"

"Seriously. They asked if you could hop on a call next week. I said you were booked solid, but you could probably make time."

I press a hand to my chest, heart fluttering like an anxious moth. "I—wow. Yes. I can definitely make time."

"Excellent. And Diane? I read the last chapter last night. The ending made me ugly cry. In a good way."

I blink hard, looking at my painted self, eyes calm and unafraid. "Thank you," I manage.

We talk logistics for another minute. I hang up in a daze, the whole house tilting on its axis. Suddenly, I don't know what to do with my hands, or my face, or any part of myself.

Nathan's voice cuts in from across the room. "Everything okay?"

I nod, not trusting myself to speak. But he's already seen my expression, and he crosses the hall in three strides. I barely get the words out: "The publisher wants the book. They want to see it all."

His reaction is instant and physical. He lifts me up and swings me in a slow circle, careful not to crash into any furniture. I laugh, breathless and shocked, and when he sets me down, he kisses my forehead with all the ceremony of someone who knows how important this is to me.

Cassie and Amaya look up, the photo album forgotten.

"What happened?" Cassie asks, running over in her socked feet.

I crouch to her level. "Remember the book I was writing?"

She gives me a look. "How could I forget? It took you, like, forever to write it."

"Well, somebody wants to publish it. Like, for real."

She blinks. "Are you going to be famous?"

I laugh. "Probably not. But maybe I'll get a better desk."

She nudges me with her elbow, then, in a burst of affection, hugs me tightly. Amaya joins in, and for a minute we're a tangle of limbs and giggles.

Nathan watches, hands in his pockets, head tilted. When our small huddle breaks apart, he reaches for my hand. "Proud of you," he says.

It feels like the room is swelling. I look around at this strange little scene—my partner, my daughter, her best friend, and, of course, Rolo. I think of Sara. The thought is sharp but not unlivable. I wish she could see us like this, messy and hopeful, unfinished but so stubbornly, beautifully alive.

Later, when breakfast is over and the girls are off searching for sand dollars on the beach, Nathan and I wander out to the back porch. The sun is just beginning its ascent, splattering the horizon in pink. The air is cool and carries with it the salt of the sea. We're both quiet, lost in our thoughts, but it's comfortable. The kind of comfort you only have with someone who's seen you at your worst and still thinks you're worth the sunrise.

"I always knew you could do it." He reaches for my hand, entwining his fingers with mine. "You deserve this."

I chuckle, bumping my shoulder into his affectionately. "You're a good liar," I tell him.

"I'm serious, Diane. You're brilliant... We all knew that. It was just a matter of time everyone else caught on."

I squeeze his hand in reply, too overwhelmed by emotion to form words. And in that moment, I realize that not only is my story not over, but I can't wait to see how it ends.

CHAPTER 46

DIANE

December

The weather is unseasonably warm, and the house is full of sun, salt, and the anticipation of people. I have the front windows thrown wide for the cross-breeze, but also because it feels wrong to trap anything inside on a day like this. I imagine Sara's voice, amused and dry, narrating my every move. "You'll let in all the gnats, and half the neighborhood's going to see you fussing in your pajamas." She's not wrong, on either count.

But today is hers, so the gnats can come, and so can the neighbors. I float from room to room with my checklist, balancing a ceramic pitcher of flowers on one hip, a roll of painter's tape in the other hand, and a mind full of instructions I didn't write down. Cassie is at the dining table, tongue between her teeth as she carefully scripts names on card stock. Her handwriting is a mess of loops and sharp angles, a code only she can read, but I have learned it, because mothers always do.

Nathan is in the living room, up on the stepladder, putting the topper on the tree. He hums as he works, something tuneless and persistent, and even from across the house, I can feel the rhythm in my chest. Above the fireplace hang five stockings, meticulously arranged in a perfect line. Three for us, one for

Sara, and another for Rolo, a doggie stocking decorated with a tiny bone.

I set the pitcher down on the console in the hall. The flowers are all wrong—dahlias, poppies, bachelor's buttons, a handful of ragged roses. Sara would have chosen something elegant, lilies or maybe peonies, arranged in color gradients. I like the disorder of mine. It feels like the way I remember her, wild and sudden and a little bit too much. I pluck a dead leaf from one stem and smooth the blooms into a shape that will never be perfect, but will last the day.

From the kitchen, Cassie calls, "Can we use the seashells on the table, or is that weird?"

Judy sticks her head around the doorframe. "Not weird. Very on-theme with a coastal Christmas." She tries for a smile, but the sight of the shells, the worn and glossy ones Sara picked on walks, some with handwritten dates in her tiny, looping script, refuses to let it materialize.

Cassie eyes her sidelong, all teenage intuition. "I'll only use the little ones," she says and drops three purple coquinas into the bowl with practiced care.

The house is still mostly Sara's, even four months after her leaving us. Her books line the shelves, each with a faint crease along the spine from where she stopped and thought. Her blankets, hand-knit and shedding, drape the backs of every chair. There is an entire cupboard in the kitchen devoted to herbal teas, most of which taste like soap or sadness. But the house is also ours, now. Nathan's toothbrush is in the bathroom, Cassie's ridiculous collection of enamel pins are stuck to the corkboard above the stairs, and my own Post-its are stuck to every flat surface. Judy has claimed the bedroom at the north end, the one with the best view of the lighthouse, but only when she comes to visit.

At eleven thirty sharp, the first guest rings the bell. I'm still in bare feet, but at least my pajamas have been swapped for a festive sweater and dark jeans. Nathan wipes his hands on a rag and hurries to open the door.

It's Barbara, resplendent in navy blue and pearls, her hair set like spun sugar. She arrives with a Tupperware of lemon squares and a hug that almost knocks the air from my lungs. "You look beautiful, dear," she says.

Cassie comes to stand beside me, arms crossed, wary but present. She is bracing for the parade of grown-up emotions about to flood the house.

Barbara beams at her. "If your hair gets any longer, you'll need a whole team of hairdressers to tame it." She offers Cassie a warm smile. "A beautiful young lady you are growing into."

Cassie blushes, mumbling her thanks and darting back toward the kitchen.

Other guests filter in, and soon the house is alive with the sound of voices. Everyone brings something. Scones, a bottle of wine, homemade cranberry sauce. The food piles up on the sideboard, an accidental buffet of memories and carbohydrates.

By noon, the house is full. Voices bounce off the beams, laughter threads through the rooms. The light, filtered through Sara's favorite curtains, casts everything in a forgiving glow. I stand in the kitchen, watching in awe the people who have become our family, the life we have built from what was left.

Nathan comes up behind me, slides his arms around my waist, and rests his chin on my shoulder. "See? Told you this was a good idea."

I nod, and it's the truth.

The last guest to arrive is Roger, the mailman, who helped

Sara plant her garden before his back gave out. He hands me a letter addressed to me in Sara's handwriting. "What's this?"

"I was given specific instructions not to give this to you until now," he says. "It didn't feel right to drop it in the mailbox."

I thank him, tucking the envelope away for later when I can be alone.

Gradually, the party concentrates in the dining room. I herd everyone toward the large oak table, laden with mismatched plates and cutlery that I've amassed over the years. Cassie watches from the doorway, a look of quiet satisfaction on her face as she takes in our motley crew of friends and neighbors gathered to celebrate the holidays and remember Sara.

"Is it time?" she asks, voice half a dare.

I glance at Nathan. He's still, attentive, waiting for my cue.

I clear my throat and step forward, feeling the weight of every gaze. "Thank you for coming," I say, and my voice wobbles but doesn't break. "I know Sara would have loved this. All of you, together in her home. The first time I met her, she told me that this house was once the center of the universe. I didn't get it at first, but standing here now, I think I do. It's not just the wooden beams or the creaking floors that make a home, but people, laughter, shared memories. This house, our home"—I pause here, swallowing hard against the lump in my throat—"has become the center of our universe because of you. Because of Sara, who loved this place and each one of us."

Barbara raises her glass of sparkling water. "To Sara," she says. The rest of the room follows, a dozen hands in the air, a chorus of "To Sara!" that fills the space to the rafters.

Cassie sidles up next to me, her head just reaching my shoulder now. She leans in, all sharp elbows and affection. "You did good," she says, and I nearly lose it right there.

Nathan squeezes my hand, anchoring me.

It's not until everyone has plates in hand, drinks poured, that I can finally sit and take in the room. From my chair, I can see Cassie, the corners of her mouth twitching toward a smile. She's holding court with Amaya and a couple of others from school, their voices mixing with the scraping of cutlery and the lull of conversation.

Across the table, Judy is locked in an animated debate with the mailman over the best way to grow basil. From her gestures, it seems she's advocating for a south-facing sunlight, while he insists on regular water. They both wave forks and napkins as if conducting invisible orchestras.

Nathan is beside me, alternating between bites of food and sips of wine. His eyes wander around the room, absorbing the chaos with an unreadable expression.

"Regretting your decision to move here yet?" I tease, nudging him gently with my elbow.

He chuckles. "No way. They're all mad and it's wonderful."

After everyone has eaten, Barbara stands up and clears her throat. "I think Sara would want us to share stories," she says, and before long the house fills with voices, some somber, some ridiculous. *Sara once broke a window trying to swat a fly. She knew the Latin names for every wildflower in the county. She argued with telemarketers for sport, and once got banned from the town pool for skinny-dipping after hours.*

The stories make their way around the room. Some guests laugh until they cry. Others just cry, and it's okay. No one tries to stop it.

As the light fades and the tide creeps up the shore, I wander into the kitchen to breathe. The envelope is still on the counter. I take it, slip out the back, and walk to the cottage where I can be alone. Now that we're in the main house, the cottage feels small and strange, like an echo of a dream. I sit at the little desk by the window, the one where I wrote my first chapters. The ones Sara read. In the dim light cast by the little desk lamp, I open the envelope with careful fingers. Inside is a letter, dated three weeks before Sara died. I read it sitting down, heart in my throat.

Diane,

If you are reading this, you have made it through at least a few months of living without me. Which means, the worst is behind you. I know you, and I know you think you're doing everything wrong. You're not. You're better at this than I ever was. Please, for the love of God, stop baking so much. And tell Cassie I'm sorry about the time I ruined her ant farm. She was right; they are technically livestock. Give Nathan hell if he ever hurts you. And tell him if he ever thinks of painting a portrait of me, not to make my nose too big. If you're reading this at a party, or a memorial, or any kind of gathering, I want you to remember one thing: You are allowed to live, to love, and to be happy. It doesn't mean you've forgotten me.

Love, Sara

I hold the letter to my chest, laughing and crying at once. When I return to the main house, I fold myself into the empty armchair in the living room—Sara's armchair—pull Cassie into my lap, and let Nathan rest his head against my knee. Around us, the stories spin on.

It is still her house, but it is also ours. The ocean wind

carries voices out to the porch, into the evening, and for a long time, I listen. I want to remember all of it.

The ache is still there, but it feels less like a wound and more like a place to begin.

EPILOGUE

5 Months Later

It's always colder than you think, first thing in the morning. Even in May, even this far south, the air pinches at your bare arms and wrists, the wind threading itself into the spaces between your bones. I have my knees hugged to my chest, my toes buried in the cool, uneven sand, and I watch the sunrise turn the Atlantic into one of those color-gradient T-shirts Cassie used to wear when she was little, a mix of topaz, flamingo, then the faintest powder blue. I'm not sure I'll ever get tired of it.

Nathan sits beside me, so close our shoulders nearly touch. He's wrapped in one of Sara's old blankets, the one with the faded paisley pattern and the fringe that tickles my arm. His sketchbook is open across his lap, and he's hunched over it with the kind of concentration that makes him oblivious to everything except the arc of graphite in his hand. If I look quickly, he could be anyone, but then I see the scar at his jawline, the way his foot makes tiny, absent circles in the sand, and he's only ever Nathan.

A few yards down the beach, Cassie is a streak of blue and silver, her hair even wilder now that she's let it grow out for summer. She's bent double, examining something at the water's edge, and every so often she stands, shell in hand, and yells to us. Usually, it's some untranslatable mix of Latin taxonomy and pure, unfiltered excitement.

I have my own notebook open, the pages already damp and stippled with sand. It feels different this time, the act of writing. Not just because the first novel is out there in the world, but because I can finally believe that every word might matter to someone who isn't me. I draft the chapter headers in neat columns, circle a phrase, double-underline another, then scratch it out again. The motion is familiar now, almost routine. I don't have to apologize for taking up space in the world, or in this family. I just do it.

The waves break in their practiced way, shushing the beach in soft, regular exhalations. Above, a single tern glides low over the surf, then veers inland, chasing some invisible pattern on the wind. Nathan looks up from his sketchbook, catches me watching, and smirks.

"Don't judge," he says. "This is a no-pressure zone."

"I would never judge a man wrapped in a paisley blanket," I reply.

He makes a show of wrapping the blanket tighter around himself. "It's growing on me."

"Or just growing something," I say.

He snorts and leans back, bracing himself on his hands. His fingers are stained with charcoal, the skin just above his knuckles permanently creased from years of this exact posture. We sit like that for a minute, watching Cassie work her way down the shoreline, her stride stubborn and unhurried. The sun is higher now, pulling itself free of the water, and the whole sky is streaked in the kind of pastels you only see on tourist postcards.

"Did you get anything good?" Nathan asks, nodding at my notebook.

I flip the cover closed, feeling a strange surge of pride. "I think so. There's a voice emerging."

He grins, all teeth and gratitude. "Yours, or the character's?"

"Why not both?"

He laughs. This is what passes for flirting these days: who can be more earnest, who can say the truest thing without blinking.

Cassie jogs up, arms loaded with a haphazard pile of shells and a perfectly intact sand dollar balanced on top. She's barefoot, her feet already pink from the cold water, and her shorts are damp in a line that says she misjudged the size of a wave by at least a foot. She plops down beside me, scattering her treasures onto the sand.

"Look," she commands, and we do.

There's a razor clam, a few pale coquinas, and something that might be part of a whelk. The sand dollar is pristine, its center marked with a five-pointed star. Cassie turns it over, inspecting the underside with reverence. "Did you know these are technically the skeletons of sea urchins?" she says.

Nathan raises an eyebrow. "You're sure about that?"

She sniffs. "I am the reigning champion of marine trivia in this family."

I reach over and ruffle her hair, and she submits to it for once, still distracted by her findings. "Can I keep it?" she asks, holding out the sand dollar.

"Of course," I say. "It's yours."

She grins, then looks at Nathan. "Are you still drawing, or did you give up?"

He holds the sketchbook aloft. "I did not give up. I pivoted."

Cassie snorts but takes the bait. "Can I see?"

He hands her the book. On the page, a loose, gestural

drawing of the beach at dawn, the shadows exaggerated, the clouds a wild scribble of gray. I recognize the outline of Cassie, half-crouched at the shore, hair whipping sideways like a flag.

She studies it, then shrugs. "Not bad," she says, but she's smiling.

Nathan leans toward her, bumping her shoulder. "High praise from the marine life champion."

Cassie grins wider, then turns to me. "You should write a book about us," she says. "You know, the family that collects dead things on the beach."

"Maybe I will," I say, and it gives me an idea.

She squints at me, then at the water. "We should do this every Saturday."

"We will," I say.

Nathan looks at me over Cassie's head, his expression serious now. "You really mean it, don't you?"

"About the beach, or the writing?"

"Both," he says, and something in my chest flares up—gratitude or relief or just the small, ordinary miracle of being seen.

I let the feeling fill me, like air after a long swim.

For a while, we sit there, the three of us, arranged in an uneven row. Cassie sorts her shells into piles, categorizing by color and size. Nathan sketches Cassie and me from new angles, quick lines and big swathes of negative space. I outline chapter three, then lose myself in the act of watching them, the way their heads tilt in tandem, the way their hands brush as they reach for the same broken shell.

The wind shifts, carrying a cold spray that stings my cheeks and makes Nathan shiver. He pulls the cardigan tighter, then wraps an arm around my waist. The gesture is easy, almost unconscious, but it anchors me in the present, in this exact version of reality.

I lean into him, close my eyes, and listen to the waves, to Cassie's running monologue about mollusks and beach glass, to the scratch of graphite on paper. The sun is high now, the light a little harsher, but I feel warm all the way through.

I am not waiting for something to go wrong. I am not bracing for the next loss, or the next goodbye. I am here, on this patch of sand, with these two people, and I am happy.

When I open my eyes, Nathan is watching me, his gaze soft and unguarded. He leans forward, then kisses my hair, just above the temple.

"You look peaceful," he says.

I surprise us both by laughing. "I am."

"Gross," Cassie says, but there's no heat in it.

Nathan smiles, and the three of us dissolve into easy, morning laughter, the kind that fills up all the empty space.

The tide creeps closer, lapping at our feet, and the day stretches ahead.

I turn back to my notebook, flip to a clean page, and begin again.

***

We last a good hour before Cassie gets bored. She tries to hide it, poking at a horseshoe crab shell with the toe of her foot, but she keeps glancing up to see if we're watching. When Nathan takes a break to shake out his hand, Cassie pounces.

"So," she says, "have you actually decided when you're doing it?"

"Doing what?" he asks.

Cassie groans, flops backward in the sand. "Getting

married."

I'm too surprised to deflect. "We were going to talk about it after—well, after things settled."

"Things are settled." She says it with the force of fact, not wishful thinking. "You're both here. I haven't run away to join the circus. We have a dog that only pees indoors sometimes. If you don't set a date, I'm going to die of suspense."

Nathan looks at me, eyebrows up. "She's not wrong."

"I'm aware," I say, and it is just like every old argument, except no one is yelling and everyone is smiling.

Cassie sits up, gathering her shells into a neat pyramid. "I want to be the flower girl," she says, not looking at either of us.

I blink. "Don't you think you're a little old for that?"

She shrugs. "I'll wear a suit. Or a lab coat. Amaya can be the other flower girl. We'll scientifically optimize petal distribution."

Nathan starts to say something, then just shakes his head, grinning.

I dig my toes deeper into the sand. "I don't want a big thing," I say, more to myself than to them. "No tent, no band. Just...us. Here."

Nathan's hand finds mine. "Beach wedding?"

The words sound made up. Like a joke, or a movie pitch. But I like them. "Why not? Everyone we love is in a twenty-mile radius. And the sand is free."

Cassie bounces on her heels. "Can we get a dog tuxedo for Rolo?"

"We can get a dog tuxedo for every dog on the beach," Nathan says.

Cassie whoops, already planning logistics.

I turn to Nathan, suddenly self-conscious. "Is that okay

with you?"

He nods, smiling so wide the scar at his jaw deepens into a dimple. "It's perfect."

I tear up, just a little, and Cassie rolls her eyes so hard I think she might sprain something. I look at him and then at Cassie, her face scrunched up in mock disgust but also smiling.

"Sara always knew we would end up together," I say, and it comes out steadier than I expect.

Nathan nods, slow and certain. "She did."

Cassie leans in, dropping her voice to a conspiratorial whisper. "You're definitely going to cry at your own wedding."

"Absolutely," I say, not ashamed.

Nathan laughs. "Then I will, too. We'll be a mess together."

Cassie sifts through her shells, selects the sand dollar, and sets it on my knee. "You should use these for decorations," she says. "We could glue them to, like, everything. It would be on theme."

"That's actually brilliant," Nathan says, and Cassie glows.

We fall into planning—real planning, not just jokes and hypotheticals. Who to invite. What time of day. Whether you can actually get a marriage license from the same courthouse where Sara used to work. Nathan wants to write the vows together. I veto, on the grounds that I don't want him to see mine in advance. Cassie demands a sandcastle-building contest for the reception. Nathan volunteers to build a driftwood arch. I suggest borrowing folding chairs from the high school.

It's all so ordinary, so sweetly absurd, that I want to bottle the feeling for later, when everything will inevitably feel harder and messier. I want to save it for Cassie, for myself, for the version of us that doesn't know how this turns out.

We lean together, heads almost touching, until the sun is

high enough that the sand no longer feels cold.

Nathan tucks a strand of hair behind my ear. "It's settled, then," he says. "Beach wedding. Minimum chaos. Maximum us."

I nod. "Perfect."

Cassie claps once, loudly. "I am going to make an epic spreadsheet."

Nathan and I look at each other, then burst out laughing.

And just like that, the future starts to come into focus.

We sit there for a while, shoulder to shoulder, a little trio in the vast morning. I watch Cassie make her final survey of the tide, hands sifting the sand with reverence. She's taller now, braver. I see traces of Sara in her, but also so much of the girl she's become—the girl we've made together, in a way I never could have planned or even wanted, back when everything felt temporary and the future was a wall I couldn't see over.

A pair of seagulls squabble overhead, and somewhere out past the breakers, a boat motors slowly by. The wind has teeth, but the sun is strong enough to blunt it. I close my eyes again, listen to the hush and rush of the waves, the sound of my daughter's voice, Nathan's even breathing beside me.

I think about all the ways we've reassembled ourselves, about the space we've made for the old, the new, the things we lost and the things we never thought we'd find. I think about Sara, and how the last gift she left wasn't a memory, but a direction—forward. Always forward, even when it's hard. Especially when it's hard.

I reach for my notebook, open it to a blank page. At the top, I write:

For Sara, who saw what could be and pointed the way.

Then I close the cover, let it rest against my thigh. The

sun climbs higher, the water sparkles, and Cassie runs back to us, arms full of sand dollars, laughing so hard she can barely breathe.

Nathan wraps one arm around me and the other around Cassie. We're not exactly a family. Not yet. But it's close enough to fool the heart. And for now, that's more than enough.

THE END

ACKNOWLEDGEMENTS

As always, I would like to thank the individuals who played key roles in shaping this story into what it is today.

To my agent, Katie Monson, thank you for your continued support. To Meredith, Jordyn, Victoria, Jennifer, and the amazing team at Page & Vine, it has been an absolute pleasure working with you on this story.

A special shoutout to my beta readers, Jeanette, Roxi, and Amelia, for their time in scrutinizing this manuscript and helping make it the best it can be.

I must also thank my wife, Josette, for her patience and understanding as I expanded this universe. None of this would be possible without your love and support.

And last but not least, to my readers, your unwavering support is what keeps me writing. You're the best!

ABOUT THE AUTHOR

Buck Turner is the bestselling author of nine novels, including *The Keeper of Stars, A Thousand Distant Shores, Promises Promises,* and *The Long Road Back to You.* A former IT professional turned writer, he lives with his family in Northern Kentucky, where he spends his free time golfing and drawing.

ALSO BY BUCK TURNER

The Keeper of Stars

A Thousdand Distant Shores

Unspooling Honey

Promises Promises

The Hearts We Leave Behind

The Long Road Back to You

Losing Adam

Evergreen

UNSPOOLING HONEY

Coming July 2026

A poignant love story about two people who think their wounds are too deep to heal, until a random act of kindness changes their lives forever.

Nick Sullivan used to believe in happily ever after, but that was before he lost his wife and daughter in a car accident. Five years later, the thirty-eight-year-old widower lives a quiet life in the East Tennessee mountains where he spends his days harvesting honey and nights battling the ghosts of his past.

Across town, Dr. Eve Gentry has just started as a professor of English at Lincoln Memorial University. After a recent divorce, Eve is eager for a fresh start and the opportunity to prove that she can make it on her own.

Ready to put down roots, Eve searches for a place she can call home. When a mysterious flyer lands in her faculty mailbox, it leads her to a property that appears too good to be true.

Soon, Nick and Eve become neighbors. As the seasons change, something shifts between the two. Nick, once withdrawn and hardened by the cruelty of fate, starts to soften under Eve's gentle persistence. Meanwhile, the woman who once vowed never to depend on anyone again, finds herself gradually letting down her guard.

Their wounds run deep, but can they find something beautiful amidst their shared sorrow, building a bridge between their hearts along the way

PROMISES PROMISES

A NOVEL

BUCK TURNER

PROMISES PROMISES
BUCK TURNER

PAGE & VINE

PROMISES PROMISES

Available Now

A sentimental romance about a woman who thought she had it all—fame, success, and wealth—until she attends her best friend's wedding and discovers her own chance at a happily-ever-after.

Harper Emery has always lived in the shadow of her best friend, Sidney Westwood. While Sidney's outgoing and charming personality draws people towards her, Harper prefers spending time alone, often hidden behind a sketch pad or sewing machine, dreaming of a future as a fashion designer. Despite their differences, the two are often inseparable, bonded by their love for nature and an unspoken connection that runs deep between them.

But everything changes during a trip to Destin, Florida. After a near-death experience, Harper finds herself being pulled from the waves by Cameron Spears, a lifeguard who gives her a taste of the limelight and the exhilaration of a whirlwind romance.

A decade later, the memories of that unforgettable summer, the love that followed, and the inevitable heartbreak still haunt Harper. Despite seemingly having it all—fame, success, and wealth—thirty-year-old Harper still feels like a failure when it comes to love. But when she agrees to be maid of honor at Sidney's wedding, little does Harper know that her own happily ever after may be waiting right around the corner.

www.buckturner.com